The Widower

ALSO BY D.L. FISHER

THE
WIDOWER

D.L. FISHER

JOFFE BOOKS

Joffe Books, London

www.joffebooks.com

First published in Great Britain in 2025

© D.L. Fisher 2025

Cover art by Nick Castle

ISBN: 978-1-80573-220-4

To my readers, I wouldn't be here without you.

PROLOGUE

The shot rang through The Estates with the bold certainty of a church bell. If only it were so benign.

In pure Estates fashion, every neighbor ran to their windows and peeked out of their doors to see what had disturbed the quiet April morning in their sleepy community. The neighborhood, only recently untroubled, once again hummed with nervous activity. The gunshot was a spark igniting a blaze, and news of it spread like wildfire through the community.

As it often does in a place like this, the rumor mill churns twenty-four hours a day, seven days a week. But the rumor mill was not the most accurate of sources, with details added here and omitted there. Within minutes, every resident gathered in the center of Main Street, desperate to know what the commotion was about. The residents of The Estates were no strangers to tragedy.

But no one could have imagined what they would discover on that crisp spring day.

The body lay unmoving, shrouded in a thick blanket of red, a once familiar face now barely recognizable. It didn't take long to figure out what had happened — the horrible bang that sent residents scurrying from their homes like mice, the pool of blood, and the shell casings from a .22 revolver. The image would be forever imprinted in their minds.

1

A nosy neighbor dared to creep closer for a better look. She confidently reported back to the crowd, all equally curious, the way one might recount a simple fact — a single gunshot to the head.

Neighbors gripped one another, sharing their fear, offering support and impossible reassurances. How much tragedy can one community endure? Hadn't *this* community suffered enough?

They all knew who was lying there. It was one of them. A neighbor. A friend.

Dead.

In the back of their minds, a horrifying question lurked: was this just the beginning?

CHAPTER ONE

"Happy Anniversary, Carrie Winter!"

"*Excuse* me?" I stare into the phone, my eyes feeling as though they're about to pop from my head. For a moment, I think I've won a trip or a prize. Something, *anything*, other than what I sense is coming next.

"With the three-month anniversary of the Mark Black murders approaching, we've chosen *you* for an exclusive interview . . ."

I immediately hang up and throw my phone across the room. It hits the wall and slides dramatically down to the floor, almost in slow motion. I wrap my arms around my body as though I might be able to shield myself from whoever was on the line.

These calls. I can't. I seriously can't.

Making matters worse, *Dateline* is airing our episode, 'Back from the Black,' *again*. It must be at least the third time in the past two months. It seems people never grow tired of hearing about the havoc Mark Black wreaked on The Estates, our prestigious gated community nestled into the safe and idyllic hamlet of Armonk, New York.

Don't get me wrong, I never grow tired of listening to Keith Morrison — his voice is as smooth as melted butter — but unlike them, I don't need to watch the episode for the third time.

I lived it.

And though permanently evicted from The Estates, Mark Black will forever live rent-free in my head.

I try to dislodge the thoughts of my dead psychotic neighbor. I head into the kitchen and begin layering ingredients in the Crock-Pot for the *Best Pot Roast Ever* recipe that I've honed over the past two years. My husband, Bennett, and stepson, TJ, are obsessed with it. It's a labor of love — all the time and energy that goes into making it. *Anything* to take my mind off the past three months.

"Morning, Carrie."

I glance up at my stepson. He's dressed to the nines, the spitting image of his father. Same thick, dark hair. Same piercing blue eyes. It's *Bring Your Kid to Work* day at Bennett's law firm. At nineteen, TJ's probably a bit old to sit at Bennett's desk, coloring by numbers and playing games on an iPad while his father conducts important legal business, but TJ has expressed a strong interest in following in his father's footsteps and becoming a lawyer. He's enrolled in classes at Westchester Community College, which is a definite step in the right direction. Overjoyed by this development, Bennett has vowed to support his son every step of the way.

They've come a long way from their estranged relationship and TJ showing up on our doorstep out of the blue. There I was, getting ready to celebrate our one-year wedding anniversary. And there he was, a child I never knew existed.

"Look at you," I say, abandoning my post by the Crock-Pot and approaching TJ. I straighten his tie and then pat him on the chest. My own chest squeezes with a jolt of affection for my stepson. "Perfect." I beam with pride. I haven't known TJ long, but I've jumped head first into the role of loving, supportive stepmother. It's a hat I wear pretty darn well.

"Are you excited?" I ask. "Nervous? It's your first day in the office, after all."

"A little of both." TJ shifts from foot to foot, his apprehension radiating off him in waves.

"I'm sure you'll do great. And if you decide law isn't for you, there's always culinary school." I toss him a playful wink.

TJ laughs at what he thinks is a joke, but I'm dead serious. My stepson is a phenomenal chef. He first snared me with some maple-caramelized bacon and the fluffiest scrambled eggs ever. That feels like a lifetime ago — waking up to TJ cooking me breakfast the day after he turned our lives upside down.

I think back to that moment, remembering how *big* the TJ problem felt. Catastrophic. Insurmountable, even. TJ arrived, and less than twenty-four hours later, seventeen-year-old Sofia Swanson was found floating face down in the community pool. Two days later, Lila Lockwood was discovered drowned in the creek. Then Sienna disappeared, and the punches just kept on coming.

Punch. Punch. Punch.

Sometimes, it feels like they'll never stop coming. Like I'm just waiting for the next fist to land.

I shudder at the memories. If Mark Black had had his way, I would have joined Sofia and Lila among the dead. I very nearly did. I finger the scar on my face, a permanent reminder of a past I'll never forget.

My breath quickens — the beginnings of an anxiety attack. It's hard not to be anxious when you have a past like we do. Just as I start to hyperventilate, I feel my husband's muscular arms wrapping around me from behind, shielding me from the awful, unbidden memories. "I wish it were *Bring Your Kid AND Wife to Work* day," Bennett says, kissing my neck and instantly turning my palpitations into flutters. At times like these, I can't help but wonder how long the honeymoon phase lasts. Two years in, Bennett's touch still ignites an explosion in my chest. I take a slow, deep breath, steadying my pulse as I marinate in my husband's comforting scent.

"Get a room," TJ laments, rolling his eyes.

I break out in a full-face grin. Despite getting off to a rocky start, we're starting to feel like a real family.

My phone pings from where it landed on the floor, jolting me back to attention. I quickly pick it up, finding a text from my best friend and neighbor, Marnie Black.

Marnie: *What's taking you so damn long?*

My lips quirk up. It's still early — not even 7 a.m. The sun is barely up, and the sky is still a moody blue from the waning night. But Marnie doesn't like to be kept waiting.

Me: *Sorry, seeing Bennett and TJ off.*

I tap my fingers on the screen, waiting for a response.

Marnie: *TJ? Way to rain on my parade . . .*

I roll my eyes. I can't so much as mention my stepson without setting Marnie off. She won't tell me why, either. I've asked, and asked. Oh God, have I asked.

Why do you hate TJ?

What is it?

Has he done something to you?

My questions are typically met with noncommittal grunts and a swift subject change.

I place my phone down on the table, and can't help but think how bizarre it is that TJ feels the same way — just the mention of Marnie to my stepson causes him to break out in a full-blown rash.

Oh well, I huff silently. This is all the thought I'll give to the Marnie-TJ dilemma today. While TJ is busy shadowing his dad at work, I'll be spending the day with my best friend, and with dinner in the slow cooker, I've got nothing but time on my hands.

A smile creeps across my face as I consider my agenda with Marnie today: good, old-fashioned surveillance.

A new neighbor is moving into The Estates. Someone was apparently crazy enough to buy a house where a teenager went missing only to be found dead in the creek butting up to said house. And Marnie and I are keen to find out just how crazy they might be.

As if on cue, another text from Marnie comes through on my phone.

Marnie: *Did they leave? Are you ready yet???*

Me: *Yes, and am I ever!*

I glance out the window at the SOLD sign standing proudly in the Lockwoods' sprawling front yard. I wasn't exactly sad to see them go, but I am anxious to meet our new neighbor.

Perhaps it's just the knowledge of the heinous crimes our former neighbor, Mark Black, committed right under our noses that has me slightly on edge. It goes to show — you never *really* know anyone.

CHAPTER TWO

From her bedroom window, Marnie has a perfect view of the house where the Lockwoods resided, the house they shared with their daughter, before Mark Black callously ended her short life.

And after two months of anticipation and speculation — and all the "ations," — the new neighbor is finally moving in to the very same house.

Once TJ and Bennett are packed into the Porsche with home-made lunches and Yetis full of hot coffee, I head straight across the street to find Marnie anxiously awaiting my arrival.

"I made mimosas," she announces, shoving a delicate glass flute overflowing with champagne and orange juice into my hand before I've even removed my shoes. I lean against the door frame as I awkwardly attempt to untie my sneakers with one hand while balancing the drink in the other. I may actually *need* a drink after all that work.

"How was last night?" I ask, still struggling with a double knot.

"Meh." Marnie rolls her eyes. "Book club was at Florence's house. She always picks the worst books. How many historical fiction books can one person read?"

"I guess it depends on the person. But if I were hosting, we'd be reading *Verity*." I give Marnie a wry smile.

"Yeah," she agrees. "But you know how our neighbors hate penises."

I snicker at Marnie's forthrightness. I'm *so* glad I quit book club.

I expect a laugh to meet my own, but instead, Marnie taps her foot against the floor, her tight expression a stark contrast to the more cheerful topics of penises and the bubbly in our hands.

"Oh no, what's wrong?" I ask.

"Did you see *her*?"

"See *who*?" I feel my eyebrows furrow. Not for the first time in our years-long friendship, I have no idea where she's going with this. Only that it's not going to end well for whoever has pissed her off. It rarely does.

She rolls her eyes as if I should already know. "Nikki Lang. Her dog just crapped on my lawn."

I glance out the window, searching for the offending dog poop, but all I see is a velvety carpet of green. "Did she pick it up?"

Marnie eyes me up and down as if I've gone crazy. "Yes, but that's not the point."

"Well, you know what they say, when you gotta go, you gotta go." I try to inject some lightness into our conversation, but it does little to soothe the look of annoyance on her face.

"Not on *my* lawn." Marnie crosses her arms in front of her chest. "I've already emailed her a fine. And as of this week, she's kicked out of book club."

What a terrible loss for her, not, I remark inwardly. I step closer to Marnie. "You did what you had to do," I tell her outwardly, attempting to mirror her seriousness at this gross infraction.

Her face relaxes. "I thought you'd agree. That's what's great about us, Carrie. We always have each other's backs."

"I wouldn't have it any other way." And I meant it — I'd have a death wish if not.

9

A glint of light on her breastbone catches my attention. "You're wearing the necklace again, I see." This is the first time I've seen her wear it — *the* necklace, the floating diamond on a thin strand of gold — since Mark's death.

Marnie fingers the jewel clinging to her neck. She exhales evenly at my remark. "It reminds me of how much I've overcome."

I nod sympathetically, even though it reminds me of the necklace I once had hidden in my nightstand, the one that had graced the neck of Andrea Winter, Bennett's ex and TJ's mom. The necklace I'd found bloodied and tucked into a corner of the dead woman's stairwell. That identical necklace, gifted to Andrea by her killer, now sits in an evidence box at the Armonk Police Department.

Like a twisted joke, Mark Black bought the exact same necklace for his wife and lover.

I'm slightly thrown off at seeing it again, but a small smile plays on my lips. I'm glad my best friend is trying to move on.

Besides, we've got much more important matters to contend with.

"So . . . ?" I ask, hoping Marnie takes the bait.

"Moving vans parked outside all morning. No sign of the new owner yet."

"Darn it." We are all dying to know who's moving into that house — pardon the expression.

Marnie pulls me by the arm. "Come, let's go have a look." She leads me up the winding staircase to her bedroom. Marnie once told me she does her best work in her bedroom. Considering Mark Black was sleeping with any seventeen-year-old with a pulse and an address in The Estates, I'd venture to guess her best work did not involve her husband.

Case in point, Marnie quickly replaces the mimosa in my hand with a pair of binoculars. I turn them over in my hands — the lens is solid, scratch-free, and there's a fancy range-finder feature. I'm pretty sure these binoculars cost more than my car. *This* is what Marnie meant by her 'best work.' I guess you don't become HOA president by *not* knowing every last detail about the people living in your development.

It just so happened that the annual elections fell a week after Mark Black's death. The timing couldn't have been better for Marnie. The sympathy vote alone was enough to get her elected, and Ryan Altman, the former HOA president, ousted. Altman didn't stand a chance, not after two teenagers were murdered and a sadistic, sociopathic serial killer had run amok in our development under his so-called watchful eye. Not that any of that was his fault, but residents of The Estates are all about appearances, and it would appear they felt it would look better if the development went in a *different direction*.

Disregarding the fact that the sadistic, sociopathic serial killer was Marnie's husband, the general consensus was that nothing like that would happen again with Marnie in charge since she is a no-bullshit kind of gal. Just take her earlier incense at Nikki Lang's gross dog poop infraction. If Nikki has checked her email, she would likely agree with the aforementioned characterization.

"Oh, oh, oh," I hoot, nearly dropping the binoculars in excitement.

"What is it?" Marnie grabs the binoculars to look for herself.

After a few seconds, she pulls them away from her eyes, her lips twisting in disappointment. "That's one of the movers, Carrie."

I take them back from her. "No, I don't think he is." I gesture toward the house, where the sun is reflecting off of the silver, metal roofs of the two large moving vans that are pulling away. "Either they left one of their workers behind, or *that* is our new neighbor."

My jaw is on the floor. Even from a hundred feet away, this guy is something to look at. He so does *not* have one of those dad bods I've grown accustomed to seeing around here, like our previous next-door neighbor, Steven Lockwood. His lawn mower had a permanent indent from the beer gut that rested on it while he groomed his estate every Saturday at 2 p.m. This new guy is *deliciously* shirtless. Beads of perspiration drip down his chest as he chugs a beer on the front porch. He looks like he's shooting a Budweiser commercial. Marnie attempts to grab the binoculars, but I'm not finished. This guy is hot, and not just from the exertion of moving furniture and boxes into an eight-thousand-square-foot house.

I move the binoculars lower — no, no, not *that* — to examine his left hand. A ring is conspicuously absent from a certain finger. What can I say? I'm a firm believer in neighborhood watches, especially if it involves watching a neighbor who looks like this. As the freshly anointed HOA president and town gossip, Marnie, of all people, should appreciate the desire to keep my finger on the pulse of The Estates. But I don't have to look up to know that she's giving me the stink eye instead of appreciating my careful consideration. I reluctantly hand the binoculars over.

Marnie fiddles with the zoom lever to get a closer look. "Holy shit, Carrie. Is this a joke? Did you hire a stripper for my birthday?"

I giggle at the thought. "Um, sorry, but no. Your birthday was two months ago."

One month after I accidentally killed your husband.

Do I regret that it happened? Not one little bit. That man was a sadistic, sociopathic serial killer. And for the record, it was self-defense. He would have killed me first had my bedroom door not fallen off its hinge and buried him.

Marnie pouts momentarily before the corners of her lips curl back up, her thoughts far away from her dead husband. What a glorious place to be. I'm jealous. "Well, whoever he is, he's absolutely freaking perfect."

She's not wrong. He is *absolutely freaking perfect* — physically, anyhow. But I can't help but wonder if there's something else. Something I can't see. I mean, what brought him to our infamous development? As a general rule, people tend to avoid tragedy, not run head first into it.

So, as my gaze fixes on the stranger across the street, I find myself wishing something was visibly wrong with him. A beer belly. A bad toupee. Better, a third nipple. Something to warn us of what he's doing here. Of what he might be capable of.

But no, there's nothing remotely unsavory about him. He's got a perfect body, perfect dark, thick hair, and two perfect nipples.

I take a deep breath, crawling out of the rabbit hole Mark Black dug. It's a beautiful day in the present. The sun is shining brightly, casting a warm glow on our development. The sky is crystal blue, without a cloud in sight. There's a chorus of bluejays chirping from their nests in our oakwood trees. It's certainly not doom-and-gloom weather.

I'm sure there's nothing nefarious to see here. The newest resident of The Estates is probably a perfectly normal, run-of-the-mill, abnormally good-looking guy.

The worst is behind us.

Everything will be fine.

"We should go over there," I suggest, because we can't just sit around all day staring at him. What if he has his own binoculars and catches us spying? Too creepy. Besides, now is as good a time as ever to meet this guy. Taking a page from the Marnie Black playbook, my inner busybody will not shut up until I give it what it wants: to meet this freakishly attractive stranger.

"Come on," I continue, warming more to the idea. "Let's go introduce ourselves. Welcome him to the neighborhood. I mean, you are the HOA president now."

"Yes, yes, yes," Marnie squeals, taking my ego stroke and running with it. "Let's do it." She throws the binoculars onto her bed (as if they don't cost more than a freaking *car*) and races toward the door, spinning back to face me. Her jet-black hair cuts through the air like a whip. "Are you coming or *what*, Carrie?"

I don't remind her that it was *my* idea to go over there in the first place. *It's better to be kind than right*, I have found myself repeating a lot lately. My mantra of 2025. Though, considering what we've been through, my mantra really should be, *don't trust your neighbors*.

"Coming," I call out.

It takes us all of three minutes to walk across the street. I'm not sure you'd even call it walking — it's more of a swift, snappy jog, with me trying to keep up with Marnie so we can show up at his door and welcome our new neighbor to the community together. In our nearly two years of friendship, I've never seen her run so fast. Come to think of it, I've never seen her run at all. I trip over a loose shoelace and narrowly avoid a faceplant on the street while trying to shorten the distance between us.

Spoiler alert: we do not arrive at the front door together. Marnie doesn't even wait for me to catch up before beginning the introductions.

I'm still a few paces back, watching as she holds out her freshly manicured fingers and shakes his hand, clutching it for a beat too long. Unless I really did trip over my shoelaces, hit my head, and become concussed, I look on in disbelief as she blatantly flirts with him.

This is terrible to say, but a part of me thought maybe Marnie was dead inside after everything that happened with Mark. Apparently not — alive and kicking at the first fresh whiff of testosterone that presents itself.

I introduce myself once I've arrived, huffing and puffing like I've run a marathon. I don't know how Bennett does it. He runs ten miles like he's casually strolling down the driveway to grab the mail, but I can barely jog ten feet.

"Yes, I'm *the* Marnie Black," I hear her say as I arrive at the front door.

"Damian Brown," the man standing before us offers, a twinkle in his mahogany eyes. I slip my hand into his, forgetting momentarily about my husband. I'm not sure if it's from the man or the movement, but my heart is beating obscenely loud in my ears.

Marnie dissolves into giggles, tears streaming down her face. It takes me a moment to catch on, and I lightly chuckle. I suppose it is *slightly* amusing — Mr. Brown and Mrs. Black. It's like, amid all of the absurdity, we've tumbled into the pages of a Dr. Seuss book.

No, that's not entirely accurate. More like a Dr. Seuss book with Stephen King as the ghostwriter.

"I have a confession," Damian admits once Marnie has calmed down. "My last name is actually Mankiewicz."

I shoot Marnie a puzzled look — surely, this has to be a joke — but she's not looking at me. She's still staring at Damian as if he's Dave Chapelle.

"Any relation to the *Dateline* reporter?" I venture.

"Afraid not."

"Cute *and* funny," Marnie says, twirling a strand of stick-straight hair with a finger. I don't think I've ever heard her laugh so hard at a statement that wasn't even remotely funny. But I can't help but smile widely at my friend, who is clearly getting her flirt on. Good for her. She's been through so much over the past few months. If a hot new neighbor is what it takes to put a pep back in her step, far be it for me to deny her that.

Damian's cheeks redden at Marnie's compliment, although it could also be from the heat. It's unseasonably warm today, and the humidity drapes heavily over us like a thick blanket. Even the trees are sweating. My eyes wander down Damian's toned torso, landing on his biceps. Plus, with all the furniture he just moved despite having movers . . . it's getting pretty dang hot out here.

"Can I interest the two of you in a drink?" Damian motions toward the inside of the house. I've been inside that house before — it's another model, slightly smaller than ours — but this feels different. It *is* different. I think about my former neighbor, how I thought I knew him so well. I can't even count the number of couples' dinners we shared, vacations . . .

Perhaps that's what has me so rankled. We don't know *this* man at all. He's a complete stranger, albeit one with a chiseled chest.

I don't allow myself to finish the thought. Damian Mankiewicz could be anything. I'm concerned about the ease in which Marnie is falling under his spell. Like, *give it a minute, girl!*

And then there's also the fact that I'm not sure how Bennett would feel about me hanging out inside this strange man's house. As good as I'd feel, I expect, if the roles were reversed and the new man in town was a half-naked, drop-dead gorgeous woman. "Erm . . ." I grumble, hesitating.

As it turns out, I don't have to decide because the decision has apparently been made for me. Marnie is already halfway through the door. At the rate things seems to be going, I can't say I'm surprised.

I quickly debate what to do. I can't very well let her go in there alone, *can* I? We came together, and we should leave together. I'd never forgive myself if something happened to her, especially after the Mark situation.

I feel the cool breeze blowing from inside Damian's house. My eyes flit to the empty street, where the sun is practically melting the pavement. I step one foot inside the doorway. Maybe I'm just being dramatic. I'm sure Damian is fine.

We'll be totally fine.

CHAPTER THREE

Bennett and TJ should be at work for the next few hours, so what my husband doesn't know . . . I shove whatever guilt my conscience is entertaining to the side. I'm just trying to be a good friend here and stare at something other than bell peppers in my garden for the next six hours. And to keep Marnie safe. I'm just here to keep Marnie safe.

I step inside, removing my shoes at the door.

A cursory glance at the furniture and boxes tells me Damian Mankiewicz has no kids. The lack of a ring on that finger confirms he likely does not have a wife, either. I would never be so presumptuous as to ask.

"Is it just *you* in this big old house?" Marnie bats her eyelashes, and I can almost see the gears in her head going into overdrive. She's practically moved herself in already. I guess she's lonelier than I thought.

"Yeah," he says, looking down for a moment. "I'm a recent widower."

Recent? I reexamine Damian's ring finger. There's not even the slightest hint of a ring line despite the fact that he's like a bronze statue.

"Shut up!" Marnie slaps Damian on the chest, apparently forgetting (though how could you forget?) that he's shirtless. *Ouch.*

Her cocktail ring leaves a large mark on his chest. *See, even Marnie is wearing a ring!* Shortly after Mark died, Marnie began wearing the giant bauble on her left hand in place of her wedding band. She said she felt naked without *something* there. The ring is beautiful — a large round sapphire encircled by pave diamonds — but a little much for everyday wear, especially if she's going to be slapping people with it on.

"I'm a widow, too." She pauses, clearly for effect, before adding, "I know what you're thinking — she's too young to be a widow, but I swear I am. We totally have that in common."

Damian visibly recoils. His eyes widen, and he takes a sharp step back, putting some space between himself and Marnie. That is probably *not* what he's thinking. I imagine it's more along the lines of: *what have I gotten myself into?*

"Looks like we have lots to commiserate about," she adds, her face flushed.

I almost laugh out loud. I'm sure this guy totally wants to relive losing his wife with the widow from across the street that he just met. Not.

Damian clears his throat. "Yeah, so I'll, uh, go get us those drinks. Why don't you ladies find a seat somewhere? Feel free to throw some boxes out of the way. I haven't started unpacking yet."

"I can help you!" Marnie calls out as Damian's back disappears from view.

"Marnie!" I slap her hand. "You're acting like a thirteen-year-old boy who's just discovered porn."

"Too much?" she asks, flicking on her phone's camera to check her reflection. Marnie smooths out her jet-black hair with a hand, then reaches into her pocket and pulls out a tube of blood-red lipstick, running it across her mouth. She sucks in her lips, making a loud puckering sound as they shoot back into place.

Red lipstick? It's like nine in the morning and eight million degrees outside. I roll my eyes. "Yes, way, *way* too much."

Marnie, with a pout, turns her attention to me and huffs, "You didn't lose *your* husband, Carrie."

Ouch. Point taken. Flirt away.

"Gosh, Marnie, I just meant—"

Marnie throws up a hand to dismiss my explanation before wiping a finger under her eye as if brushing away a tear. I guess losing Mark has hit her harder than I've given her credit for. And now I feel awful.

But I don't know what else I could possibly say. So I let it lie, an uncomfortable silence settling over us. It feels like hours, but it's likely only minutes before Damian returns with three beers and a shirt on. *Oh well.* He hands us each a beer, angling a cardboard box into a makeshift table.

"To neighbors," he toasts.

Once again, my thoughts turn to my former neighbor. A fresh wave of anxiety washes over me, an uneasiness I can't seem to shake. Somehow, with trembling hands and sweaty palms, I manage to bring my bottle to meet his. "To neighbors."

We clink our beers together, and Damian sits down on one of the many boxes packed into his living room. He's got a lot of boxes for a single guy. But then, it is a huge house, *especially* for a single guy. My eyes flit to a medium-sized box tucked into a corner of the room — *DO NOT OPEN* is scrawled across the top and sides in Sharpie. I wouldn't be surprised to find it written on the underbelly of the box as well. The box sticks out like a sore thumb. It's the only one moth-eaten and labeled. The rest of the boxes appear brand new and neatly sealed with tape.

"So, what brought you here?" I ask, unable to dismiss the agitation I've felt since the house sold.

"Oh, you know, this and that." Damian waves a dismissive hand through the air. I follow it with my eyes, expecting to see *this* and *that* manifest in the room with us, but all I see are white walls and a shit ton of boxes. This room looks like a cardboard city.

"I know what you mean," Marnie says with a giggle. I shoot her a side-eye. *She knows what he means?* Marnie Black had her name on the waitlist the second The Estates went up for pre-sale. *This* and *that* wasn't enough to bring her here. The Estates, touted as one of the most exclusive gated communities in Westchester County, had a little more something to do with it.

But Marnie Black learned the hard way that living in this development is not all it's cracked up to be. We all did.

House values have taken a nosedive, but The Estates is *still* one of the most sought-after communities in the county, at least in terms of the press attention it garners. Three months after the horrific events that rocked our small hamlet and even smaller development, reporters *still* camp outside our gates, day and night. I refuse to give any interviews or spend even a moment of time or energy rehashing the past in the public eye. Marnie, on the other hand, now has an agent and has thrown around the possibility of starting a blog or a podcast. To be honest, I'm pretty sure that, if given the choice, she wouldn't trade all the fanfare to bring Mark back. Though judging by her performance today, she's definitely in need of some male companionship. Maybe, just *maybe*, even grieving. That said, Marnie is very much enjoying her fifteen minutes of fame.

Fame. I can't help but wonder if that's what brought our new neighbor here. Maybe he thinks he can somehow capitalize on all the media attention — launch an acting career or get work as an underwear model perhaps. My thoughts flash back to his sweat-streaked abs glinting in the sun. Damian could *definitely* get work as an underwear model. Logic yields no other possible explanation. You'd have to live in a bubble not to have heard about The Estates. You'd have to be a little crazy to want to live here after what happened.

Then again, you'd have to be a little crazy to *stay* here after what happened.

And yet here we are.

But I have to ask him. I *need* to know. "Have you not heard what happened here? About the family who lived here before you?"

There's a moment of awkward silence as we simultaneously look around the room, the airy open floor plan and polished wood floors a stark contrast to the unspeakable horrors the former owners lived through. Well, two of them *lived* through. Lila Lockwood wasn't as fortunate.

Damian's eyebrows scrunch together, painting his face with a look of confusion. Is it possible he really *doesn't* know? Maybe he moved from out of state. Doesn't watch *Dateline*. Doesn't read the freaking newspaper. It's possible, I guess.

"Of course, I know, Carrie. It was international news. A terrible tragedy, really. But the house was so dang cheap. You'd die if I told you what I purchased it for." He leans in closer, propping his elbows on his knees. "Do you want to know?"

Every muscle in my body stiffens as Damian's rich, deep eyes bore into mine, waiting for a response. Somehow, I manage to shake my head. Damian's bargain-basement deal is not something to celebrate. It surely won't help with the crash in property values we've faced. And besides that, no, I *don't* want to die; I've already evaded death once before. Once is enough, thank you very much.

He continues, "I couldn't turn down a once-in-a-lifetime opportunity because of something bad that happened here. It's not like someone was murdered *in* this house."

True, that's not quite how it played out. Lila was murdered in the creek *behind* the house. But still, *I* wouldn't buy this house.

You couldn't pay me to live here. I can barely stomach living next door to it.

"Besides," he adds, pausing to take a long swig of his beer. "Bad things happen *everywhere*. And . . ."

And? My eyebrows shoot up as I wait for what's coming next. Like maybe there was a serial killer and double homicide in the last development he lived in.

"Lightning never strikes in the same place twice."

Damian winks.

CHAPTER FOUR

I ponder Damian's strangely prophetic words. I hope he's right because it feels like a bolt just shot straight down my back. It's rendered me rather speechless.

But thankfully, Marnie appears undeterred. "What do you do for a living?" she asks, playing with her hair.

I stare at Damian, inexplicably afraid of what he might say. If it's, *oh, you know, this and that,* I'm putting our house on the market. Because that could mean, well, just about anything, and given what we've seen here, I'm going to need a tad bit more transparency from the guy living next door. The guy whose house I'm sitting in *right now.*

Damian takes another swig of beer and smiles widely. His brown eyes crinkle around the corners, and deep dimples form on each cheek. I couldn't place it before, but now I see it. Eddie Cibrian — that's who he looks like. The actor who left his wife after falling in love with LeAnn Rimes while filming a Hallmark movie. The resemblance is so uncanny, he could be a body double. My cheeks color even though I don't say this out loud.

"I flip houses," he offers nonchalantly.

I unclench my fists and exhale a deep sigh of relief. There's nothing nefarious about house flipping unless, of course, you're burying bodies beneath a freshly poured foundation. He's probably not doing *that.*

23

"Sounds fun." I jump back into the conversation. "Are you on one of those HGTV reality shows?" I'm only half kidding. He *should* be on one. Suddenly, all I can picture is a shirtless Damian with a sledgehammer in his hand and an untouched canvas of drywall begging to be demolished.

I blush at the mental image. What the hell is wrong with me? I need to escape from these thoughts, and this house. I try to picture Bennett in his underwear, but somehow, that makes me think of Damian in *his* underwear. *Again.* I fan myself absently with a loose hand. Goodness, it feels like someone has cranked the heat up to a hundred degrees.

I throw out a logistical question to steer the conversation in a less sexy direction. "Where was the last house you flipped?"

"Just finished one up in Yonkers."

The relief I felt just moments ago instantly vanishes, replaced with an emotion akin to dread. The smile slides off my face, and I freeze. *Yonkers.*

I'm instantly transported back to TJ's childhood home. The place where his mother was brutally pushed down the stairs to her death. My mind fills with images of the peeling paint and the broken glass. My nose fills with the unmistakable stench of death.

Months ago, Andrea Winter's house went into foreclosure, pushing TJ to our doorstep. I suddenly can't remember whether I heard it had sold to the highest bidder or not. Could Damian have been the highest bidder? It's a Gumby-sized stretch, but something won't let me let it go so easily.

I'm probably just being paranoid. There are, like, eighty thou-sand-something housing units in Yonkers. Really, what are the chances that it's *the* house? Eighty thousand to one? It's not possible.

Despite his easy smile, I can't quite explain it — something about Damian Mankiewicz's sudden arrival this morning rattles me deep to my core.

I glance at Marnie, expecting to find my friend grappling with the same sick possibility, but TJ and Andrea Winter are the furthest things from her mind right now. She's too busy eating up Damian's every word as if she's fresh off a fast.

"Yonkers, huh?" My voice comes out as a rattle. I have a gazillion questions. *Do you know who the previous owner of that house was? Can you provide the address so I can cross-check it with Andrea's?* I open my mouth, but the words don't fall out. This really could mean absolutely nothing. A coincidence — just like the coincidence of TJ showing up and all hell breaking loose. I hardly want to alienate my next-door neighbor on our first meeting.

That, and I seem to have lost the ability to speak.

"Is that what your plans are for this house? Flip it and move on to the next one?" Marnie juts out her lower lip like a disappointed child. I have a feeling I will have to drag her by the shirt sleeve from this house with her feet flailing when we've overstayed our welcome. That is if she doesn't wrap her body snugly around Damian's leg and refuse to let go.

"Nah," he says, a broad smile spreading across his lips. His eyes gently crinkle around the corners again. "I think I'll stick around. See what kind of trouble I can get into." A wink.

My body tenses. I glance down to find my hands shaking. *Trouble?* When I look back up, Damian catches my eye. He saw my trembling hands, too.

Damian laughs. "Gotcha. I swear, I'm a pretty boring guy."

Let's hope so.

I force a conciliatory giggle, though my insides are twisting and turning. I try to ward off the incoming spiral, enjoying my ice-cold beer as we make casual conversations that don't revolve around serial-killer husbands and murdered seventeen-year-old girls.

Before I can stop what's happening, one drink stretches into two, into three, as is often the case when Marnie is involved. I don't have quite the same tolerance as my friend, which is probably why I have tingles spreading through my fingers and toes. And since when could stark white walls spin?

I'm not sure how long we've been at Damian's house, only that it's been *too* long. It occurs to me that I haven't checked on dinner all day. I'm sure it's fine in the slow cooker, but a little shake here and there helps prevent too much browning on the base of the roast. I *really* should go. Saved by the bell, my phone starts buzzing in my pocket. When I hazard a glance, Bennett's face is smiling at me from the screen. But I guarantee he's not smiling right now. He's probably frowning — scowling, even — questioning if he should jump in the car, turn the twenty-minute drive into ten, and make sure I'm okay.

Things have mostly returned to normal here over the past few months since Mark Black committed all those atrocious crimes. While Mark is physically gone and will never, ever be coming back, the mental and emotional damage he inflicted has proven a bit harder to shake. God forbid, if I'm unaccounted for, even for a minute, Bennett thinks I've been kidnapped and stuffed in a trunk or met with some other foul play. It wasn't like this before. I wonder if every household in our development is like this now or if it's just ours. It's a little excessive. I get that he's worried, but I bet if I let him, Bennett would have me microchipped like a dog.

My husband, though, is back in the office, back to doing his thing — his miles-long runs, depositions, and client meetings. Though I don't know how he gets any work done with all the time he spends checking up on me. I guess there are worse things one could have than a husband who cares too much.

I could have a dead, sadistic, sociopathic serial-killer husband like Marnie.

I excuse myself and step outside to take Bennett's call. My gaze flits toward our sprawling property next door, the grass a brilliant shade of emerald green. The grass seems contently hydrated despite the heat of the day.

But Bennett, I'd venture to say, is not very content right now. To be honest, I'm borderline shocked that my husband isn't pacing around the front lawn with an angry, gesticulating hand slicing through the air.

My voice quivers. "Hello?"

"Carrie? Can you hear me?"

I can, but not well. Noise filters through the background — male and female voices, drowned out slightly by what sounds like *live* music. Since the back seat of the Porsche is barely big enough to fit a toddler, I suspect they are not in the car on their way home after all.

And Bennett doesn't sound all that upset. To the contrary, the lightness in his voice would suggest he's blissfully unaware of and unconcerned with what I've been up to today.

"Where are you?"

"We're at McAlister's. Everyone in the office really took to TJ. We're grabbing a few drinks and a bite to eat. Do you want me to bring something back for you?"

I feel a stab of something unfamiliar and unwanted. I can practically smell my pot roast marinating in the slow cooker at home, mixed with buttery potatoes and carrots, hand-delivered from the local farmer's market. It took me hours to prepare the perfect seasoning for that pot roast. I weeded through our rosemary shrub to find the brightest, most fragrant bunch. I let the pot roast sit overnight so the flavors could fully seep in.

It's Bennett and TJ's favorite. I made it *just* for them.

Like the pot roast simmering in the slow cooker, rage begins to boil within my gut. I'm so glad I put in all that time and energy so they could dine out.

I huff an annoyed breath. Dinner *without* me? When did I become the third wheel in my own family? Bennett didn't even ask if I wanted to join them.

I stare at my house, with its Grecian columns and picturesque shutters, fighting against the resentment bubbling within. There's no point in going home now.

Not alone.

CHAPTER FIVE

I slip back through the entryway of the house next door, following the sound of uproarious laughter to the living room. I find Marnie bent over a box, clutching her side.

"Ahem. What did I miss?"

Marnie jerks up dramatically. Her hair flies through the air like she's shooting a commercial, complete with a fan blowing straight at her. I want to tell her she's trying too hard, but I wouldn't dare.

"Damian was just telling me about all the crazy housewives in his last neighborhood," she murmurs, in a breathy Marilyn Monroe sort of way. "Tell her, Damian." Marnie drapes a hand over Damian's bicep, letting it linger for an obscenely long time. I awkwardly wait for her to remove it, but she doesn't, and Damian doesn't flinch or even hint that he wants her to remove it. They've gotten awfully friendly. I check the time on my phone. How long was I out there for?

Damian's cheeks color. "It was a little scary when it happened, but laughable now, I suppose."

My eyes widen. This guy has no idea what scary looks like.

My silence spurring him to elaborate, Damian explains, "Let's just say I had a bit of a fan club. I woke up on a few mornings to several pairs of women's thongs on my porch. You'd think I was on

29

a Mötley Crüe reunion tour." He chuckles to himself, seemingly lost in the memory.

I blink owlishly, then raise an eyebrow. "Where did you come from, Damian Mankiewicz?" If women were leaving underwear on his porch, why the heck wouldn't he stay? Surely, that's every straight man's dream. I mean, maybe not while he was married, but now . . .

Damian's laugh cuts through my thoughts, dimples forming on his cheeks. "Well, as you might imagine, I was not super popular among the husbands in my old development. Then this house came on the market for such a steal, and I couldn't resist. Sometimes in life, you need a fresh start."

I nod in understanding but can't help wondering if *this* is the place best for a *fresh start*.

I don't imagine Damian will be super popular among the husbands here, either, if the way Marnie has embraced him is any indication. It's safe to say Damian can expect to find her *entire* wardrobe waiting for him in the morning. Surely, there must be something in the HOA bylaws about scattering underwear on front porches.

But that's not my concern. I'm still thinking about the amazing meal I slaved over that my husband and stepson have chosen to skip. I don't even like pot roast, for Christ's sake! Bennett and TJ can have their lukewarm drafts and McAlister's frozen beer-battered fish sticks for all I care.

I'll be busy having an impromptu dinner party.

"What are you two doing for dinner tonight?"

"DoorDash," Damian replies with a sheepish grin. "There's no food in the fridge, and even if there were, I'm not too optimistic about finding the pots and pans tonight, or the plates and silverware for that matter. I probably should have labeled the boxes before the move. It all just happened so fast." He scratches his head. "Yeah, it's going to take me a *long* time to unpack."

Well, you certainly found time to label ONE of the boxes, I don't say.

Instead, I turn to Marnie. "And you?"

"Let me check my calendar." She pulls her phone from her pocket and begins fake scrolling through dates. I know she's fake scrolling because I know her schedule better than she does. Besides her sporadic media appearances and monthly HOA meetings, the girl has less going on than I do. We both know that, but I suppose Damian does not.

Marnie pokes frantically at the screen. To an untrained observer, it looks like she's moving things around to make herself available. I guarantee she's playing Candy Crush. Either that or prematurely updating her Facebook status to "In a relationship."

"I moved some things around," she declares.

Yeah, pieces of colored candy. I fight the urge to roll my eyes when she turns to me, as if reading my mind.

Perhaps I'm being too hard on her. I feel a twinge of guilt. Marnie deserves happiness after everything she's been through. Maybe Damian Mankiewicz can be the one to give that to her. Let's just hope our new neighbor doesn't have a treasure trove of kill trophies or a human skull in that ominously labeled box.

Damn you, Mark Black.

"Great," I announce, grinning widely. "I would love to have you both over."

"Can I bring anything?" Damian asks, glancing at the mountains of boxes lining his living room. That one box, in particular, grabs my attention again. Damian's gaze meets mine on the *DO NOT OPEN*. Or maybe I'm just imagining it. I quickly blink and look away.

Someone should tell him that '*don't look here*' kind of screams, '*look here, look here!*'

"Just yourself."

"I'll bring the wine," Marnie offers.

"Perfect, thanks. I just need an hour or so to whip something together. I should probably get going."

To my surprise, Marnie agrees to leave without a fight. "I'll leave too, Carrie. I need to go home to freshen up."

As I make to leave, I case one more sidelong glance at our new neighbor. *You're welcome, Damian's leg.*

"Six p.m.," I tell them, walking quickly toward the front door. "I'll see you then."

There's much to prepare for.

CHAPTER SIX

I'm not going home to get dinner ready.

The pot roast has been cooking all day — nine hours of melt-under-the-knife perfection. All I need to do is spoon that bad boy onto plates, and *voila*, dinner is served. Marnie is bringing the wine. Damian is bringing himself. We've got all the ingredients for a perfect evening.

If I can shake this unease prickling at the back of my neck.

Marnie and I part ways in front of my house with plans for her to return in an hour. The sun is already starting to set, painting the sky a canvas of pink and purple hues, though the temperature has yet to fall. Or maybe it's nerves that have me feeling like I've been set on fire.

Once I'm convinced Marnie is tucked inside her home across the way, I throw on a baseball cap and sunglasses, and slip into my BMW. Instead of turning right out of the driveway toward the front gates as I typically would, I push deeper into The Estates, toward the lesser-used service gate hidden in the back of the development. With paparazzi camping out day and night at the front as if waiting for Taylor Swift to show up to a Chief's game, I'm hoping the back entrance will get me out of here, unseen. And the hat does make me look incognito, if I do say so myself. But doubt suddenly creeps in. Maybe I should have ditched the mirrored Ray-Bans if I didn't want to draw attention.

That, and the press know my car by now.

I hope no one will be there, but that's unfortunately not the case. A lone wolf with a camera spots my BMW, and the flashes commence — bright, blinding stabs of light. *Great.* My flustered image will no doubt be plastered across the front page of tomorrow's issue of the *Westchester Sentinel* because Carrie Winter leaving The Estates is B-I-G news. I cover my face and speed past. An open hand bashes against the driver's side window — the last thing I see as my development fades into oblivion.

I huff quietly to myself, annoyed. Assaulting my car? *Seriously?* I can't believe how aggressive these people are, like freaking vultures who can barely wait for the roadkill to die before pouncing. You'd think they'd take heed of what happened to that poor reporter from the *Westchester Sentinel*, Jessica Jones (another casualty of one Mark Black), and be a tad more cautious. You truly don't know what people are capable of when cornered.

It's almost as if they're challenging me to show them.

Things have only gotten worse here since 'Back from the Black' first aired on *Dateline*. These reporters have even taken to regularly calling and hanging up — from unknown numbers, of course. I don't know how they've gotten my number in the first place. It's unlisted, for Christ's sake! My grip tightens on the steering wheel. What's the point of paying for an unlisted number if people can get hold of it?

At first, I chalked the calls up to a wrong number or a prank — reporters wanting an interview. But then, when the heavy breathing started, *that* felt a bit more personal. I've already changed my number twice, and now I'm seriously considering changing it *again* for a *third* time. I drive my foot down on the accelerator. I've been holding out hope that, at some point, these salacious newspapers and gossip magazines will lose interest because, surely, they must. I mean, it's only a matter of time before something unfathomably terrible happens somewhere else. *Anywhere* else. Hopefully, sooner rather than later.

It takes a few minutes for my heart rate to recover from the encounter, the remnants of the sweaty palm print clouding my peripheral vision like an insidious fog. Seriously, what the hell is wrong with people? I'm tempted to take the car for a wash or report this encounter to the police, but I don't have time — not with company arriving at six.

What I do have time for, however, is a scenic twenty-minute drive down the Taconic, across the Saw Mill River Parkway, to Yonkers, New York.

Andrea Winter's former residence, here I come.

I don't plan on breaking into her house like I did the last time I rolled through this part of town, though. Despite the heat of my earlier anger still enveloping me, a shiver courses through me as I recall that escapade. It was then that I discovered Marnie's late husband, Mark, had a dirty little secret.

The very thought of Mark Black makes a thick line of perspiration shoot across my hairline, down to the small of my back. I break into a chilled sweat as if I've taken a cold plunge. I try to banish him from my mind. *You can't move forward if you're constantly looking back, Carrie,* I reassure myself. But that's easier said than done when it comes to Mark Black.

He's not someone easily forgotten.

And driving toward Andrea Winter's house is only making it worse.

If only I could leave well enough alone. As I stop at a light in Yonkers, I run a quick search on my phone on Andrea Winter's house. Did Damian purchase and flip Andrea's home? At a minimum, I should be able to see if he's the one who purchased it (and then moved into her ex's development). Except, unfortunately, there's no buyer information for the listing, which only tells me that whoever purchased the home likely paid for it in cash as mortgages are of public record. I quickly run another search — on the deed, this time — but it shows the house was purchased under a trust. All super unhelpful. And also slightly suspicious. Why would the new owner go to such lengths to hide their identity?

Now, I *really* need to confirm that my suspicions about Damian Mankiewicz aren't true. My foot pushes deeper into the gas pedal, propelling me down Andrea Winter's pleasant tree-lined street so I can see for myself.

I pull up in front of her house, my jaw dropping in shock. I think back to the state of dilapidation it was in the last time I was here — with bold *CAUTION* tape draped across the dented door and blowing around the cigarette-stained front lawn.

Except, that's not what I find.

Flickers turn to flames as I find the last thing I was hoping for — a *FOR SALE* sign standing proudly on the greenest lawn I've ever seen. The ground looks like it's coated in a soft blanket of brand-new sod. The house is pristine, not a speck of flaking paint in sight. It's a lovely soft yellow color, unlike the urine-stained exterior that covered it before. Whoever did this must have worked awfully hard to create what can only be described as the perfect shade of buttercup.

A charming bungalow stands in place of the poor excuse for a home where TJ's mother was murdered.

A loud honk jolts me back to attention and I realize I'm stopped in the middle of the street. I wave a quick hand of apology and press my foot to the gas, pulling over to the side of the road even though I don't need to see any more. I've no doubt the inside is even more spectacular than the outside. I bet someone even washed the dirty dishes in the sink, shredded the stack of unpaid bills, and cleaned the blood stains off the stairs.

Was this house renovated and flipped?

My heart is beating unreasonably hard in my chest. So what if Damian Mankiewicz is flipping this house? I mean, he literally told us that's what he does for a living. He flips houses. Why should Andrea Winter's house be different from any other house?

Perhaps because she was murdered in it? Maybe because that would mean he's now associated with two houses that murdered women resided in? One would be more easily dismissed. But TWO?

I'm not great with math, but even I know that would have to be one heck of a ginormous coincidence, like some impossibly ridiculous statistic. As I try to wrap my head around it all, I continue staring at the house with my mouth agape, unable to tear my eyes away.

If it's not a coincidence, it could well mean Damian knows much more about our past than I'm comfortable with, especially when we know practically nothing about him.

I draw a deep breath and wrap my hands tightly around the steering wheel, taking one last look at the house before pulling back onto the road.

My encyclopedia's worth of questions will have to wait. I can't sit here any longer, not with Damian and Marnie showing up for dinner in twenty minutes.

CHAPTER SEVEN

I roll up at my house at 5:55 p.m., having made record time. My chest thrums with fresh panic and I'm finding it increasingly difficult to breathe, my inhales coming in quick gasps. How the hell am I going to pull this off tonight? 'Act normal' seems like a ridiculous hyperbole right about now.

I barely have time to compose myself. With Damian and Marnie showing up in five minutes, I have to figure out a plan.

I toy with the idea of sharing my suspicions with Marnie, but something tells me I shouldn't. Maybe she won't care. Perhaps she'll think I'm trying to ruin her second chance at happiness. Or flat-out refuse to believe what I have to say. The truth is, I have no idea how Marnie will react.

Besides, how can I tell her when I've no idea what's going on myself? There's zero proof that Damian has done anything wrong.

Watching Marnie interact with him this morning, I have no doubt she will *not* want to hear that our new neighbor may have ulterior motives for moving into our development.

And then I wonder: *what would his ulterior motives even be?* It's all just speculation that could mean absolutely nothing. Just a really strange coincidence.

I take a grounding breath. My mind is made up. I'll find out everything there is to find out about Damian Mankiewicz on my own before I let him casually waltz into our lives.

But not before I let him casually waltz into my house. Perhaps inviting him to dinner wasn't the brightest idea, in hindsight. Damian may live next door to me, and we may have shared more than a few drinks today, but I'd say I know my gynecologist better than I know him.

Trust him more, too.

Still, there's nothing better than a few glasses of wine to loosen the mood and get someone talking. My eyes flit to the bottle of Diamonte tequila, displayed on the glass table in our foyer. Truth serum. Maybe this will be easier than I thought. And perhaps there really is nothing to see here other than a devastatingly handsome man who knows his way around a sledgehammer, and has an unconventional method of (not) labeling (most) boxes.

Let's hope I'm right, because I can't begin to process what this could all mean if I'm not.

Thankfully, I don't have time to process anything other than the doorbell heralding the start of our evening.

I tell myself it will all be fine. A night of drinking with my best friend and new neighbor may be just what I need to shake the spiral I'm rapidly barreling toward, even if Damian Mankiewicz is something of a catalyst for it.

I wipe my sweaty palms on the legs of my pants and make my way to the front of the house. I pause at the door, listening to the sound of friendly banter from outside.

It looks like Damian and Marnie have arrived together. Staring through the peephole at them, I'm not going to lie — they do make a handsome couple, especially against the backdrop of a moonlit, star-filled sky.

Great, now I feel like the third wheel for the *second* time today.

I plaster on an easygoing face, one that certainly does not match my inner angst, and swing open the door.

"Hey!" Marnie chirps enthusiastically, handing over a bottle of Pinot Noir that nearly matches her lips. She reaches in for a hug, planting a blood-red kiss on my cheek.

"Long time no see," Damian adds with a wink.

"I'm so glad you both could make it. Come in, come in."

I step aside, letting Damian and Marnie into the house. They've barely made it inside the foyer when Damian observes, "Wow, Carrie. Your house is amazing. I've never seen anything like this." I follow his eyes as they graze across the alabaster walls, up the winding marble stairs, and overhead to the two-hundred-pound crystal chandelier.

I bite my lip at his remark. Now, I won't deny our house is an architectural masterpiece, but if you flip houses for a literal living, surely you've seen it all, right? But judging by Damian's widened eyes and partially agape mouth, he *truly* has never seen anything like this. This makes me wonder if he made up the whole house-flipping career on the fly, not wanting to tell us what he *actually* does for a living, what really brought him here.

But that would be crazy.

I internally roll my eyes. I can't even take a compliment without spiraling.

Damn you, Mark Black.

I try to shake the thoughts of my old neighbor, focusing my attention on my new one. He looks quite handsome this evening in his dark, straight-legged jeans and a fitted khaki tee that brings out specks of amber in his brown eyes. I totally get what Marnie sees in him.

"Bennett, my husband, deserves most of the credit," I explain, the mention of my husband bringing me back to earth so I can tear my eyes from Damian. "He definitely has a flair for interior design. He's an avid art collector." That and more — a high-powered attorney, marathon runner, philanthropist, and loving husband. I'm so freaking lucky, and I know it.

Stop drooling over the new neighbor, I chide myself. I quickly motion for Damian and Marnie to follow me to the kitchen, not so I can show off more of our priceless art and decadent decor, but so I can open this bottle of wine. I could certainly use a hearty glass to loosen the knot in my stomach.

An angry bang and a rapid succession of clangs blast from the front door, stopping us short. Instant panic sets in whenever the doorbell rings like that. I suppose that's a natural reaction, considering. It seems we have a revolving door of life-shattering visitors.

My eyes catch Damian's. Maybe our new neighbor is not Mr. Perfect. Could he have a scorned wife? A jealous girlfriend? A jilted lover?

Damian shrugs, wordlessly conveying that whoever's at the door isn't here to see him.

"Marnie," I ask. "Did you invite anyone else to dinner?"

"What, and get in the way of me . . ." She clears her throat. "I mean *us*, spending the evening getting to know Damian better?" Marnie bats her eyelashes at Damian. It's as if I'm not even in the room. Another round of furious banging overwhelms what would be an exasperated chuckle from me.

Were they home, Bennett and TJ would come in through the garage. Nobody *should* bang on my front door like it's a matter of life or death. With the pit growing in my stomach, I approach the door, feeling as though I'm walking a plank. I press my eye against the peephole.

Lydia Berman?

I recoil, momentarily shocked. What in the hell is *she* doing here?

I haven't spoken to my neighbor in months. Not since she invited me over to show me her daughter Sienna's journal and accuse my stepson of kidnapping and murdering the teenage girls of The Estates. To make matters worse, she never did apologize despite being so very, very wrong about TJ.

And it sure doesn't look like she's come to apologize now. Her lips are pinched in a tight line, her shoulders hunched, and her bony hands are balled into tight, angry fists.

Against my better judgment, I reluctantly open the door. Something tells me she won't stop creating a ruckus until I do.

"Where is *he*?" Lydia seethes before I've had a chance to say a word.

Damian and Marnie appear at my side. Adding to the great first impression I've made with my new neighbor, I now have another neighbor accosting me at the door. That's just great.

"Where is *who*, Lydia?"

"Your stepson, Carrie," she responds mockingly, making my cheeks color.

I've officially had enough of this day. And more than enough of this crazy neighbor. "First of all, Lydia, why would I tell *you*," I bite, "of all people where TJ is, considering how you treated him? Second of all, he's not here."

Lydia glares at me before swiveling her head toward Marnie and Damian. Apparently forgetting what brought her over here in the first place, she huffs, "Who is *that*? Wow, you didn't wait very long, did you, Marnie?"

I let out an audible gasp. Lydia should know better. *No one* talks to Marnie like that and lives to tell about it.

My body tingles with anticipation for a fight. Marnie does her best snipping through gritted teeth. "This is our new neighbor, Lydia. I don't appreciate your insinuations. And—" she pauses a moment for effect — "your presence in our book club is no longer needed." Marnie then plasters on the fakest Stepford-wife smile I've ever seen. "Fucking psychopath," she adds, just loud enough so we all hear her.

Damian gives an awkward wave and a half-smile. "Hey. Just moved in next door. I'm Damian."

"Welcome to The Estates," I mutter under my breath.

Lydia runs her hands over her bobbed hair in a futile attempt to compose herself. "Welcome to the neighborhood," she says before turning to Marnie. "I'm sorry for the misunderstanding, Marnie. I hope you'll reconsider."

Marnie chews on a cuticle, flicking her eyes up to leer at Lydia. "I will most certainly *not* reconsider."

"I realize you're upset right now . . ."

"Oh, just cut the crap, Lydia. We all know you don't even read the books. You're out."

I tried to stifle a cringe. How unfortunate for Lydia. Getting kicked out of book club is like getting blackballed. Lydia should just go ahead and move at this point.

Except, in classic Lydia Berman fashion, she just can't help herself and fires back, "This isn't about you, Marnie. It's about the Winters. *TJ.*" She whirls on Damian, a twisted expression on her face. "And our new neighbor. You should that know you're in the home of a kidnapper. A *murderer.*"

Well, *that* was unexpected.

Marnie grips Damian's arm as if she's about to faint. My jaw drops. *The meddlesome, troublemaking, accusation-throwing . . .*

"Enough, Lydia!" I scream in my neighbor's face. "You have ten seconds to tell me what this is all about."

"You want to know what this is all about?" Lydia stabs a finger at the air between us. "Sienna is missing. And your stepson had something to do with it!"

I feel the color drain from my face, and my mouth goes bone dry.

Holy shit, here we go again.

CHAPTER EIGHT

"*Missing?*" I arch an eyebrow in disbelief. "What do you mean, she's missing?" I feel incredibly nauseous, my vision blurry. It's almost as if I'm watching this play out on a movie screen, like it's happening to someone else. I think about Damian's earlier reassurances — *lightning doesn't strike twice*. He may want to rethink that. It sure feels like lightning has just struck *again*.

Lydia holds up a hand, rattling off a list with her long, bony fingers. "She hasn't been home in two days. She isn't returning my phone calls. Her phone is going straight to voicemail. I reached out to her father, and once he finally got back to me, I found out she wasn't with him. Now here I am."

I regard her skeptically. "Did you call the police?"

"You bet your ass I did."

"So, why are you here, Lydia? What am *I* supposed to do about Sienna not calling you back? Have you checked with her friends? Maybe she just needed a break . . ." *From you*, I restrain myself from adding. I turn to Marnie apologetically, and then back to Lydia. "Mark Black is dead, Lydia. That chapter is over. I'm sure Sienna is fine."

"She hasn't even posted on social media!" Lydia folds her arms across her chest and releases an angry breath.

I raise an unconvinced eyebrow. I hadn't realized Sienna was an influencer. But I do know this girl is a runner.

"Maybe her phone died, Lydia."

"And if it did — if she's *okay* — where is Sienna that she couldn't charge it?"

I don't have an answer for that. A silence settles over us. With the door still ajar, the air inside the room has grown sticky, stagnant. I struggle to find a calming breath.

Seconds, maybe minutes tick by. Finally, Lydia shakes her head, a seething look in her eyes. "It's TJ. He's finally done something to her. I just *know* it."

I narrow my eyes. "What makes you think TJ did something to her, Lydia?"

"I've seen them together, Carrie. I'll tell the police. I'll tell everyone!"

I open my mouth to say something, but Marnie speaks first. "I've seen Sienna with *a lot* of boys, Lydia. Sorry to break it to you, but your daughter has developed quite the reputation here." Marnie rolls her eyes as she says this. She's definitely *not* sorry. And I'm definitely not complaining.

I shoot Marnie a grateful glance. Then I rub my fingers against my forehead, struggling to ward off a Lydia-induced migraine. "You've seen TJ and Sienna together? When? Where?"

"That's not important. What's important is that I saw them together and soon everyone will know the truth about your family!" Spittle flies from Lydia's mouth.

"You're delusional," is all I can manage. What else does one say to a completely deranged woman? I should tell Lydia that Sienna is probably hiding out again, just like she did before. Given her track record, that's the most logical explanation. There's no reason Sienna should hide out again in the absence of the neighborhood serial killer, though.

But a voice in my head starts to scream.

Unless she's not hiding out.

Unless something bad has actually happened to her.

The Bermans have made their fair share of enemies around here over the past few months. The mother and daughter duo have been unnecessarily vocal since Sienna came out of hiding, making wild claims that the police only got it half right. *Yes, Mark Black was having affairs with underaged girls. But no, Mark Black did not kill them.* I assumed Sienna was half crazy like her mother, but now, I can't help but question: what if she's not? What does Sienna know? And is someone trying to silence her?

I push those thoughts further to the back of my mind. The police spent more money and manpower investigating the homicides in The Estates than they did in the federal Whitewater controversy. They couldn't have gotten it wrong.

That inner voice whispers again: *could they?*

No, it's not possible.

It's also not possible to win an argument with Lydia. You can't argue with crazy. I've watched this woman's madness play out before. I don't care to witness it again, especially not with our hot new neighbor looking on.

So, I do the only thing I can think of — I slam the door in Lydia Berman's face.

Crass? Perhaps. But I can't just stand here letting her hurl unfounded accusations at me. I know my stepson much better now than I did when he first showed up on our doorstep. He's out there trying to build a future for himself, not kidnapping the daughter of his deranged neighbor.

"So, now that we have that settled," I chirp as I turn back to Marnie and Damian, but my cheeks burn with embarrassment. *Welcome to the neighborhood, Damian.*

"Well, that was intense," Damian says, cutting through the stunned silence that has settled over the room like a thick cloud of smoke.

"I take it you had not met the Bermans yet." My voice quivers as I say this. In a perfect world, none of us would have met the Bermans yet, or *ever*. Then again, you can't always pick your neighbors.

"Oh, don't worry about her," Marnie says casually. "She's batshit crazy. Sienna has just run away again. If I had a mother like Lydia, I'd disappear, too." She turns to me. "You can breathe now, Carrie."

I exhale audibly. "Yeah, that tracks. She's certifiably insane," I agree. Though I believe this to be true, it doesn't make me feel better about the situation. Who the hell wants an unhinged woman with your family in her vendetta-fueled sights? An unhinged woman who lives two doors down, no less. The only thing worse would be living directly next door. *My condolences, Damian.*

"Well, I'll be sure to keep my distance, then," Damian chimes in. His face is more than a few shades lighter than when we met this morning. The poor guy looks like he's just seen the ghosts of Christmas past, present, and future all rolled into one.

I nod voraciously in approval. "If you know what's best, you won't go near her with a ten-foot pole." If he knew what was best, he might've thought twice about moving here.

"Wine. We need wine," I mumble, hobbling on wobbly legs to the kitchen. I pick up the bottle and it quivers in my grasp. I can just barely make out the footsteps of Marnie and Damian following me over my heart thumping into my head.

A hand on my shoulder makes me jump. "Ignore her, Carrie," Marnie says, clearly sensing how unsettled I am from the encounter.

"I just . . . I don't know why she has it in for TJ."

Marnie's face scrunches into a scowl at the mention of TJ. She shrugs and takes the bottle from me. My knuckles are white, and my fingers numb from clutching it so tightly. She places the bottle on the countertop and uncorks it with a satisfying pop. With trembling fingers, I grab three glasses from the cabinet and place them on the island in front of her. My mouth waters as she fills each glass. I've never needed a drink so badly in all my life.

"Cheers," Damian says, holding out his glass.

I pull mine, already half emptied, from my lips. I swallow down the wine, and we clink glasses. "Cheers." I gulp down the rest of my glass, and the warm, crimson liquid floods my veins with a momentary sense of relief.

Only momentary.

No sooner have I begun to relax than the hammering on the door resumes.

I freeze in place, glass suspended in midair.

"Jeez," Marnie laments, the corners of her lips dipping. "You're going to need to get a restraining order against that bitch. She's a real psychopath." She's not wrong about that. What are the chances of having two psychopaths in the same development — assuming Sienna Berman isn't a psychopath like her mother, because that would make three. There must be something in the water here.

"I need to call Bennett," I mutter, fumbling around the island in search of my phone, but I can't find it. It doesn't help that my hands are shuddering, as if I've just recently given up caffeine.

Bang. Bang. Bang.

"Let me talk to her," Damian offers. Marnie and I stare at him as if we're in the presence of yet another lunatic. One does not simply talk to Lydia Berman willingly.

"Look," Damian presses, "there's obviously a history between you all. I'm new here. She doesn't have any reason to question my motives. I'll be gentle with her."

Before I can argue in favor of simply ignoring her, Damian disappears from the room as quickly as he appeared in our lives this morning.

"Wow, he's quite charming, isn't he?" Marnie's nut-brown eyes are wide, staring into the space where Damian just stood.

"Seriously, Marnie? I'm getting harassed, and the first thought that comes to mind is how charming our new neighbor is?"

"Jeez, Carrie. I just meant he would probably be able to talk Lydia off the ledge, is all. Get her to leave you alone." She sniffs at me. "I didn't know you'd get all twisted in a knot about it."

"I'm sorry, I . . . I completely misread that." I feel bad about upsetting Marnie, but there's little else I could think. "You can't go to someone's door and accuse them of something that isn't true over and over again."

"Unless it *is* true."

Marnie says this so quietly, I almost miss it. *Almost.*

I round on Marnie. "What's that supposed to mean?" I eye my supposed best friend in disbelief. Maybe I didn't misread anything at all. "Seriously, what is your problem with TJ?"

"Nothing, nothing . . . I just meant *she* obviously thinks it's true."

My shoulders relax because even if she hates him, surely Marnie couldn't *actually* believe TJ had something to do with Sienna's umpteenth disappearance.

"What's gotten into you, Carrie?" Marnie folds her arms across her chest. "It's like you can't even have a rational conversation."

I don't have a chance to defend myself or respond to her observation. What Marnie thinks or doesn't think is the least of my problems right now as Damian charges into the kitchen and announces, "It's not Lydia. It's the police."

CHAPTER NINE

"That bitch." Marnie slams her glass on the island. Wine splashes over the sides, pooling on the marble like drops of blood, but the glass doesn't shatter. The last time the police showed up at the door with news of Sienna Berman's disappearance, Marnie shattered a wine glass all over our bamboo floor, and cut up her hand.

My eyes flit to the sleek, black clock on the stark white kitchen wall — 7 p.m. Bennett called over two hours ago. He should hopefully be home any minute. I consider leaving the police waiting at the door — let the lawyer deal with the law.

"Carrie?" Damian's unnervingly calm voice rips me from my scheming. My eyes meet his. I open my mouth to say something, but no words come out. It's as if I've forgotten how to speak.

"Do you want me to see if they can come back later? I could tell them you're in the shower or something."

Marnie scoffs. "In the shower, Damian? Why would she be in the shower with company over? They'll think she's just had sex. With *you*." Marnie points an accusing finger at him. "We wouldn't want *that*, would we?" There's a palpable edge to her voice, sliced through by more banging coming from the door.

I round on Marnie, stunned. "*That's* what you're worried about, Marnie?" I bet Marnie wouldn't mind if the police thought he was having sex with *her*, though.

"I wouldn't want this to get back to Bennett, Carrie. Would you?"

"You wouldn't want *what* to get back to Bennett? I didn't *do* anything." I slap a hand against my forehead — *duh*.

Marnie's eyes drag up and down my body, looking unconvinced.

"You two literally came over here together! We haven't even been alone!"

She raises a disbelieving eyebrow.

I've had enough of this conversation. Talking to Marnie when she's set her mind to something is like talking to a wall. Come to think of it, a wall would likely be more receptive to reason.

Damian interjects, "Ladies, whether the police think I'm having sex with either of you or your dog right now doesn't matter—"

"We don't have a dog."

"You're missing the point. The police are not leaving until we tell them something. And just for the record, I don't like dogs. I'm a cat person."

"Oh, I *love* cats, Damian," Marnie purrs.

My head whips around, and I stare at Marnie. It's the first I've ever heard of this. It's an interesting development, considering she's freaking allergic to cats.

"Cats, Marnie? Really?" This entire conversation is getting out of hand.

Marnie clenches her jaw, her lips stretching into a thin, angry line. Though she doesn't say anything, there's a warning in her eyes. Like, *try me*.

"Whatever, fine!" I throw my hands in the air and drag myself to the door, more than ready to remove myself from this circus in my kitchen. The last time I had a night like this, Marnie wound up grinding against my husband before intimating she might expose my secrets to him. In the grand scheme of things, my secret — initiating a 'chance' meeting with Bennett — doesn't seem like the most significant issue we've had to deal with. But it certainly did at the time. I wasn't sure how Bennett would take to finding out we weren't quite the fairytale he'd thought us to be. Thankfully, there are no secrets now.

None that I'm keeping.

My supporting cast of morally gray characters, on the other hand . . . debatable, at best. I flash to the ominous box inside Damian's house, to Lydia Berman's accusations.

"I'm coming," I yell, the words strangled in my throat.

I press my eye against the peephole. A man's balding head glistens under the porch light. My eyes find the gun, just barely hidden by the paunch of his stomach. I recoil from the door, feeling sick to my stomach.

Seriously, was there no one else?

I take a deep, calming breath. It does absolutely nothing.

I twist the lock and open the door with trembling hands.

"Mrs. Winter, long time no see."

"Detective Johnson," I reply through clenched teeth, barely opening my mouth. I'm going to need an ice pack after this conversation. My jaw already hurts.

"Where's your partner?" I ask, looking around the front porch for Detective Young. It feels like yesterday that the duo first showed up at our door with news of Sofia Swanson's disappearance. The duo that had tried to crucify TJ without any real evidence.

"She quit the force," he responds casually. "You know what they say: if you can't take the heat . . ."

I regard him quizzically.

"The whole investigation in your development really messed her up. Last I heard, she took a job at Rikers Island as a prison guard."

So, apparently, Rikers Island is less troublesome than the multi-million-dollar Estates. Let's hope *that* juicy tidbit doesn't make its way into the welcome packet.

"May I come in?"

We've done this dance before. Whether I say yes *or* no, Detective Johnson will keep coming back. Or he'll camp out across the street, watching our every move. Apparently, all very legal, Bennett explained back when TJ was public enemy number one.

No, you cannot come in, not without a warrant, I screech internally. Or, at the very least, not until Bennett gets home. With TJ. *Oh God.* Instead, I croak, "What can I help you with, Detective?"

"I'm sure you've heard Sienna Berman has been reported missing." He raises a thick eyebrow, waiting for my response.

"Yes, just like I'm sure *you've* heard, Lydia Berman came over here throwing around wild accusations about my stepson." I shiver despite the warmth of the stagnant nighttime air. A bolt of lightning shoots through the sky. It looks like a storm is rolling in.

Detective Johnson's focus remains firmly fixed on me. "Where is TJ, Mrs. Winter?"

My eyes bulge. They feel like they're about to pop from their sockets. "This is a joke, right?" I look around the lawn for a camera crew, but all I'm met with is impossibly green grass.

"Lydia Berman seems to think TJ is behind her daughter's disappearance."

"Based on what, Detective?"

"Look, I'm just doing my job, Mrs. Winter. I have to take her allegation seriously. Investigate it. I just want to speak with him, that's all."

I shake my head, annoyed. This isn't Detective Johnson's first rodeo. Surely he knows by now that the woman is insane, and that Sienna has a history of hiding out. Someone should get this guy a 'World's Greatest Detective' mug. But I'm not volunteering.

"I understand that you're doing your job, but you do realize she's run away before, *right?*" I cross my arms over my chest. "This girl is the definition of a flight risk! So why are you treating this time as something different?"

"We are exploring all possibilities, Mrs. Winter — your stepson being one of them."

"Fine," I huff. "Give me a moment." I turn to open the top drawer of the mirrored accent table adjacent to the door. I pull out a business card and hand it to Detective Johnson.

"Call my husband," I say before closing the door.

In other words, call my lawyer. If Sienna doesn't surface soon, I sense TJ is going to need one.

My eyes flick down to the entryway table. Well, what do you know? My phone has been sitting there all along. I pick it up and hit the speed dial for Bennett's cell phone.

Every nerve ending in my body screams at me to call him — *warn* him — before Detective Johnson gets to him.

CHAPTER TEN

Bennett's phone goes straight to voicemail. I collapse against the door, my heart thrumming like a snare drum in my chest. I drop my head between my knees to ward off the dizziness wrapping itself around me.

Surely, TJ had nothing to do with this. Surely, Sienna Berman is fine. Because this can't be happening again — I still can't believe it happened the first time. It feels like it was all just a bad dream. *I wish.*

"So, um . . ." Damian's husky voice breaks me from my panicked thoughts. "I should get going." He looks down at his feet, hands shoved deep in his pockets.

I try to catch his gaze, but the once gregarious Damian seems to be avoiding eye contact at all costs. I can't exactly blame him. This is *a lot* for his first night here — the police, a missing girl, and a neighbor who's already Googling wedding venues. But what did he expect? The Estates has become notorious for these types of things.

"Please don't leave on account of this. I'm sure it's all just a big misunderstanding." Like the last time. Well, at least the TJ part. The dead and missing girls — *that* was no misunderstanding. I laugh to ease the tension, but it comes out sounding strained.

"I don't want to be in the way," he responds. "You obviously need to talk to your husband and son."

"*Step*son," Marnie interjects with a razor edge to her voice. I try to push down the bile rising in my throat. No surprise there, though I would have hoped she would temper herself in front of our guest.

This impromptu dinner party is turning out to be a bona fide disaster.

My cheeks color. "Can I at least send you home with some food?" I motion desperately toward the kitchen where my made-from-scratch, home-cooked meal simmers untouched in the slow cooker.

"I . . . uh . . . I should go. Rain check?" If there were an award for the worst first impression to be made, I've earned it twice over. Damian can't get out of here fast enough.

And apparently, neither can my best friend.

"Would you mind walking me home, Damian?"

"You're leaving *too*?" I narrow my eyes at her.

"I have an early morning." *No, she doesn't.* "And to be honest, I don't want to be here when TJ gets home." Marnie wraps her arms around her body as if suddenly chilled. She casts a simpering look at Damian as though she's actually afraid. As though TJ poses a *threat* to her. I scoff inwardly — that's rich. Maybe she *should* try to stretch her fifteen minutes of fame until it breaks. Marnie Black is one heck of an actress.

"Thank you for being so warm and welcoming, Carrie. It's been great getting to know you today."

"You too, Damian." I force a weak smile.

At least one of my about-to-get-the-hell-out-of-Dodge guests is kind.

I wait for my so-called best friend to apologize, but it never comes. Not surprising. Marnie Black doesn't apologize for anything or to anyone.

I bet she would kick me out of book club right now, if I hadn't already quit.

I awkwardly move aside so she can storm out the door without so much as a *goodbye* or *thanks for having me*. Damian follows her, surely relieved to be out of the home of a suspected kidnapper. He shoots me a sympathetic albeit nervous glance before departing like a sheep to the slaughter.

Don't let the door hit you in the ass on the way out.

What an awful turn this day has taken, and I struggle to comprehend how we even *got* here.

I flash back to when I first moved in with Bennett, a happier time when I'd open the door on the first ring without even checking who was on the other side. According to The Estates' *Dateline* episode, 'Back from the Black,' our brochure used to boast that the community was *so* safe that neighbors left their front doors unlocked. Crime was unheard of in this neighborhood. And as for even a whiff of foul play — wholly inconceivable. It's so freaking ironic I almost want to laugh. Long gone is the feeling that nothing can touch us here.

If I could, I'd permanently cement the front door shut and slap a great big *Caution: Attack Dog* sign on it to keep the evil forces at bay. Or move. I honestly don't know what's keeping us here anymore.

The click of the garage rips me from my thoughts, which are racing faster than I can keep up with.

It's about freaking time.

I fill with a mixture of relief and irritation. I could have avoided this debacle of an evening had Bennett invited me to dinner with him and his son in the first place. Or, better yet, he could have just come home after work like he was supposed to and eaten the perfectly amazing meal I'd slaved over. The meal that is probably congealing in the Crock-Pot, the liquid now a gelatinous mess, thanks to our unexpected visitors this evening.

"Carrie?" Bennett's voice travels loudly through the foyer as father and son make their way inside from the garage. I can practically smell the beer on his breath from my post at the front door. Jealousy tugs at my insides as the easygoing conversation and light laughter grow closer. They must not have noticed the police vehicle parked outside. They wouldn't be in nearly as festive of a mood if they had.

"I'm by the front door," I answer through gritted teeth, trying to temper the edge in my voice.

"There you are," Bennett says, a wide grin spreading across his face, but the slur to his words isn't very endearing. "I missed you today. Didn't we miss her, TJ?"

"Sure did," TJ agrees. "You should have met us at McAlister's."

I fold my arms defensively across my chest. "The invitation must have gotten lost in the mail."

"You're so cute," Bennett says, tapping a finger on the tip of my nose before wrapping me in an embrace.

I gently push him away. "And *you're* so buzzed. You need to sober up. Both of you. Who drove home, anyway?"

Bennett and TJ glance at one another and snicker, but neither says a word. It's as if they're in on some inside joke I'm not privy to.

I don't suppose that matters right now.

"Detective Johnson came by." I change the subject, my expression stone-cold sober. "He was looking for TJ."

The smile slides off TJ's face. "Looking for *me?* Why would he be looking for *me?*"

"Sienna Berman is missing."

"*Again?*" Bennett shouts, a large vein pulsing on the side of his neck. "Is this some sort of sick joke?"

"That's what I said. But no, Lydia Berman came by here earlier as well. She's convinced TJ has done something to her daughter."

"Why in the world would I do something to her daughter?"

"Again, that's what I said. Sienna probably ran away again. But Lydia won't listen to reason. She's one stop away from the loony bin."

"This is just great," Bennett huffs. "TJ wasn't responsible the first time Sienna disappeared, but this time he is? I can't believe I pay fifty thousand a year in taxes to deal with this bullshit."

As if on cue, the doorbell rings.

CHAPTER ELEVEN

"I'll leave you to it," I say, unwilling to see Detective Johnson for the second time this evening. Once was plenty. None would have been ideal.

I hurry out of view as my husband opens the door and greets the detective — *greet*, of course, being used in the absolute loosest sense of the word. Bennett's lips are turned down, his expression hard. TJ is shaking as if he's gotten an electric shock.

Damn you, Lydia Berman.

Damn you, Mark Black.

The knot tightens in my stomach. Voices carry through the foyer, informing me of what I already know — Sienna Berman is missing, and her mother believes TJ is the one responsible for her disappearance.

Normally, I would loiter around the corner and eavesdrop, but there's something I need to do. Besides, I already know Detective Johnson is here on account of the rantings of a crazy lady and a (hopefully) repeat runaway.

I hurry upstairs to the bedroom, gripping my phone tightly. I may not own pricey binoculars, but I am just as good an armchair detective as Marnie.

And I'm going to prove it.

I tap away on my iPhone, typing 'Damian Mankiewicz' into the search bar. He's living in the Lockwood house and has potentially flipped Andrea Winter's house. And now Sienna is missing again. It can't be a coincidence.

The phone instantly fills with hits. My finger flies across the screen as I search for *the* Damian Mankiewicz, who lives in the house next door to mine. I breathe a loud sigh of relief as I find a link that reads, *'Damian Mankiewicz, Redeveloper.'* That must be a fancy term for a house flipper. So he *was* telling the truth. That still doesn't explain how he wound up *here* after flipping Andrea Winter's house, but at least it's something I can work with. A balm for my frazzled mind.

Except . . .

When I search for Damian's profile on the website, there are no pictures of him on there. Not a single one. Damian Mankiewicz is possibly the sexiest man I've ever met in person (with the exception of Bennett). Surely that would help drum up business. If I were him, I'd have billboards erected all over town. At the very least, a picture of himself should appear on his "about" page.

It doesn't make sense.

My mind races as I try to figure out what to do. Where to look.

I log on to Facebook, typing Damian's name into the search bar, my breath hitching in my chest. I tighten my grasp around the phone, hands quivering so badly that I'm afraid I might drop it. Things are only getting worse. Not only is there *no* picture on Facebook, there's not one Damian Mankiewicz. Nothing.

It's almost as if he doesn't exist.

My heart is beating so hard, I can see it through my shirt. It feels like it might explode in my chest.

What the hell?

I skip over to LinkedIn, and my fingers tremble as I type in his name. Everyone with a business has an account on LinkedIn. Don't they?

Oh God.

Apparently, everyone *except* Damian Mankiewicz.

Every cell in my body is screaming that our new neighbor isn't who he says he is.

"Carrie?"

My phone flies from my fingers like it's been set on fire. I lift a trembling hand to my chest. My heart is beating wildly, and I sense it's not from Bennett appearing out of nowhere and scaring the crap out of me.

It's what I found, or rather, what I *didn't* find, that has me so on edge.

"What did he say?" I ask, perching on the edge of the bed. Damian Mankiewicz and his ghost protocol will have to wait. For now.

Bennett walks over to the bed and sinks down beside me. He loosens his tie and runs his hands through his hair. His shoulders slump, defeated. His anxiety is palpable, contagious, and I find myself riding a fresh wave of panic.

"I'm filing a restraining order against Lydia Berman."

I exhale the breath I've been holding tightly. "Better late than never," I say, rubbing a hand across Bennett's back.

"But . . ."

"But what?"

"The police are taking Lydia's accusations seriously. It's only a matter of time before Detective Johnson comes back with a warrant to search our house, our cars, and — oh, my God — my *office.*"

"Your office?"

"I told you, everyone really took to TJ. They offered him a position interning. He starts tomorrow."

"What about college?" I interject. "He has classes."

"Switched him to online courses last night, after you'd fallen asleep."

I don't bother correcting him. That shimmer of pride clouds over, replaced by a look of disquiet. "This is really bad, Carrie. I'm afraid there is nothing I can do to stop Detective Johnson from flipping our lives upside down again."

"Based on the rantings of a crazy lady?"

"You said Lydia claimed she *saw* TJ with Sienna, right?"

I nod, though still not understanding how *anyone* would trust *anything* Lydia Berman has to say.

"Well, that could be enough for them to finagle a warrant. She's so convinced TJ has done something, I wouldn't put it past her to lie about what she supposedly saw."

For the briefest of moments, I allow myself to consider the possibility that Lydia *did* see TJ with her daughter, that she's *not* making it up. I shake my head as if to toss the thoughts from my mind. "I have the absolute worst case of déjà vu ever. Do you think Sienna's run away again? Or . . ." I can't finish the thought out loud.

"Yes. No. *Probably?*" Bennett stammers and shrugs. "I have no idea if she's run away again, or if something has happened to her. Either way, I can't believe TJ would do something to her. He's my blood."

It shouldn't hurt, but I feel the sting — the exclusion — nonetheless. TJ may not be *my* blood, but I don't want to believe it either.

"Well, what did TJ tell you?" I ask, goosebumps pricking my skin. All I can picture is Lydia Berman's accusatory finger stabbing the air between us. "And the *police?*" I choke on the word as if it's poison. It may very well be for our family.

"TJ said he hasn't spoken to Sienna Berman, let alone done anything to her. He said he avoids the Bermans like the plague."

I take my husband's hand in mine, running my thumb soothingly across his knuckles. "Then we have nothing to worry about." I try to look and sound confident, though I can't help but chew on my lip.

Assuming, like last time, my stepson is telling the truth.

CHAPTER TWELVE

When the alarm goes off at 6 a.m., I pretend not to hear it, instead trying to cling to the sleep that evaded me. I tried everything to settle down — warm milk, melatonin, guided meditation. I even counted non-existent sheep, for goodness' sake. But I was too restless, flopping around like a fish out of water, my mind frantically turning over the eerily familiar events of last night. I had naively believed the worst was behind us.

Yet trouble seems to find us irresistible.

Bennett doesn't attempt to rouse me. He creeps around the room quietly like an intruder, readying himself for another day at the office with his son. In the aftermath of last night's intense conversation, I've thought all night about what TJ interning for his father will mean. For our family dynamic. For the missing-person investigation. Despite my jealousy that TJ will be spending even more time with his father than I will, I would still be bursting with pride if there weren't this giant Sienna-shaped cloud hanging over our heads.

I'm sure Bennett isn't too keen to talk, not with all the uncertainties choking the air like smog. In the six months I've known Bennett's son, he's been at the center of not one but *two* police investigations. That's two more than the average law-abiding citizen.

My heart squeezes the more I think of TJ. I need to talk to him one-on-one. I want to look my stepson in the eye to see if he is telling the truth about having no contact with Sienna Berman, as he told his father and the police. TJ has a killer poker face, yes, but I am confident I can read him better than when he first showed up at our door. I'd like to believe I'd know if he were lying.

But that challenge will have to wait.

I wait patiently in bed until the garage emits a series of satisfying clicks. The hum of Bennett's Porsche trails him and my stepson down the street as they move farther away from the house. And then there is nothing — just silence. I've never been so grateful for quiet.

I tug my phone from the charger and press my thumb against its side, resurrecting it. I crack my neck and take a deep breath. I am so *not* looking forward to this. *She* should be calling first.

"Hello?"

"Hey, Marnie," I say. "Are you home?"

"Where else would I be?"

The edge to her voice is palpable. She definitely sounds like she's pissed at me. I was just trying to feed her and our new neighbor, for crying out loud. How was I to know dinner would be served with a side of Lydia Berman and Detective Johnson? I struggle to suppress an exasperated sigh. It's going to be a long day.

Instead, I roll my eyes and grit my teeth. "I'm sorry about last night." I'm most definitely not.

"It was *very* uncomfortable," Marnie responds. "Here I am, trying to welcome Damian to the neighborhood, and then . . ."

How is any of this my *fault?* I'd love to scream into the phone before throwing it across the room dramatically. But I can't afford to make her even more upset. Not when I need her help.

"Listen," I interrupt, swallowing down the anger building inside me, along with what's left of my pride. I have to keep

Marnie on my side. No matter what. "I have an idea, a way to prove TJ had nothing to do with Sienna's disappearance. We can end this nonsense once and for all." Hearing no protest on the other line, the words begin to fly out of me. "Maybe when this is all said and done, we even launch a petition to force Lydia Berman to sell her house and leave The Estates. I'm sure we can find some bylaws that she's violated. I mean, have you seen her mailbox? It's covered in bird poop. And I'm pretty sure one of her shutters has been missing since 2023. Plus, I know for a fact that Lydia let Sienna drive their golf cart *before* she turned sixteen. That's quite a laundry list of violations, wouldn't you say?" I'm talking so fast, my words tumble over one another. What I'm saying sounds ridiculous, even to my own ears, but *this* is just the sort of shit that Marnie lives for.

To prove my point, her voice softens subtly as if she's just enjoyed a steaming mug of hot tea with honey. "I'm well aware of the golf cart, Carrie. Amanda reported it."

"Amanda *who?*"

"You know, the one all over Nextdoor who complains about *everything*. Always trying to stir the pot. Anyway, what's your point?"

I draw a deep breath, trying to calm the fizzle in my veins. "Right. So, according to TJ, he's never spoken to Sienna Berman."

"Well, according to Lydia Berman, he abducted her."

"True, but . . . Either one of them is lying, or the other is very misinformed. How far does security footage go back?"

"Thirty days, and then it automatically deletes."

"Okay, so if TJ did have something to do with her disappearance — which, for the record, I don't believe he did — we should expect to see him somewhere on the video footage having some sort of contact with Sienna Berman, right? Maybe in or near the clubhouse?"

There's a brief pause before Marnie ventures, "Unless they met outside The Estates."

I hadn't thought of that. "Well, there's no way to prove or disprove that unless we can gather CCTV footage from all around Armonk and the surrounding areas." *Which the police are probably doing as we speak.* "But we can at least check *your* video footage, don't you think?"

"Sure, Carrie, whatever you want."

I'm not sensing Marnie shares my enthusiasm for this brilliant idea. In fact, I don't think she could sound any *less* enthusiastic. I nonetheless press on undeterred. "So, can I come over? Can we look through the footage together?" I'd much rather look through the footage alone, but pigs would sooner fly before Marnie would hand that over to me.

If there's something incriminating to be found, you can be damn sure she's the one who wants to find it.

CHAPTER THIRTEEN

Twenty minutes later, I'm freshly showered and standing on Marnie's doorstep. I've already rang the bell three times, but she hasn't answered. She must be even more worked up over last night than I thought.

I press my face against the rectangular glass, but I don't see any movement inside — not a light on, not a shadow. Nothing. Strange, since I told her twenty minutes ago that I was coming over.

My eyes flick to her bay-window curtains. When she's not in her bedroom, you can find Marnie on the couch perched beneath the large bay window, looking out on the development with a cup of tea (glass of wine) in hand. But the curtains are tightly drawn and deathly still.

Marnie is nowhere to be found.

A few loud knocks, and worry starts to thrum deep in my chest. First Sienna Berman, and now this . . .

No, no, no, I chide myself inwardly. *Sienna Berman ran away. Nothing has happened to her.*

Carrie, meet spiral.

"Boo!"

I whip around, my hands flailing through the air as I prepare to fend off an attack. Marnie, who's appeared out of freaking nowhere, starts howling, clutching her side. It takes a minute to register what's happening. A joke. A fucking joke. I shouldn't be surprised. This isn't the first time Marnie's pulled a shenanigan like this. If scaring the living daylights out of me were an Olympic sport, she'd be all in.

"What the *hell?*" I manage, struggling to catch my breath. I want to scream. I want to cry. I want to scream, cry, curl up in a ball, and roll away in embarrassment that I let her scare me like this *again*.

The first time, when there really was a killer on the loose, Marnie thought it would be amusing to jump out from behind my front door and startle me as I opened it. She's lucky I didn't grab an umbrella and whack her over the head. This time, however, it somehow feels worse.

"Just trying to lighten the mood," Marnie chirps. "I think I was a little hard on you."

"So you thought sending me into cardiac arrest was the best way to say I'm sorry?" *How about flowers? Chocolates? A bouquet of balloons?* If my heart weren't so busy rattling against my ribcage, I would round on her. "Where have you been? I thought something happened to you!"

Marnie makes a face, pursing her lips and lifting a brow, as if I'm being dramatic. "I ran over to Crumbl to pick up your favorite cookies." She pulls out the unmistakable pink box from behind her back. "Surprise! Death by chocolate," she adds with a giggle and a wink.

I blink owlishly at her choice of words. *More like death by crazy neighbors.*

Once my heart rate has returned to normal, I thank Marnie for the cookies and step aside so she can let me into the house. In retrospect, I should have grabbed her spare key from under the potted plant and let myself in. You'd think after what happened here, she'd be a little more cautious.

But what can I say? We're creatures of habit. And we know each other all too well.

Like the fact that the classic milk chocolate cookie, which I'm now holding an entire box of, is my absolute favorite. Well, not the entire box. I'm already licking crumbs off my fingers before we've made it to the kitchen. It is a welcome, short-lived distraction from what I've come here to do, which is hopefully to find *no* evidence linking my stepson to the missing girl.

"Do you want a drink?" Marnie asks, opening the fridge to retrieve a bottle of chilled wine.

"Marnie, it's, like, eight in the morning."

"You should," she insists, pouring us both a generous glass. "I think you're gonna need it."

I suddenly find myself rooted in place.

Marnie carries the drinks to the kitchen table and pulls out a chair. "Come here, you're gonna want to sit down, Carrie."

Why won't she just spit it out already? She's giving me more anxiety than Damian's *DO NOT OPEN* box that I can't stop thinking about opening.

Marnie takes a seat across from me. She folds her hands under her chin, holding my gaze but not saying a word.

"What is it?" I ask, moments away from a full-blown panic attack. Someone is going to need to call me an ambulance if she doesn't say something soon.

It would appear Marnie's not planning on saying anything any time soon, and I may be imagining things, but it almost seems like she is enjoying this. It's the way she's watching me — eyes wide, a slight curl to her lips. My hand instinctively reaches for the stem of the wine glass, eager for something to grip. Dear God, does she want me to beg? Marnie pulls her phone from her pocket and slides it across the table slowly. And then, after what feels like an eternity of her sharp, blood-red nail hovering over the device, she finally taps the screen.

Every muscle in my body tenses as video footage fills the frame. It's from outside the clubhouse, date stamped two days ago. The video is crystal clear thanks to the brand-new, high-definition cameras the HOA splurged on after the previous cameras were smashed to smithereens.

The benefit, or issue, with the picture-perfect images on the screen, is that there's no mistaking what or *whom* you're looking at. There's not the usual grainy footage where it's difficult to distinguish a human being from a bobcat.

I know who I'm looking at, and sure as shit, TJ is outside the clubhouse, deep in conversation with the person he supposedly never speaks to. Evidently, avoiding the plague is a euphemism for facing it head-on.

At one point, Sienna tries to turn and walk away, but TJ grabs her forcefully by the shoulder and pulls her back. TJ seems to look straight at the camera, eyes crazed, mouth twisted. Then Sienna storms off, and TJ follows until they've both disappeared from the frame.

And I'm left wondering what happened to Sienna after that, as will anyone who watches this video.

Numbness suffuses my senses.

"Can I get you a refill?" Marnie's clipped voice cuts through my stupor.

I'm not sure how long I've been staring at the screen, but I can't seem to pull my gaze away. I nod without looking up at her, my eyes transfixed on the spot where my stepson and the missing girl were just moments before.

Marine places a second glass of wine on the table before me. I drain it in a single, desperate gulp.

"Is there anything else?" I ask. "Or is this it?"

"Well . . ." She pauses, drawing a deep breath. "There's also a video of Sienna slapping TJ across the face."

"Oh my God. There *is?*" The room spins as though I'm on a roller coaster, and my stomach plummets to my feet. My imagination fails me when I try to conjure up what my stepson could have possibly said to make Sienna slap him across the face.

"Well, not that I've seen yet," Marnie says, interrupting my third spiral of the still very early day. "But there *could* be. This is all I've found *so far.*"

It takes every last ounce of willpower not to wrap my hands around Marnie's neck and squeeze the life out of her. Toying with me like a cat that's caught a helpless baby bird is just cruel.

Although she was joking (if you could call it *that*), the reality is that there may truly be more.

And if there's additional footage of TJ and Sienna, Marnie has it. Thankfully, she's the only one with access to it. Back when she was Vice President of the HOA, Marnie was assigned the job of monitoring the tapes, a job she has held on to tighter than a pair of Spanx. Unless she offers up the footage, it's unlikely anyone will think to ask for it.

Except maybe the police. But there's a good chance that the police may not be aware that the security cameras are now operational. Last time they were here, all that was left of the cameras were shards of broken glass and scattered pieces of battered metal. Detective Johnson doesn't exactly run an airtight investigation, either.

My eyes snap to Marnie's. I can't quite read the expression on her face — an inscrutable, unsettling mix between empathy and triumph.

"It's not possible. TJ wouldn't do something like this," I state, but the words sound empty. I'm not sure who I'm trying to convince — Marnie or myself.

Videos don't lie, even if people do. Still, just because he was arguing with Sienna doesn't mean he did something to her.

"Carrie . . ." Marnie places a cool hand on mine. "I know you don't want to believe your stepson could hurt someone, but maybe it's time you admit to yourself that TJ is not who you think he is."

The realization slices through me like a cold gust — I *don't* know who my stepson is. I only know that I need to speak with him. Evidently, two days ago.

"Marnie, please. I'm begging you . . . you can't show this to anyone."

Marnie rolls her eyes and flips her long, dark hair over a shoulder. "You're so dramatic, Carrie. The police don't even know this footage exists. And do you honestly think I give a shit about Sienna Berman? She slept with my husband, remember?"

When she puts it that way . . . True, but still. It really feels like we *should* give a shit about Sienna Berman. If, in fact, something terrible has happened to her.

"I'm sorry, Marnie." I apologize, for lack of anything better to say.

Her face momentarily softens. "It hasn't been easy, Carrie. Having to watch Sienna living her best life when she ruined mine."

It's better to be kind than right, I remind myself. I don't point out the fact that it's actually *Mark* who ruined her life. Sienna was just a child. Instead, I say, "I know it must have been hard losing your husband." In every sense of the word. Even the memories of their marriage are completely tainted, down to the diamond pendant ghosting Marnie's collarbones.

"Oh, I don't miss Mark at all," Marnie clips, her expression darkening. "But I do miss having *someone*. It's no fun being alone. And now, I've been given the chance to try again with someone new. Someone who actually cares about me. As long as TJ stays out of my way, we're all good. And I'm sure there'll be ample opportunity for you to repay the favor." Marnie winks and my blood turns cold.

"So you'll delete the footage, then?"

"Sorry, no can do."

"But you said you don't care."

"I *don't* care, Carrie, but I can't delete this for another twenty-eight days. According to Section 12A of the HOA guidelines, all video footage must be retained for twenty-eight days before deleting." She shrugs. "Rules are rules."

The sinews in my jaw tighten reflexively. This isn't the Constitution we're talking about here. "You won't show anyone, will you?" I finally manage to grind out. "I'll talk to TJ to figure out what this is all about—"

Marnie cuts me off. "Look, all I know is that according to Lydia, Sienna hasn't been heard from in two days. This video footage is from two days ago. You do the math, Carrie. TJ may have been the last person to see Sienna. Do you honestly think he'll tell you the truth?"

That gives me pause. I'm not sure, to be honest. But I won't tell Marnie that.

For now, I just need to keep her quiet for twenty-eight more days while I figure out what the hell my stepson has been up to.

CHAPTER FOURTEEN

I take another hearty gulp from what is now my third glass of wine, and it's not even 9 a.m. Liquid courage, they say, though it doesn't seem to be working. I certainly don't feel very courageous. Just utterly confused and slightly remorseful.

I glance over at Marnie, who's sitting quietly, fiddling with the stem of her own wine glass. Maybe I overreacted about Damian last night. I try to put myself in Marnie's shoes. She's obviously lonely, and it's clear she really likes this guy, even if she barely knows him. "I truly am sorry for making you uncomfortable last night."

Marnie tucks a strand of dark hair behind her ear. "I guess it wasn't *really* your fault."

That's as close to an apology as I'm going to get. I'll take it.

"Damian really seems to have taken to you."

"You think so?" A brilliant smile breaks across her face.

"Oh, I'd say, more like, I *know* so. He couldn't keep his eyes off you."

I'm not lying. I caught Damian staring at Marnie multiple times during our impromptu day together. I don't know him well enough to decode his expressions, but I imagine the wheels were turning in his head as well as hers. Maybe the whole widow thing *is* bringing them together.

"He invited me over tonight," Marnie gushes, pulling her seat closer to mine.

"That's awesome," I say, returning her smile with a genuine one. Hopefully, Damian will keep her busy.

Busy enough that she doesn't have time to think about Sienna and my stepson. And of what my stepson might have done to Sienna.

"O-M-G!" Marnie slaps my hand, halting my umpteenth spiral of the morning. I believe I've lost count.

"What is it?" I cry out, wincing from the pain. *That damn cocktail ring.* I'm pretty sure it would be considered a lethal weapon in at least forty of the fifty states. She might as well wear brass knuckles.

"You and Bennett should *totally* join us tonight. It'll help break the ice a bit. You'll do that for me, won't you, Carrie?" Marnie purses her lip while waiting for me to respond to what is clearly more of a directive than a request. I've always had a hard time saying no to Marnie. And now, knowing she has incriminating footage of my stepson, it feels damn near impossible not to bend at her every request.

But I try to be tactful. "Do you honestly think Damian wants to hang out with us after what happened last night?" I picture the look of horror on his face as he practically sprinted out the front door of my house. He was in such a hurry that he couldn't even be bothered to take a doggie bag with him, despite my offer. If I were him, I'd hardly be jumping at the opportunity to hang out with me again. It's anyone's guess who'll show up the next time.

"Oh, definitely," she affirms, though her expression screams, *maybe.*

"I'd love to join you, Marnie, but why don't you run it by him first?"

"Great idea. And why don't you ask Bennett if he's planning on coming home tonight or going out with TJ again? Wouldn't want you to feel like a third wheel!"

How considerate. I fight to keep the corners of my lips from dipping. That was pretty dang low. I'm not sure what Marnie's issue is with *me*, but clearly there's something.

"I should get going. A million things to do today," I lie. I'm actually slightly intoxicated and will probably go home to take a nice, long nap. "Let me know what Damian says, and I'll check with Bennett."

"Sounds good." Marnie jumps to her feet to escort me out. I clutch the box of cookies tightly to my chest like a life preserver.

There's nothing good going on here. I've got information that, in hindsight, I don't want, and a best friend with an attitude I don't need.

And so, so many questions for which I have no answers.

* * *

No sooner have I reached my front door than a text from Marnie comes through.

Marnie: *All good for tonight.*

I roll my eyes. That was *too* fast. I wonder if she even asked Damian about us coming over. I don't suppose it matters. What's he going to do — kick us out onto our own street? Make us walk next door to get home? Not the worst thing that could happen here . . .

I twist the knob and let myself into the house, closing the door behind me. The silence, which I found so comforting this morning, now rattles me. A chill skitters up my spine. You'd think I'd appreciate the quiet with all the noise this development has to offer. But truth be told, I've gotten used to having TJ around. Between the deathly silence and marble everything, I'm starting to feel like I'm trapped in a mausoleum. I pull my cell phone from the back pocket of my jeans and type out a message to Bennett, suddenly desperate even for the company of a text.

Me: *Our new neighbor invited us to dinner tonight. Marnie is going as well. Will you be home?*

I leave out the part, *actually, Marnie invited us, and I said yes so she won't release incriminating footage of your son fighting with Sienna before she disappeared.* Not something best shared over text.

Almost immediately after sending the message, my phone pings with a response.

Bennett: *Wouldn't miss it. I miss you.*

My shoulders sag in relief. I know I tend to make too much out of nothing, and that's obviously what I did last night. I was being selfish and unfair. My husband is entitled to spend time with his son. He missed out on eighteen years with him. It's not all about me all the time.

My phone rings, and I quickly accept the call.

"I miss you too," I say, love dripping from my voice like honey from a comb.

A few beats of silence.

"Hello?"

More silence.

"Hello? Bennett? Are you there?"

And then the breathing starts. Deep, horror-movie inhales and exhales. I rip the phone from my ear, checking the number on the screen.

Unknown.

I end the call and fight the anxiety welling inside me. A fresh bout of dizziness hits me like a tidal wave. I bring a hand to my ribs to stop my heart from beating out of my chest.

It's just a call, I reassure myself, and I wish I believed it. *Just a call.* I take a deep breath. *Sticks and stones may break my bones, but crank calls will never hurt me . . .*

Unfortunately, I can't say the same for the sharp sound of glass breaking in my kitchen.

CHAPTER FIFTEEN

I don't move. I don't breathe. I don't even blink. It's as if I'm frozen in time.

Bennett and TJ are still at the office, and since the housekeeper comes on Tuesdays, no one else should be here.

But yet, I hear *someone*. I'm ninety-nine percent sure I'm not imagining it.

Crunch.

Make that one hundred percent. There's someone in our kitchen, someone who is *not* supposed to be there.

Shit. Shit. Holy shit.

With my pulse pounding in my ears, I propel myself toward the front door. The only other sound I hear is hasty footsteps headed in my direction. Isn't adrenaline supposed to give you superhuman strength? Mothers lifting cars to save their children, strength? Is that a *myth?* It seems to be having a paradoxical effect here. I'm moving so slowly I might as well be trudging through quicksand. It feels like my feet have been dipped in cement.

Finally, my hand finds the knob. I twist it—

"Carrie?"

Oh my God. My hand flies off the doorknob to my chest. My heart is beating so fast that I'm certain I must be having a heart attack. A stroke. An aneurysm. Maybe a combination of all three.

"*TJ?*" I manage to splutter, still gripping my chest.

Oh, thank God. But a barrage of questions begins to assault my conscience like the rapid beating of my heart. I suck in a sharp breath. "What are you doing here?"

"I live here," he jokes with a half-smile. When I don't respond, because I'm still desperately trying to temper my shock, he adds casually, "I didn't go into the office today." The serious expression on his face does not match the lightness in his voice. His shoulders are raised, his posture tense. My eyes shoot down to his hands which are opening and closing into tight fists.

"But you *did* go into the office today," I reply slowly. "I heard you leave with your dad this morning."

"Nope, never left."

TJ's eyes dart between mine as he waits for me to say something. He folds his arms across his chest. I can't put my finger on it, but I don't love how he's staring at me. His brow is furrowed, lips dipped into a frown. It feels like he knows that I know he's done something wrong. I've never had a reason to ever feel afraid of my stepson — thoughtful TJ — before.

Not like I am now.

TJ raises a hand, and I reel back as if he's about to bring it across my face. He instead runs the offending hand through his hair, looking at me like I've lost my freaking mind. And maybe I have. Clearly, I'm a nervous wreck.

This must be some big misunderstanding. Maybe we'll even laugh about it one day. Just not today. TJ thrusts his hands onto his hips.

Definitely not today.

"You're awfully quiet, Carrie. Is everything okay?"

No, everything is not *okay.* I find myself moving slowly away from TJ until my back is flush against the front door. There's nowhere to go.

I almost feel ridiculous. TJ wouldn't do anything to hurt me. He wouldn't hurt anyone. At least, I don't think so.

Flashes of the video — TJ's twisted expression, and the forceful grab of Sienna's arm — suddenly streak through my mind like meteors, burning as they go.

"I have to ask you a question, TJ. And I need you to be honest with me."

"Of course. What is it? You're scaring me, Carrie."

I'm scaring *him?*

"What happened between you and Sienna?"

I search TJ's face for some sign of deceit. Am I imagining things, or did a muscle in his jaw just twitch? Perhaps, but I'm definitely *not* imagining the sheen of sweat on his forehead. The kid looks like he went to town with my liquid highlighter.

TJ clenches his jaw. He looks down at his feet before returning his gaze to meet mine. Isn't that *the* oldest tell in the book — avoiding eye contact? But he's looking at me now as he says, "I already told Dad and the police that I avoid her. Why are you asking me about this again? Did the police come back?"

I watch through narrowed eyes as he wrings his hands together. Why is he so nervous about the police coming back if he hasn't done anything wrong?

Unless he *has.*

I know for a fact that TJ was with Sienna — I saw it with my own two eyes. His lies land like a smack in the face. After everything I've done to protect him. I've believed in him. I deserve the goddamn truth.

My legs feel like they're about to buckle. I want to run, but there's no way I could get out of the house with TJ standing so close to me. Flashes of Mark Black chasing me up my stairwell render me paralyzed. Where would I go anyway if I managed to escape? *Marnie's? With how she's been acting?* Thanks, but no thanks.

I'm driving myself crazy. Adding to my sense of unease, the kitchen . . .

"What happened in the kitchen?"

"I broke a glass."

I'm not sure what I thought it was that I heard, but my shoulders sag in relief.

"I'll help you clean it up," I offer, desperate for a distraction as I hobble toward the kitchen. For a way out. *I could bolt through the back door if I have to. The garage . . .*

I stop short as I enter the kitchen. TJ nearly tumbles into me. There's no glass to clean up. Didn't TJ just say he broke a glass? The kitchen is spotless. If it was Tuesday, I'd understand, but . . . I spin around to look at TJ. "Where's the glass?"

"Already cleaned it up," he says.

"Well, where is it?" I ask as I walk over to check the garbage can.

"The garage," he replies, folding his arms across his chest. "What? You don't even believe me that I broke a glass? Really?"

"I . . . I . . ."

Worry lines stretch across TJ's forehead, as his defensive expression turning to concern. "You look like you need to sit down, Carrie."

He's right. I *do* need to sit down. I sink down onto a chair at the kitchen table. "This . . . I . . . we need to talk." My body buzzes with nervous energy. I feel fragile. Like I'm about to break.

"Well, what is it?" TJ sits down across from me and folds his hands in his lap. Despite the casual gesture, they're shaking.

"There's no easy way to say this." I inhale sharply. "There's footage, TJ, of you and Sienna arguing outside the clubhouse."

TJ rests his elbows on the table and drops his head into his hands. I watch as his back rises and falls, his breath quickening. "Oh God," he mumbles.

I sit stock still as I wait for TJ to recover from the blow, to talk to me. As I stare at him, his head shifting back and forth on the table, a part of me wants to go and offer comfort. He's my stepson, for goodness' sake. But I don't. I can't. All I can do is watch as he processes what I've told him and hope that he tells me the truth. I fold my hands in my lap, anxiously waiting.

TJ's head suddenly flies up from the table, startling me. "I can explain," he says. "Sienna has been terrorizing me, Carrie. Following me around, threatening to get back at me . . ."

"Get back at you for *what?*"

"I don't know. She's crazy. She thinks I did something to her friends. She keeps telling me she has proof."

Proof? I consider this for a moment. "What kind of proof could she possibly have if you didn't do anything?"

"I have no idea. All I know is that I told her to meet me so I could make her see that I didn't do anything to her friends and that she needs to leave me alone. I don't want any trouble. That was it, I swear."

Was it? I've given my stepson every opportunity in the world to tell me the truth, but I can't shake the feeling that he's still lying through his teeth. If there were such an innocent explanation for the footage, I shouldn't need to drag it out of him.

"We argued, and then I left. I haven't seen or heard from her since."

I consider what he's telling me, but there's something I just don't understand. "Why didn't you tell the police all this?"

"You think they'd believe me?"

Of course not. I'm not even sure if *I* believe him.

"Well, why didn't you tell me or your father about Sienna harassing you? Surely your dad could have done something to help."

"I *did* tell him about that. He knows."

It feels like I've taken a punch in the gut.

"Oh, I see," I manage, my tone clipped.

TJ regards me with raised eyebrows, studying my face for a reaction. When I don't say anything further, because I *can't* say anything further, he adds, "I'm so sorry, Carrie. I just assumed he'd told you."

Well, he didn't.

CHAPTER SIXTEEN

I'm not sure how long we sit in silence as I attempt to process the bomb my stepson has just dropped at my feet. Why didn't Bennett mention this when we spoke about TJ last night? He made out like TJ hadn't talked to Sienna *at all*. His *deception* sends me reeling.

My thoughts turn to back to TJ, standing lamely in front of me. I almost want to smack the boy upside the head for being so darn foolish as to get caught on tape. Unless the possibility of getting caught on tape never crossed his mind. Maybe he genuinely wasn't doing anything wrong. If that's the case, how could he possibly have known that Sienna Berman would vanish, and that their heated conversation right before she went missing would come back to bite him in the ass?

My head is spinning so hard and fast, I feel like I might pass out. The room tilts. Thank God, I'm sitting down.

"Carrie?"

TJ's voice rips me from my spiral and brings me back to the present and the monumental problem we currently have. If the police catch wind of that video, my stepson will be absolutely screwed. Bennett may be one of the most successful professionals under forty in Westchester County and a top-of-his-class prose-cutor and litigator, but there's not a chance in hell he'll be able to talk TJ out of this mess if Marnie decides to release the video. She said she wouldn't.

But some small, fearful part of me isn't so sure.

I take a deep, grounding breath to steady my trembling hands. Until there's categorical proof of my stepson's guilt, I guess I *have* to trust TJ. I'm not sure Bennett would forgive me if I didn't.

Speaking of whom. "I guess I should call Bennett," I announce to myself, as much as to TJ, reaching into my pocket for my phone. While the sting of my husband's lie by omission lingers, I feel my confidence returning. Bennett will know what to do. As the call connects, I turn to TJ and whisper, "We need to figure out a plan — what you're going to tell the police if . . ." *If they find out you lied and are potentially the last person to see Sienna Berman alive and well,* I don't say. I silently pray she isn't dead.

Bennett answers after the first ring. "Carrie? Is everything okay?"

His voice quivers with uncharacteristic insecurity. Bennett checks up on me regularly, but when my husband is at work, I let him do his thing. I text when I need him. We both know I wouldn't be calling if everything was okay.

And I tell him as much. "No, Bennett, everything is *not* okay. I'm with TJ. We need to talk. When will you be home?"

Without a breath of hesitation, he replies, "I'm on my way."

* * *

Twenty minutes later, the garage door clicks open. TJ and I have said maybe twelve words to each other, and that's a generous estimate. At some point, my stepson asked if I was hungry. TJ is a phenomenal cook, yes, but even a *hint* of a thought of food threatens to make me gag.

At the sound of Bennett's *hurried* footsteps, we both jump up, even though we've been fully expecting him.

"What's going on?" Bennett blows into our kitchen like a bat out of hell. He's completely disheveled — breathless, tie askew, and his hair wild as if he'd been running his hands through it repeatedly on the ride over. He probably was, in between slapping his palm against the dash and squeezing the steering wheel so tightly that his knuckles lost all pigment.

"You should sit down, Bennett. We need to talk about what's going on with Sienna," I say, fighting to keep my breathing steady.

He fidgets in place. "I'll stand, thanks. Have they found her yet?"

I shake my head.

"Did Lydia come back? Detective Johnson? I'm going to have to file a restraining order against *both* of them. Surely, there's another detective in Westchester County capable of investigating this case." Bennett's fingers curl into a fist. Like father, like son.

"No one has come back. It's just—"

"What?" He interrupts. "What is it?"

"Some new information has come to light. Information that does *not* paint TJ in a favorable light." As if on cue, a bright stab of sunlight streaming in through the kitchen window cuts through the table like a knife. How awfully perfect.

The sudden blare of Bennett's ringtone prevents me from saying more.

He quickly checks the number and answers. Holding up a finger, he mouths *Detective Johnson* as he listens to whatever is being said on the other end. I wish we could hear what Detective Johnson is saying, but all we can do is guess it's *not* good based on the concern braiding itself into Bennett's expression.

Bennett finally speaks, and I take back what I just said — I wish I didn't know about this conversation *at all*.

"Fine. I'll bring him to the station now."

With that, Bennett hangs up and stares at his son.

"Detective Johnson wants you to come down to the station for a formal interview and to take a polygraph."

"A polygraph? Why do they want him to take a polygraph?" My eyes dart nervously between father and son as I wait for him to answer.

"It's just for precautionary purposes, Carrie. Trust me, the police do this all the time to rule people out."

"Or to rule them *in*. You know that's what they're trying to do. Do you really think this is wise, Bennett? As TJ's dad? As his *lawyer?*"

Bennett walks over and rests his hands soothingly on my shoulders. But any semblance of calm heartily avoids me. "This isn't a bad thing, Carrie. It's a way to take the heat off him, so the police can get back to doing their job and try to find Sienna. We both know TJ hasn't done anything wrong. I think he's earned the right for us to believe him after the last misdirected manhunt."

I get what he's saying, but . . . "Bennett, TJ *was* with Sienna. That's what I was trying to tell you." My voice cracks as the words finally tumble out.

All the color drains from Bennett's face.

"The clubhouse," TJ says, throwing a worried glance at his father. "I told her to leave me alone, like you said."

"Okay . . . you did the right thing, son."

"Right thing, perhaps. But the wrong place," I interject. "The clubhouse cameras caught their exchange — it was heated."

"Heated? You didn't say it was *heated*. What the hell does that even mean?"

Red splotches bloom on TJ's neck. He drops his gaze. "We were arguing. She wouldn't listen to reason."

"And did you do anything *other* than argue?"

The tension in the room crackles like an electrical charge. I swear I hear it thrumming in my ears, pulsing through my veins.

TJ crosses his arms. "Like what? You think I *hurt* her?"

Bennett reaches for TJ's arm, but he pulls away from his father angrily. "I'm not saying you hurt her. I just need to know . . ." His voice trails off. His eyes glaze over, his gaze suddenly unfocused and far away. He almost looks catatonic standing there, and I worry that he's gone into shock. Then suddenly, as if coming back to life, he turns to me. "Detective Johnson didn't mention anything about having footage."

"The police don't have the footage," I tell him.

"So *who* does?"

"The gatekeeper," I say lightly, though the words fall heavy like bricks. "Marnie said she'll keep quiet for now."

"For *now?* What the fuck is that supposed to mean?"

"I don't know what she meant by that, Bennett. All I know is she won't delete the footage for another twenty-eight days. HOA rules. And, she wants us over there tonight. Something tells me we need to do whatever she wants."

"Then that's what we'll do." Bennett's shoulders relax. "Well, now that we're all on the same page, TJ and I should get going."

"We are *not* on the same page!" I screech, panicked. We're far from even being in the same book, let alone the same *genre*. I may have gotten used to the little thriller that is our lives, but this is pure, bone-chilling horror. "Please tell me you're not going to go through with this, Bennett. You can't let him take a polygraph."

"Carrie, if we decline, it will look like TJ has something to hide."

"But he *does* have something to hide. Even if he didn't do anything, he was with Sienna before she went missing." Was quite possibly the last person with Sienna before she went missing.

Bennett places his hands back on my shoulders and stares at me intently. "You need to trust me. I'll coach him on the way over. It'll be fine. These tests are meaningless anyway."

I throw my own hands up in frustration, my stomach churning with dread. If these tests are so meaningless, I can't help but question why TJ needs to take one in the first place. But another question, dark and heavy, slinks through the back of my mind and settles there.

Just what *will* my stepson reveal?

CHAPTER SEVENTEEN

I don't know how Bennett can be so stinking calm at a time like this, and without his miles-long run, no less. Second to lawyering, my husband spends most of his time running. Apparently, when you live in a place like this, you've got plenty to run from.

I guess there wasn't enough time for that today, though, with Bennett so graciously agreeing to bring TJ down to the station for a lie-detector test — a freaking lie-detector test when we already know he *is* lying!

I'm not quite so cool about it. I'm feeling more like the conductor on the hot-mess express. I massage two fingers over my eyelids in a futile attempt to ward off a migraine. My head is pounding, the knot in my gut tightening by the second.

I need *something* to take the edge off. But I don't overeat. I don't smoke. I don't drink . . . okay, I *do* drink, but socially, so for argument's sake, that doesn't count.

My only solace when I'm stressed out is baking. If there were a contest for stress-baking pastries, Carrie Winter would be a blue-ribbon competitor.

So that's precisely what I do after Bennett and TJ slip out of the kitchen, into the garage, and venture off to the police station. I heave the mixer from the cupboard, placing it not so gently down on the counter. I huff a frustrated breath. I'm not sure why no one ever listens to me. This might be the worst idea ever. Polygraphs may mean nothing in a court of law, but if TJ slips up even slightly, it will mean *everything* to Detective Johnson. I shake my head, my shoulders loosening slightly as I pull the ingredients from the fridge and cabinets.

I guess it doesn't matter what I think.

I refocus my nervous energy on my charge: a spongy strawberry shortcake with fresh strawberries and hand-whisked whipped cream. I was planning on bringing it to Damian's house tonight. Assuming, of course, I'm not otherwise detained, bailing my stepson out of jail. I'm stirring the flour, sugar, and butter, plumes of flour drifting from the bowl, when a loud rap sounds at the front door. *Not again.*

I wipe my hands on my apron and hurry to see what unwanted visitor awaits me this time.

Oh God. She's back.

Lydia *freaking* Berman.

I should one hundred percent unequivocally *not* open the door. I should pretend I'm not home. Run upstairs and hide under my duvet. Call Bennett.

Do something, *anything*, other than open that door.

Maybe she's come to tell me that Sienna has come home and that this was all just some terrible mistake. Or (*gasp*) that she's sorry. But that's wishful thinking for a more naïve woman. Not believing it for a second, I foolishly open the door. And it's abundantly clear from her seething expression that she has *not* come to tell me any of that.

Sienna has *not* come back.

This was *not* all just some terrible mistake.

And Lydia Berman is most definitely *not* sorry.

I glance down at Lydia's hands, and my stomach somersaults because I now know exactly what this visit is all about. Lydia is holding her daughter's journal. I am quite familiar with it, having read entry upon entry when Sienna went missing the last time. In it, Sienna talked about TJ when it was actually Mark Black.

This time? My stomach clenches. I can't even begin to imagine what it says to bring her over here again, especially after having the door slammed in her face last night.

I also can't imagine sending her away now that I know that TJ has, in fact, had contact with Sienna. This time, there actually could be something in there that names him. If I shut her out again, Lydia Berman will go straight to the police station with this.

I can't let that happen.

I glance around to make sure no nosy neighbors are eavesdropping. I'm not crazy enough to invite the psychopath in. My eyes flick to Marnie's bedroom, then to her bay window to make sure she's not watching this exchange, binoculars clenched tightly in hand. All clear.

"What is it, Lydia?"

"I have evidence, Carrie!" Lydia waves the journal in my face. I fight the urge to roll my eyes. What I want to say is: *hey, remember that one time you accused my stepson of harming your daughter, and she was actually on the lam?*

But I don't.

If she actually has evidence, the last thing I want to do is piss her off. So much so, in fact, I'm about to offer to pull some strings and get her back into book club.

I step outside, closing the door behind me, motioning toward the custom-made all-weather couch on the front porch. We both sit, and Lydia frantically licks her thumb before flipping through the journal with alarming speed.

"Look," she says, poking her finger against a page like she wants to murder it. The manic look in her eyes is borderline terrifying. My breath quickens as a chill runs through my body.

"Why are you here, Lydia? Why bring this to *me* of all people?"

"So you can see what a monster your stepson is," she hisses.

I inhale deeply, attempting to keep my blood pressure from spiking. "May I?" I ask, manifesting calm as I reach for the journal. I wonder what Lydia would do if I jumped up and ran with it.

Lydia hesitates, pursing her lips while she considers my request. It's almost as if she knows what I'm thinking. She reluctantly hands it over, and my gaze falls to where her finger just lay. There's a date at the top from exactly two weeks ago.

Dear Diary,

I can't take this anymore. He's been following me every-where — like some sort of sick stalker. I don't know what he wants from me. I just know I need to stay away from him. TJ Winter is dangerous. I don't care what the police say, I know he killed Sofia and Lila. I just know it. And he's going to kill me, too, if I don't stop him. I have to stop him.

My heart wails in my ears as I turn the page. Good God, there's more. This time, one from a week later.

Dear Diary,

I found a note on my golf cart this morning, folded into a neat little square in the cupholder. It said: if you don't stop digging, you'll get buried. It's from TJ. He's going to kill me.

Just when I think I can't take any more, I foolishly read the final journal entry. It's from just three days ago.

Dear Diary,

TJ told me to meet him at the clubhouse. He said he wants to talk . . . that it's important. I feel like I'm making a mistake, but I need to know the truth once and for all . . .

Disbelief claws at my stomach like a desperate, rabid animal. This can't be. I blink rapidly, trying to make it all disappear. But Sienna's words linger in front of me, all there in black and white. TJ told Sienna to meet him at the clubhouse. And no one has seen her since.

Maybe Sienna Berman isn't crazy. Maybe TJ is a psychopath.

Oh, God. It feels like my entire world has been shaken. I'm dizzy, nauseous. Lydia tries to grab the journal from my hands, but unfortunately for her, my fingers have atrophied around it. "No," I tell her, pulling the journal tightly into my chest. *Over my dead body*, I nearly add, but stop myself. You should be careful what you wish for in a place like this.

Lydia's jaw drops. "What do you mean *no?*" She seethes, baring her teeth as if she might eat me alive. If Lydia Berman could expel venom and kill me on the spot, I've no doubt she would.

"Can I borrow this?" I ask.

Her eyebrows shoot up in horror. "You're joking, right? Do you seriously think I'm going to let you *borrow* my daughter's journal? Are you out of your mind?"

It does sound like a crazy request when she repeats it back to me. But, "Assuming what Sienna wrote is true—"

"Are you calling my missing daughter a *liar?*"

"No, no, no, that's not what I'm saying. I swear." I hold up a hand, the one that's not clenching the journal, in a kung-fu grip. "Just hear me out, okay?"

"This is ridiculous, Carrie. Why should I hear you out? Why shouldn't I just go to the police with this?"

"Look, you obviously came *here* for a reason. If you wanted to go to the police with this first, you would have. We both know you're not being neighborly by giving me a heads up." We both know that's an understatement and a half. *Neighborly* is not a word in Lydia Berman's vernacular.

Lydia glances down at her hands, clenched into tight fists in her lap. "Fine," she says. "You have thirty seconds. Talk . . ."

"I get it, okay. You want to find your daughter. You need to trust me. If I confront TJ with the journal, maybe it will force him to admit the truth. Whatever that truth may be."

Lydia chews on her lower lip, thinking it over. It's a crazy request, of course — hand over your daughter's journal to the stepmother of the young man you believed has kidnapped her. It's so crazy, it just might work.

"Well," she says, wringing her hands together. "Since the police have been useless so far . . ."

I raise an eyebrow, encouraging her to continue.

"I don't think Mark Black killed those girls, Carrie. I think your stepson did."

I cover my mouth as I gasp. "What evidence do you have, Lydia?"

"You wouldn't understand. It's . . . it's . . . a mother's intuition."

I recoil as though Lydia has taken a dagger to my heart. The pointed words certainly feel like it.

"Anyway, I hope you'll be better at coaxing TJ to tell the truth than the police. Will you, Carrie? Will you help me find my daughter?"

"I promise, I'll try."

And I will. I'll do the right thing. If what Sienna wrote is true, I'll make sure TJ pays for what he's done. If *not*, Lydia will never see this journal again.

"Thank you, Carrie." Lydia rises to her feet and takes a step to walk away.

"Just one more thing," she says, spinning on her heels to face me.

What now? I hold my breath.

"Don't get any funny ideas. I made copies."

CHAPTER EIGHTEEN

It takes me what seems like an eternity to calm down after Lydia reluctantly leaves my front porch. I promised her I'd talk to TJ, and I will, but I'm not giving this journal back any time soon. Not until I'm certain of TJ's innocence or guilt, one way or the other.

Hopefully, she was fibbing about the copies. I'm not holding my breath, though.

I return to the kitchen, seeking solace in my strawberry short-cake. I watch as the batter thickens in the mixer, the motion hypnotic. Despite everything, the cake turns out looking and smelling dangerously delicious. My stomach is too knotted up, though, to so much as imagine eating it.

But I'll be damned if I'm not going to that dinner tonight.

I leave the cake cooking in the kitchen to check the front door, unlocking and locking it several times just to be sure that it's secured. I doubt Lydia would have a change of heart so quickly and barge into my house, but you can never be too careful in a place like this — a place where everyone *thinks* they know their neighbors. A place cloaked in secrets, with an ugly past that won't let itself be forgotten.

Confident the door is locked, I hurry upstairs to my bedroom. My eyes flit around the space. It's a gorgeous room. Once upon a time, I pictured it on the glossy pages of *Architectural Digest*.

Instead, it ended up being the focus of a two-page spread in the local paper.

The scene of Mark Black's death. Where I killed him.

I approach the bed, running my hand along the white, sateen duvet. It's also where I plan on hiding Sienna's journal, not that anyone other than myself will know about it. I already know where to place Sienna's journal for safekeeping, but I am uncertain of my end game. For the moment, anyhow. When the timing is right, I will call TJ's hand.

My plan isn't perfect. It doesn't even quite exist. But I'm not sure who could possibly plan for something like this — missing teens, murderous husbands, and mysterious stepsons.

I shake my head, trying to dislodge thoughts of all of the above and refocus on the task at hand. I bend onto my knees, burying my weight in the plushy carpeting. I slide Sienna's journal between the mattress and box spring on my side of the bed. TJ rarely comes into our bedroom, and Bennett hasn't changed a sheet in his life, so I'm guessing it'll be safe here.

No sooner have I pulled the duvet back into its rightful place than the garage door clicks, indicating my husband and TJ have returned home from the precinct.

I rush out of the bedroom, hazarding one last glance at where I've hidden the journal, keenly aware that the well-loved book of papers has the power to turn our lives completely upside down — and after we've only just righted ourselves, too. I sense there's no coming back from this, not if what Sienna wrote in there is true.

Unless it's all lies, and TJ hasn't done anything to her. I entertain the faintest possibility that Lydia wrote fake journal entries about TJ because she's convinced herself he's the culprit. I wouldn't put it past her. I'm tempted to do a handwriting comparison but am stopped in my tracks by the sound of Bennett calling my name.

D.L. Fisher

"Carrie? Where are you?"

"Coming." My voice cracks.

I approach the top of the marble staircase to find Bennett waiting at the bottom.

Just Bennett.

"Where's TJ?" I ask, my heart racing at the possibility that my stepson is *still* at the police station.

But if that's the case, why the hell does my husband look so nonplussed? His hair is back in place, tie knotted perfectly just below the collar of his shirt. He's smiling up at me, while my legs threaten to buckle beneath me.

"I dropped TJ off at a friend's house in Yonkers."

"Did you *talk* to him?"

"To who? *TJ?* Of course, I talked to him — the whole car ride over. Come down. I'll give you a play-by-play of everything that went down at the station."

"Not TJ. His friend, Bennett. Did you talk to his friend? Or his friend's mom?"

Bennett laughs. "He's nineteen, Carrie."

"He's also suspected of kidnapping a minor. Sienna is seventeen, Bennett."

I descend the stairs slowly, careful not to slip on the slick marble. Ever since I found out about Andrea Winter's death, it's become one of my worst fears – tripping on the stairs and tumbling to my death below. By the time I reach the bottom and am face to face with Bennett, there are tears streaming down my cheeks. This is all too much.

"What if the media catches wind?" I say. "The press will go crazy over this. What if they find him in Yonkers? We can't shield him from the media storm if he isn't here."

Bennett runs a finger under each of my eyes, then tilts my chin up so my gaze meets his.

"The press is not catching wind of anything, Carrie. TJ passed."

"He *what?*"

"He passed the polygraph."

I can feel the weight I've been lugging around lifting slowly from my shoulders. Maybe TJ is innocent, after all. Worry getting the better of me, though, I ask, "Did the police ask him if he's had any contact with Sienna?" Surely, they must have asked him as part of their interrogation. I should have thought it would be the first question, followed by: *Do you know what happened to her? Did you harm her?*

Bennett looks away, and I have my answer.

"So he told them he spoke to her, then?"

"Well, no . . ." My husband slowly shakes his head.

"But you said he passed. How could he possibly have passed?"

"I coached him, Carrie. He was prepared for the questions. It's going to be okay. Everything is going to be okay."

I let Bennett pull me in close and wrap his arms around me. I repeat his words back to him, trying to digest them. "Everything is going to be okay . . ." But how could it be?

If TJ could lie his way through a polygraph, how do we know what — if anything — he's telling us is true?

CHAPTER NINETEEN

I pace around the foyer for a while, the worst-case scenario orbiting my head as I try, and fail, to grapple with it. Bennett watches on silently, but the scrunch to his eyebrows is a clear tell that he's engaged in a mental wrestling match of his own.

Do I tell my husband about the journal entries? Do I wait to talk to TJ first? If something has already happened to Sienna, does it matter? My mind races down so many dark alleys that I lose all sense of direction.

"So," Bennett says, bringing me back to the here and now. "What time are we meeting this new neighbor?"

I freeze. With all the excitement between TJ this morning and Lydia this afternoon, our plans with Marnie and Damian slipped my mind. I don't even want to go, but it doesn't feel like we have a choice. I'd almost forgotten about our new neighbor and what secrets he may be hiding. On the bright side, it looks like I'll have time to focus on this potential problem now since the other, more pressing one, is out for the night.

I run my fingers down Bennett's arm to the vintage Rolex on his wrist. "Five o'clock," I tell him after turning it over to check the time. It may take Bennett only five minutes to get ready, but I can't say the same for myself. And it's already well after four. "We'd better get ready."

My husband sighs loudly, visibly disappointed. "I was hoping we'd have a little time . . ." His fingers find my waist.

I place a hand on Bennett's sculpted chest. "Me too, my love. But we don't want to be late. We need to make a good first impression." Well, a good *first* impression for Bennett and a better *second* impression for me.

"Okay, fine." Bennett slaps me gently on the rear before ascending the stairs.

I pause, not yet following him. *Make a* good *impression this time,* I order myself.

And figure out a way to look inside that box.

* * *

Twenty minutes later, we arrive at Damian's front door. Bennett looks casual yet dashing in a pale-blue button-down shirt and tailor-fitted khakis. After some intense debate, he chose a pair of HEYDUDES that perfectly complement the look. I found a stylish pair of flared jeans and a silk shirt on the bed waiting for me — a darker shade of blue to coordinate with my husband. He seems to have thought of everything.

Clearly, Bennett realizes just how much is riding on what should be an innocuous dinner date. Keeping Marnie happy is our top priority, second only to keeping TJ out of jail, though the two tasks feel impossibly intertwined. Standing here together, we look like the perfect picture of high-society neighbors. The couple anyone would want in their inner circle.

The couple with a son who isn't in love with the girl next door — but may have kidnapped her.

I wish someone would wake me from this nightmare.

Bennett rings the doorbell as we stand on the front porch, his hand wrapped snugly around mine. The weather has taken a turn for the worse. Fat raindrops fall like golf balls from the sky. The soul-crushing humidity has reached its breaking point — I have reached my breaking point. At least the temperature outside has cooled down considerably. Or maybe it's everything going on behind the gates of The Estates that has my arms lined in goosebumps.

"We got this," Bennett says, interlacing our fingers and squeezing. With his other hand, he holds an umbrella over my head. Oh God, do I want to believe him.

I inhale deeply as the door opens, then my breath catches in my chest. I have no words.

There's a brief pause of silence before Marnie chirps, "My, my, my. Did you guys plan this?"

It quickly registers that Bennett and Damian are wearing identical outfits, down to the very shoes on their feet. And they're not just any old HEYDUDES. They're special-edition Margaritaville ones, with a print reminiscent of a tropical island. They have a rebellious elegance not many could pull off.

Except, apparently, both Bennett *and* Damian.

It's weird, for sure, but at least we know they have something in common. And wearing identical outfits is certainly one way to break the ice.

"Finally," Bennett says, shaking Damian's hand. "A neighbor with good taste."

"I was literally about to say the same thing!"

The men enjoy a quick chuckle while Marnie and I look on with interest. It's like we're watching a dating reality show or something.

"Can I give you a tour of the house?" Damian offers.

Bennett readily accepts. "Yeah, man. I'd like that."

"Let's start in the kitchen," Damian says, waving Bennett inside, "so we can get you set up with a drink. Do you like bourbon?"

"Do I like bourbon?" Bennett repeats with a wide grin. "Do I ever!"

My lips curl into a wry smile despite myself. *And I was worried this might be uncomfortable.*

"Uh oh," Marnie whispers in my ear. "I feel a bromance blossoming here."

"On the next episode of *Love Connection*, from next-door neighbors to best friends. Swoon." I bring a hand to my forehead for emphasis.

Marnie smiles widely, her eyes crinkling around the edges. Someone is in a chipper mood this evening. We've almost fallen back into our old selves — the ones who gossip about neighbors instead of arguing about them. It's a glimpse of who we used to be. Sometimes, I fear we will never be those people again, but at this moment, it feels natural. I allow myself to be cautiously optimistic about tonight. *Cautiously*. Because with Marnie, the tides can turn quickly. Navigating our friendship is like paddling through the ocean with no oars and a dangerous storm looming on the horizon.

"Come in," she says, grabbing my hand and pulling me toward the kitchen. The men have already left, presumably to continue to tour the rest of the house with drinks in hand.

My eyes widen as I catch sight of Damian's gleaming kitchen with a foot-long charcuterie board overflowing with meats, cheeses, and various crudites. I stifle a snort — someone sure has kept busy today. It looks like Damian has lived here for a decade, not a day. Considering this house was like an Amazon warehouse when I came over yesterday, I struggle to comprehend how he could have unpacked *everything* in under twenty-four hours and put together such an incredible charcuterie board. That would be a lot to tackle, even with Marnie's assistance. Then again, if what Damian says is true, houses are his specialty. And he does have freakishly gigantic muscles — perfectly suited for moving things in record time.

I continue to cautiously peer around, and there's not a box in sight — not even *the* box. I cross my fingers, legs, and eyes that my new neighbor has left it where I can find it when the time is right. Though I've no idea when that will be or what I'm going to do if I find myself alone with it. Or why I can't stop thinking about it, for that matter.

It's probably *just* a box.

"Wow," I tell Marnie, trying to clear my mind of all things cardboard. "It smells amazing in here. Damian cooks, too?" *Really, what doesn't this guy have going for him?* "It looks like Bennett's got some steep competition in his reigning role as the biggest catch of The Estates," I comment.

Marnie's eyes narrow on me, her dark brows darting toward one another. "Actually, *I* cooked dinner."

Again, I have no words. And apparently, I have lost the ability to hide the shock in my expression.

"Why do you look so *surprised*, Carrie?" Marnie moves her hands to her hips while waiting for my answer.

At least a dozen caustic remarks jump to the tip of my tongue, but I keep my acidity in check. Marnie Black *doesn't* cook — like, ever. I once watched her burn a pot of noodles. What thirty-something can't boil a pot of packaged noodles? I'm afraid we're all going to wind up in the ER with food poisoning if she actually prepared this meal.

But I wouldn't dare call her out.

"You must have been very busy today. It really smells delicious," I say instead, while breathing a sigh of relief that I'll live to see another day as I spot the takeout box hanging over the rim of the recycling bin. I'm tempted to tell Marnie she should do a better job of hiding the evidence, but I'm not about to start with her. The purpose of this visit is to keep my friend contently distracted from the TJ-Sienna situation.

And that's precisely what I intend to do.

CHAPTER TWENTY

It takes a few minutes for Marnie to simmer down from my perceived insult, but as soon as Damian and Bennett re-enter the room, she spackles a wide smile on her face once again. She reaches into a cabinet and pulls out two fancy glasses before uncorking a bottle of what looks like expensive wine. I'm kind of in awe of how comfortable Marnie seems here. I mean, we met this guy yesterday. Yet the way she's moving about the kitchen, you'd think she'd been living here with Damian for years.

Marnie pours us both generous glasses of wine. "Cheers," she toasts, clinking our glasses together. The blood-red liquid sloshes around the glass. She's seemingly forgotten that she wanted to rip my head off just moments earlier. Clearly, Damian is one heck of a distraction.

"To new neighbors," Damian says.

"Better, to new *friends*," Bennett adds.

Everyone looks at me to contribute to the conversation. "To all of the above," I agree, hoping no one catches the awkward edge to my voice.

"On that note," Damian pivots, "Marnie made us all a delicious dinner that I can't wait to tuck into." He crosses the island and places his hands on Marnie's shoulders, squeezing with the kind of affection that takes years to nurture. She looks up at him, love warming her brown eyes.

"Oh, it's nothing," she says, cupping his chin with her hand. I catch the glint of the damned necklace that nearly gives me a coronary every time I see it. But it's not just the necklace that sets my mind spinning.

There's a new ornament gracing her neck, and not one she picked up from the jeweler.

"You're going to have to wait just a little longer," Marnie tells Damian playfully, batting her obscenely long eyelashes that look as though her eyelash extensions have eyelash extensions.

"It needs to cook a few more minutes."

Several eyelashes flutter from her face to the ground. Glancing down, I see them scattered like carcasses across the wooden floor. I wonder where she went to get them done. Someone should tell her they did a horrible job. Not me, though. Damian pulls one that's landed on her cheek. "Make a wish," he says, holding out his hand with the eyelash resting on his finger.

Marnie closes her eyes as if thinking hard about what she should wish for. Then she blows demurely. A wish on an eyelash extension can't be anything but cheap.

I glance over at Damian, who now pouts like a two-year-old, apparently very excited about Marnie's 'homemade' meal. "Fine," he says, rubbing his stomach. "I'm taking Bennett to the game room. Let me know when you're ready for us."

"Will do." Marnie blows a kiss in Damian's direction. He reaches up and catches it, planting it on his cheek. Somehow I've wandered out of my personal horror and stumbled onto the set of Hollywood's cheesiest romcom — something unbelievable lurks beneath their overly sweet veneer. How have things moved so quickly? Have I got amnesia and forgotten the part where Damian courted Marnie (or vice versa), and they became a legitimate couple with a penchant for PDA? I continue blinking dumbly into space, for I'm sure I've completely lost my freaking mind.

"Carrie?" I jolt at the sound of my name in Marnie's mouth, the touch of her hand on my arm. My eyes meet hers. "What in the hell is going on with you?" she asks through gritted teeth, her slitted eyes boring into me.

"Oh, nothing," I say, shooing away her question with an unconvincing flick of the wrist.

"You're acting weird. Like, really weird." Marnie shakes her head. "It's making everyone uncomfortable."

"Am I? I didn't realize—"

"Well, can you *stop?*" she snips, interrupting me.

I don't know, can you stop being such an unpredictable bitch? I chew on my bottom lip. "Yes, of course, I'm sorry. I'll try to act more normal. I'm just worried about TJ, is all."

"We should *all* be worried about TJ, if what people are saying is true."

"And what would that be?"

"That he's done something to Sienna." Marnie leans in close, her mouth practically touching my ear. I shiver despite the heat of her breath. "I don't think it's such a stretch to consider that our neighbors may be right. You and I *both* know he was the last one seen with her."

"But only you and I know that, Marnie."

Marnie rolls her eyes. "Look, Carrie. I don't want to ruin a lovely evening with talk of your stepson. He already put a damper on last night." She looks contemplative for a moment and hums before adding, "More like a major buzz *kill*, actually. So if you don't mind . . ." She moves her thumb and pointer across her mouth, indicating I should zip it.

The metallic tang of blood fills my mouth and overwhelms my senses. I've — quite literally — bitten my tongue.

Then, I take a breath. *You know what,* I reassure myself, *as long as Marnie isn't the one doing the talking, it doesn't matter what the Lydia Bermans of The Estates have to say about TJ.*

He passed the lie-detector test. Sienna's journal is hidden under my mattress, where no one will find it, and the security video footage from the clubhouse camera will cease to exist in twenty-eight days.

So there, I want to stamp my foot like a petulant child.

Still, clearly, I need to change the subject.

"Are you going to spill the tea?" I ask, lightening my tone.

"About?"

I point to her neck, to the dark red love bite above her collarbone. Judging by their canoodling, Damian is the one who gave it to her. They have gotten close in what must be record time. But my inner voice continues to indulge in wild possibilities.

Like maybe they've known each other all along.

I turn it over in my head, but no, I can't make it make sense. I literally watched them meet each other *yesterday.*

"Oh, *that?*" Marnie's cheeks color as she pulls her hair across her shoulder to cover up the giant hickey on her neck. "It's nothing. Damian and I are just getting to know each other better." She turns her back to me, turning her attention to a salad that I've no doubt came from a package. I've never seen someone so focused on tossing a pre-tossed salad. I can feel my own eyes narrowing as I study her. Marnie doesn't make salads. Wine is her favorite vegetable. Second, maybe, to Xanax, though that would be harder to qualify as a vegetable.

God, could she be any more annoyingly vague? I guess it's none of my business, but best friends are supposed to tell each other everything. She's giving me nothing. Not that I have any intention of telling Marnie about my second visit from Lydia Berman and Sienna's journal, but still . . .

"Can I help with dinner?" I ask, changing tactics again.

"Nope, I've taken care of everything."

#Doordash. With her back to me, I can roll my eyes all I want. And roll them, I do.

Just then, Marnie picks up a dinner bell and rings it.

Apparently, this conversation is over.

CHAPTER TWENTY-ONE

As if by some Pavlovian response, the men are suddenly back in the kitchen.

"You have to see what Damian has done with this place. In such a short period of time, too," Bennett says, wrapping his arms around me from behind and nuzzling my neck. I arch into him, curious what his lips will do. But all I get is a nose tickle, feather-like and sweet. An unfamiliar and uncomfortable sensation suddenly roils deep within my gut.

What the heck is wrong with me? Am I actually jealous that Marnie has a hickey? There are clearly more important things to worry about here. Like, "I would love nothing more than to see what Damian has done with this place," I chime in. But what I mean is, *I would love nothing more than to look inside that box.*

"After dinner," Marnie insists. "Could you please show our guests to the dining room, Damian?"

Our guests?

I study Damian's handsome face, with cheekbones for days. His expression is relaxed, as though this is completely normal and expected. He smiles widely at her, dimples and all, before he turns his attention back to us.

"Follow me." Damian exits the room with Bennett on his tail. I glance over at Marnie before following them, but she's busy gazing off into space with a smile playing on her lips.

Goodness, she's already so obsessed with Damian, I bet he could get the code to her safe, and a life insurance policy taken out on her if he asked. I regard Damian again — his too-easy posture, his too-calm expression. I can't explain why, but something tells me it's not her money he's after.

I wish I knew what it was. I can't imagine Damian actually likes her *this* much. Or maybe she's an even better actress than I've given her credit for, and he has no idea who the real Marnie Black is. I don't want to be there when that honeymoon ends.

I follow Damian and Bennett into a large dining room with a grand table that seats twelve. Four place settings are set out in the middle of the table, two on each side, and taper candles flicker nearby. It looks like a scene from a posh five-star restaurant, not the dining room of a widowed man who moved in yesterday.

"It looks beautiful in here, Damian." I run a finger along the mahogany wood table, eyeing the fine china and sterling-silver cutlery laid out on red silk placemats with matching napkins. Damian smiles widely and returns to his conversation with my husband. No one could argue that Damian does not have impeccable taste.

Something gnaws at me, however. I do a double take, and I recognize the placemats. Come to think of it, I recognize the silverware and fine china, too, with its bold gray-and-gold design. I suppose it's *possible* that Damian has the exact same set of china as the Blacks. I mean, it *was* a very popular wedding model in 2009. But as I examine one of the plates more closely, I spot the cracked edge from when Marnie dropped a glass of wine on it once when we dined with her and Mark. I remember us joking that the crack was in the shape of Mickey Mouse's head.

A crack the shape of Micky Mouse's head can't be explained away.

Marnie has brought the china she used from her wedding to a serial killer to her new boyfriend's house. I involuntarily shiver. This is too weird.

I glance around the room for boxes, but there are none to be found. Where is all of Damian's stuff?

Within seconds I've gone from shivering to sweating, and it's not even warm in here. In fact, it's rather chilly. A quick, clandestine search on my phone reveals a self-diagnosis of a raging case of cogombophobia — fear of cardboard boxes.

That oddly labeled box consumes my thoughts. A box that, so far, is neither in the kitchen nor the dining room. I looked up the MLS listing when this house went on the market — six bedrooms, seven-and-a-half-baths, eighteen rooms total. That leaves me with sixteen more to search through. And if the kitchen and dining room are any indication, there's the chance Damian has already unpacked the box in question, and I'll be forever left to wonder about its contents.

Maybe it wouldn't be the worst thing in the world if that happened. I mean, what if I find something troubling in there? What then? The guy literally lives directly next door to me. And is dating my best friend — that title currently pending.

Maybe it really *is* time to move.

I take a tentative seat at the table next to Bennett. Damian sits directly across from my husband. The way they are conversing and carrying on, I might as well not even be here. And when Marnie enters the room with our salads displayed on a silver platter, well, forget about it. Carrie Winter, *who*?

"To start," Marnie announces as she walks around the table and places a plate in front of each of us, saving herself for last, "we have a bed of fresh greens with crisp fuji apple slices, creamy goat cheese, pomegranate seeds, and cinnamon-spiced pecans, tossed in a maple and apple cider vinegar."

Okay, who brought Martha Stewart to the dinner party?

Bennett digs right in. "Holy shit, Marnie. This might be the best salad I've ever had."

I kick my husband under the table.

"What?" he says with a piece of arugula hanging out the corner of his mouth. "It's *really* good. Try it." Bennett jams in another bite.

I'm not eating this salad, just out of principle. Marnie didn't even make it. Jerry Seinfeld could sue her for copyright infringement, the way she's taking credit for the big salad.

I drain my wine glass as the men clear their plates, and then it's time for the second course.

"Next up, we have ravioli with heirloom tomatoes, asparagus, garlic, and herbs."

God, did she memorize the entire freaking menu when she ordered off of it?

This time, I take a small bite, if only to soak up some of the alcohol I'm sucking down. Marnie Black may be faker than this 'home-cooked' meal, but the food really is phenomenal. I'll have to dig through Damian's recycling bin when no one's looking for the name of the restaurant she ordered from.

By the time we've made it through the main course — strip steak with gorgonzola sauce, scalloped potatoes, and sauteed mushrooms (which Marnie *knows* all too well I'm allergic to) — and several bottles of wine, we are stuffed to the gills.

But there's always room for dessert.

Except . . .

"Shit, I forgot to bring the dessert."

Somehow, in the excitement of Sienna Berman's journal, the polygraph, and getting ready, I left my strawberry shortcake at home on the kitchen island. *Whoops.*

"That's okay," Damian starts to say, but it's not okay. I worked really hard on baking that cake. It's my contribution to the evening. And, my chance to get back into Damian's house alone.

"I have the best idea," I interrupt. "How about a change of scenery? We can have you over for after-dinner drinks and dessert."

"I guess a bite of something sweet wouldn't hurt after that five-star meal." He winks at Marnie. Red circles pop on her cheeks.

"Oh, it was nothing," Marnie demurs. *I'd beg to disagree. Really, she's cutting herself short. That takeout meal for four probably cost a small fortune.* "But that sounds good." She places her napkin down with a small sigh, as if relieved her hard work is done.

Bennett claps his hands. "I've got a brand-new bottle of grappa I've been dying to open."

"So what are we waiting for?" I ask, springing into action and carrying dishes from the dining room to the kitchen. I wonder if I should bring them diagonally across the street instead — save Marnie a trip.

"Thanks, Carrie. I'm wiped from all that cooking." Marnie takes a long swig of her wine, leaning back in the chair as if this is the first time she's sat down all day.

Ordering takeout and passing it off as your own must be exhausting.

I finish clearing the table *and* load the dishwasher. Being the good friend I am, I shove the takeout boxes deeper into the recycling bin.

Then, the four of us head next door to my house.

I don't plan on staying there long.

CHAPTER TWENTY-TWO

"TJ's not home? *Is* he?" Marnie leans on Damian, biting down on her lower lip in a show of feigned nervousness. She has no reason to be this deathly afraid of a nineteen-year-old boy. I mean, catching him arguing with Sienna Berman on camera before she went missing, aside. And even so, Marnie was married to a mass murderer, for goodness' sake! As far as I can tell, Marnie and TJ don't *talk* to one another. They don't even *look* at one another. Truly, her performance is borderline Oscar-worthy.

I fight the urge to roll my eyes. "No, Marnie. TJ is not home."

She breathes an exaggerated sigh of relief.

Trying to contain my annoyance, I focus on fishing my keys from my purse and unlocking the front door.

"I hope he's not arguing with any of our other neighbors," she mumbles under her breath. It's just loud enough so I can hear her, but the men are oblivious. The front door is open, and they've already taken off for the wine cellar — the grappa is waiting for them down there. I itch to call Marnie out — what if Damian *had* heard her — but that will have to wait another twenty-eight days.

I swallow an exasperated sigh. I really hope I can make it that long. With Marnie's recent diva behavior, I'm not entirely opti-mistic. But I have to do this for TJ. It's my job as his parent

117

(or stepparent, whatever) to protect him. At least, I think it is. Unfortunately for me, TJ didn't come with a handbook. Then again, The Estates did, and I'd argue it's a brochure of lies.

I shake all thoughts of TJ, the Bermans, and our twisted development loose from my mind. I need another drink. As if anticipating my (ahem, Marnie's) needs, Bennett emerges from the wine cellar with his prized bottle of grappa and a cabernet from Napa Valley for Marnie and me. Marnie perks up at the sight of the wine. It's a vintage cabernet that I was saving for a special occasion. Apparently, this qualifies as a special occasion.

Except . . .

"Carrie?" Bennett calls out. "Do you know where the wine-bottle opener is?"

I join my husband at the kitchen island, where he's already begun rummaging through drawers.

I shrug. "I'm pretty sure I left it out on the island."

"Well, it's not here. And where are all our extra ones?"

I raise an eyebrow. "No clue."

Bennett shakes his head. "Six cheese graters and not one bottle opener."

My cheeks color. "How embarrassing . . ."

Damian interjects, "Not a big deal. I unpacked mine earlier. I can run over and grab it. It's sitting on the counter."

With palms sweating, I clear my throat, before taking my chance and running with it.

"Don't be silly, Damian. You guys have already started drinking your grappa. I can get it." I arrange my features into a perfectly innocent expression, not giving Damian a chance to argue. "Keys?" I hold out a hand.

"Door is unlocked," he says, looking completely unfazed as he takes a long swig from his snifter.

The door is *unlocked*? *Where* does this guy think he is?

"Be right back!" I trill.

Marnie doesn't offer to join me, not that I'm disappointed or surprised. Ever since Damian showed up in The Estates yesterday, Marnie has been like the fly to his glue trap. Well, that's not entirely true. She left his side at some point today to pick up the takeout and her fresh set of bold, black lash extensions as well.

It takes two minutes to walk next door. My stomach twists with anticipation as I turn the knob on the front door and let myself into Damian's house. It feels weird being here without him. The house is completely silent, and my footsteps echo like thunderclaps as I walk through the foyer into the living room. My eyes quickly scour the room, but I don't see what I'm looking for.

Screw the corkscrew. I'm looking for that damn box.

I survey the rooms on the main floor, hoping Damian has stashed it somewhere else for safekeeping. Self-consciousness blooms in my chest. Perhaps he really did notice me eyeing it yesterday. Was I *that* obvious? Considering how tense things are in The Estates, it's entirely possible.

My gut tells me it must be around here somewhere. Why would you label your own box with an emphatic *DO NOT OPEN* just to open and unpack it?

Having exhausted my options on the main level, I take the stairs two at a time until I reach the landing leading to the six bedrooms. Room by room, I check in closets, bathrooms, under beds, but nothing.

Like our home, Damian's has a dormer that sits a few stairs above the bedrooms. I pause at the double-paned glass doors before twisting the knob and gently opening the door. I glance around the room, which Damian has overnight converted from a home theater into an office. It's the perfect place to stow a box.

But disappointment hits like a fist as I scour the room because, again, no box.

So I guess that's it. I'll never know what was inside that box, and I'll just have to trust whatever my neighbor tells me. Clearly, that has worked so well thus far . . .

Perhaps it's from the alcohol or running around searching this house, but my legs suddenly feel liquid and heavy beneath me. I pull out Damian's desk chair, collapsing onto the leather, and leaning my head against the headrest. I groan in frustration, momentarily closing my eyes to recalibrate myself.

The desk chair is super comfortable — one of those expensive, ergonomic ones, if I had to guess. Damian must spend an obscene amount of time on his feet if what he's told us about his professional life is true.

A jolt of panic suddenly rushes through me as it registers that I've been gone for way longer than the time it takes to retrieve a wine-bottle opener would warrant. Marnie's probably experiencing withdrawal already. I need to grab the corkscrew from the kitchen island and go before Bennett sends the cavalry out to search for me. I press my foot against the floor to push out the chair and rise to my feet.

I startle as it connects with something. It's something solid with a bit of give. I glance down, a chill crawling up my spine.

Jackpot.

CHAPTER TWENTY-THREE

Now that I've found the elusive box, hesitation fills me like a deer caught in headlights, bringing me to a sudden and chilling halt. As I weigh the levity of what I'm considering, I realize my hesitation is tinged with guilt. I can't actually go through my new neighbor's things. That's a major violation of privacy. Damian would be livid if he caught me. Bennett would certainly be pissed off, and embarrassed. And Marnie would probably try to strangle me with her own two hands.

So, I guess I'll need to be quick.

I may not have a wine-bottle opener — I hid them all earlier in my underwear drawer, the missing corkscrew a perfect excuse to get into Damian's house alone after I lured him to mine — but I do have a box cutter in my back pocket. I was sure to grab that on my way out the door.

Pulling the box cutter from my pocket, I'm suddenly in no rush to get home. I flick open the blade, feeling a shiver of anticipation as the carbon steel shimmers under the glow of Damian's desk lamp. I don't remember when or why I purchased a box cutter, only that I thought it might come in handy one day, just like the six cheese graters Bennett found in lieu of a wine opener. None of those cheese graters have come in quite as handy as this, though.

I take a deep breath as I run the blade along the packaging tape. The hairs on the back of my neck stand up as I silently slice through the box as if performing a dissection. Once the seal is broken, I gingerly place the box cutter on Damian's desk. I'm not sure what I'm expecting to find, but the possibilities are all I've managed to think about (TJ aside) for the past day and a half. Here goes nothing.

I pull back the flaps.

Oh, my God.

I stare at the contents, frozen in place. This is not what I was expecting at all. A skull? Perhaps. Trophies from a serial killer's thrill-kills? So I feared.

But *this?*

Lying inside the box I was so desperate to tear open and sink my grubby fingers into are photos — piles and piles of photos of a beautiful blonde that I presume is Damian's dead wife. How could I be so thoughtless, insensitive, and, dare I say, nosy? Of course, Damian doesn't want to open this box. I wouldn't if I were him. I can't even conceive of the tragic emotions that would escape from this Pandora's box of grief.

Oh God, Damian can *never* find out about this. I might as well throw a body-sized Band-Aid on him just to rip it off. I frantically attempt to shuffle the pictures back into place, but my hand brushes against something cool and hard — *steel.* I wrap my fingers around the object, pulling it from the bottom of the box.

A gun.

My heart pounds against my rib cage as the weight of the gun presses into my palm.

Now, *this* is unexpected.

I can't fathom what Damian would be doing with a gun, especially one buried among pictures of his dead wife. Did she kill herself? It would be pretty grisly to hold on to the gun.

Unless I have it all wrong. Is our new neighbor a grieving *widower* or someone far more sinister?

I suddenly find myself plummeting back to earth as I realize the Olympic-sized jump I'm making. But considering what we've seen here . . .

I carefully flip the gun over in my hands, and a soft gasp escapes from my lips. There are bullets in the chamber. Now that I've discovered what appears to be a *loaded* gun, Damian's red flags have red flags.

The gun slips from my fingers as shots go off in my head. I'm dizzy. My heart is doing back handsprings in my chest, beating so loudly I'm certain Bennett, Marnie, and Damian can hear it next door.

The thoughts come hard and quick, like a barrage of bullets.

Is Damian a sociopath like Marnie's last lover? This is just what we need: *another* crazy neighbor. How many crazy neighbors can you squeeze into one multi-million-dollar development at a time? Why us, *again?* It doesn't seem fair.

My phone buzzes suddenly in my pocket, and I jump up so fast I nearly knock over the desk chair.

Bennett's face smiles from the screen.

Shit. I've been here *way* too long. If I don't get back soon, one of them is going to come blazing through the door and find me going through Damian's things.

In a tremendous rush to not get caught, I open and close desk drawers, hunting for packaging tape. If I don't leave this box as I found it, there's a good chance Damian will figure out someone has tampered with it. And who else has been alone in his house other than me? Marnie, maybe, but she was too busy pretending to cook dinner to be a likely suspect.

I'm shuffling around pens and paper when bingo — I pull the tan adhesive from a drawer and quickly rip off pieces with my teeth. Once satisfied that the box looks as close to untouched as possible, I grab my things and hurry out of Damian's office, my tongue scratchy as if I've licked a hundred stamps.

I'm halfway down the stairs when the front door swings open. God, I wish I had locked the door behind me.

"Carrie?" Bennett calls, and he's not alone. I watch in horror as Damian and Marnie walk into the house behind him.

How the hell am I going to get myself out of this one?

"Hey," I call from the stairs, trying my best not to tumble down face-first. I find myself swaying in place, the alcohol deciding to kick in at the very worst moment. I grab onto the banister for support. My palms are so sweaty that I fear my hand may slip.

"What are you doing, Carrie?" Damian asks, crossing his arms against his chest.

"You're not going to believe this," I say innocently, "but I was looking for a bathroom and got completely turned around."

Bennett, Damian, and Marnie stare at me with dumbfounded expressions. We all know there are a half dozen bathrooms in every house in this development, several of which are on the main level. There is no reason for me to have gotten lost *upstairs*. Regardless, my words still feel hollow.

"Anyway," I add with a nervous giggle. "I figured it out. And you caught me just as I was about to grab the bottle opener."

You caught me. Stupid, stupid, stupid.

"Right," Damian drawls after an incredibly long and awkward pause. I am *so* obviously lying, the guy clearly doesn't believe a word coming out of my mouth. In all fairness, probably because not a word of it is true.

"I think I'm ready to call it a night." Damian lifts his arms above his head, feigning a yawn, then drops them back down. All along, his mouth remains frozen in a rigid line.

"Me too," Marnie adds, her lips twitching, because of course she does.

Even Bennett's lips are dipping down. I've really messed up our evening.

I wish I could just admit to what I was *actually* doing here. Maybe there's a completely innocuous explanation for the gun. I mean, lots of people have guns. Probably not tucked away in a box full of photos of their dead wife, but still.

I vow to myself to stay silent. I may be slightly intoxicated and a tad concerned, but I'm not stupid.

"Well, thanks for having us." Bennett reaches in to shake Damian's hand before they pat one another on the back. At least their relationship seems to be on solid ground.

As for Marnie and I . . .

I descend the stairs in full, expecting the cold shoulder from my so-called best friend. But Marnie pulls me in for a hug, which, to be honest, catches me completely off guard, given her frosty demeanor since Damian rolled into town.

"Call me in the morning," she says way too loudly, I assume, for the benefit of the men.

Because she then grabs my arm tightly and hisses in my ear, "You're going to tell me what you were *actually* doing here."

CHAPTER TWENTY-FOUR

I spend the second night in a row wide awake. Whenever I close my eyes, I picture Damian, Marnie, and Bennett's disturbed faces as they catch me descending the stairs from Damian's office. I keep thinking about that box full of photos. About the gun. And lastly, I keep thinking about the twenty-seven days I have left to keep Marnie quiet about the surveillance video.

To punctuate my sleeplessness, my phone rings promptly at 5 a.m. I hesitate to pick it up, sure it's Marnie calling to demand answers about what went on last night. But I can't tell her what exactly I was doing at Damian's house. Marnie is still my best friend, I guess, and she has kept my secrets in the past. As the incessant ringtone continues to disturb the early morning quiet, I gnaw contemplatively on my bottom lip. We seem to be in unchartered territory here. If her schoolyard-crush behavior is any indication, my confession will unleash a wicked game of telephone, and there's no doubt that Damian is the next in line. Marnie would one hundred percent rat me out to him right before giving up her safe code and listing Damian as sole beneficiary on her life insurance policy.

I realize, though, that I have to tell her *something*. The best bet is to stick with the story.

Hopefully, I do a better job than I did last night. I cringe just thinking about the awkward encounter in Damian's stairwell.

My eyes just barely register the no-caller ID as I've already swiped to pick up.

"Hello?"

Silence.

"Marnie?" I whisper, not wanting to wake up Bennett, who still has an hour left to sleep off the bourbon and grappa from last night.

My question is met with audible breaths. *Not again.* There is something seriously wrong with these people — whoever they are.

I'm about to hang up when a baritone voice warns, "Watch your back, Carrie."

Definitely *not* Marnie.

My breath catches in my throat. There's something vaguely familiar about the voice, too, though I can't place it.

I make no further attempts at being quiet. "Who is this?" I scream, my chest now a pressure cooker for my anxiety threatening to overflow.

Bennett bolts upright in bed.

"Please. Tell me who you are," I beg, desperation dripping from my words.

Bennett stares at me, eyes wild and nostrils flaring. He grabs the phone from my hand. I don't resist. He can have it. Whoever it is has already hung up.

"Dammit!" Bennett shouts, throwing the phone dramatically onto our plush white duvet, tossing down feathers into the air. "What is it, Carrie? What did they say?"

My hands are shaking, my heart is beating wildly, and I'm struggling to breathe.

It takes a few moments to get the words out, but finally, I manage. "It was a man. He told me to . . . to . . . watch my back."

These calls are nothing new. I've been receiving them for months — heavy breathing, hang ups, but never a warning. Maybe even, a *threat*.

Bennett has always told me to ignore the calls. We've pretty much accepted the fact that these reporters and rubberneckers are not above sinking pretty darn low to get what they want.

But now . . . "We need to call the police," he insists, grabbing my phone from where he tossed it.

"What are the police going to do? They'll probably blame TJ for the call." Not that TJ would ever call me and breathe heavily into the phone. That would be about as likely as Marnie apologizing for last night. Regardless, the call was from an unknown number.

"I don't know." My husband runs a hand through his thick, sleep-mussed hair. "Maybe they can trace the number. Something. Anything. They're the police."

After the way they botched things here the last time? I wish I felt half as confident as Bennett sounds.

"Fine," I acquiesce. "Call."

* * *

Twenty minutes later, the doorbell rings, and I spy Detective Johnson standing on our front porch. He's wearing his usual uniform of black slacks and a white, button-down shirt that has yet to meet an iron. His badge is proudly displayed on a lanyard around his neck. I'm starting to think Detective Johnson is the only law enforcement official in this town. Perhaps the rest of the force has joined Detective Young at Rikers Island, which is apparently like an all-inclusive resort compared to The Estates. Or maybe Detective Johnson is the one assigned to investigate all happenings at The Estates. We are certainly doing our part to keep him busy.

I'm less than thrilled to see him, but Bennett was right — if there's a way to get to the bottom of these calls, we have to at least try.

Being told to 'watch your back' is not something so easily dismissed. I'm wondering if it isn't the paparazzi after all, whether someone else is out there, harboring more sinister intentions than an exclusive interview. A chill crawls up my spine, and I imagine it will linger until we get to the bottom of this.

"Come in, Detective." Bennett opens the door widely so Detective Johnson can enter our home. It's wild that twenty-four hours earlier, I refused to let him in. Now, twenty-four hours later, we've *invited* him over. What's that they say about sand in an hourglass — days of our lives? We could reboot that soap opera and film it right here in The Estates. Starring Detective Johnson as the in-over-his-head detective.

But I'm beginning to fear that our lives took a hard left at soap opera, careening now into the Hollywood horror.

To be fair, Detective Johnson looks as excited to be here as I am to have him here. I examine his face. His eyes are glazed and bloodshot. Concern lines his forehead. I wonder if something else has happened — something other than the call that brought him here.

Have they found Sienna? Or has another girl gone missing?

I've seen this movie before. I thought we had permanently burned the ticket when I accidentally killed Mark Black. Apparently, there's a sequel. At the rate we're going, I wouldn't be shocked if this turns into a trilogy.

"Are you okay?" I ask, surprising myself as much as him by the question. Our interactions in the past have been frosty at best. I mean, we literally kicked him out of our house during a flood watch amid his last investigation, when the other girls were missing. *Dead*, I remind myself.

He shakes his head. "Actually, no. I wouldn't use the word *okay*. We found her phone."

My stomach clenches. Bile rises in my throat until I feel like I might be sick. I open my mouth to speak, but no words come out.

"You found whose phone?" Bennett asks, though the answer is pretty obvious.

Detective Johnson clears his throat. "Sienna Berman's."

Despite expecting it, hearing this doesn't make the news any less shocking. Up until now, I hadn't truly allowed myself to consider that anything bad had happened to her. I held on to the hope that she just wanted attention or needed to get away from her maniacal mother. That's not such a stretch.

"Well, that doesn't necessarily mean anything," Bennett observes.

But doesn't it? I turn to look at my husband, and I can feel the worry etching itself onto my face.

A few beats of silence pass before Bennett adds, "Maybe Sienna has more than one phone?"

I shake my head, finally finding my voice. "Like a *burner* phone? This isn't a thriller, Bennett."

"And . . . it was in the creek," Detective Johnson offers somberly.

"Oh." Bennett's face falls because, burner phone or no burner phone, that's definitely significant. The most God-awful feeling lands in the pit of my stomach. My insides twist and turn as if someone's wringing me out like a wet towel. The creek is where they discovered Lila Lockwood's deceased body. And now, somehow, Sienna's phone has turned up there.

I beg whatever higher power that might still be listening for it to be a sick coincidence.

"We are interviewing all your neighbors. Hopefully, someone has seen or heard something."

Like TJ? My stepson aced the polygraph, but now, I can't help but worry this will come back around to him again. Marnie's disingenuous face floats into view in my mind's eye, her distaste for TJ as plain as if she had sucked on a lemon. I can't help but wonder what Marnie will tell the police if questioned. Will she keep the footage under wraps like she promised?

Thoughts of Marnie take a swift turn to our newest neighbor. Flipping Andrea Winter's house, moving into Lila Lockwood's house. And then, only twenty-four hours later, Sienna Berman's phone discovered in the creek behind his home. Could Damian Mankiewicz be connected to this? Suddenly, I remember the cold steel, and the weight of it in my hand.

The loaded gun.

I feel trapped in a classic game of connecting the dots, but I just can't seem to make sense of the picture that's forming.

My hands clench into fists at my side, and I grit my teeth.

What am I looking at?

I haven't figured it out, *yet*.

CHAPTER TWENTY-FIVE

Once the shock has worn off, Bennett escorts Detective Johnson to the living room while I set off for the kitchen to brew some herbal tea for us. I'd say we could all use some to temper the chill that has settled over The Estates. Although, considering the circumstances, I doubt even a trip to the sweat lodge would thaw us out.

When I return, Bennett and Detective Johnson gratefully accept the steaming mugs, wrapping their hands around them as if they might escape our cold reality.

But I can't seem to find an escape route for *this*.

"So, go ahead and walk me through the call," Detective Johnson instructs, pulling a notepad from his jacket pocket. He raises a bushy eyebrow and taps a pen against the notepad impatiently.

I guess crank calls don't rate high on his list of priorities. As if to punctuate his disinterest, he lets out an exaggerated yawn. Perhaps he'll feel differently once he hears the scope of my harassment.

I walk Detective Johnson through *this* particular phone call, along with all the hang-ups and mouth breathing serenades that preceded it. "He told me to 'watch my back,'" I emphasize, taking a deep breath to calm my nerves.

The detective lays the pad and pen on the coffee table. He takes a long, slow swig of his tea, which, if mood alone would dictate, has no doubt already cooled.

"I wish I had better news, Mrs. Winter." Detective Johnson folds his thick hands in his lap. Again, I study the somber look on his face, the purple shadows beneath his eyes. My insides churn, as though we're standing on the precipice of something earth-shattering. "With the unknown number, seconds-long calls to your cell phone would be extremely difficult to track. And the truth is, Mrs. Winter, we don't have the time or resources to attempt to trace this call. Not with Sienna Berman still missing."

Now, that was anticlimactic.

"*Really*," Bennett drawls, a little too loudly. "Shouldn't you be taking this all the *more* seriously *because* Sienna Berman is still missing? Someone literally threatened my wife. What if it's the same person who took Sienna?"

Detective Johnson seems to consider the possibility. "Look, I understand where you're coming from, Mr. Winter, and I really wish there was more I could do. I'll file your complaint, but I'm being honest — it's not top on our list of objectives right now. There's nothing to suggest that these cases are linked, and our priority is finding Sienna Berman." Detective Johnson shifts in his seat, composing himself under the angry glare of my husband. "If you've nothing further, I'd like to get out there and do my job. In missing-person cases like these, time is of the essence."

Bennett stands abruptly, his hands curled into tight fists at his side. "I swear, if anything happens to my wife, I will hold you personally accountable."

That's of small consolation if something does, in fact, happen to me.

Detective Johnson rises from his seat and clears his throat. "Well, I'm glad we have that settled," he says, voice laced with exhaustion. "Call the station if you have any additional concerns."

Bennett sighs loudly in frustration, clearly ready to escort Detective Johnson to the door. He's been of little help. The only positive is that he hasn't mentioned TJ at all. In the short time we've known him, my stepson seems to be Detective Johnson's preferred topic of conversation.

I can't entirely blame him, knowing what I know, but he doesn't know all that. If he did, TJ would likely be sitting in a jail cell right now.

Still, I don't get the feeling Detective Johnson cares for us all that much.

I don't have time to stew on that thought as my phone buzzes on the coffee table.

I flip it over, unsurprised to see Marnie's name pop up on the screen as it's nine in the morning and we haven't spoken yet today. But I am slightly confused by her message.

Marnie: *Meet at the clubhouse in twenty minutes.*

My brows knit together. The *clubhouse?* That's super weird. We rarely go to the clubhouse. We used to visit only for community-wide events and annual elections, but there haven't been any community-wide events as of late, and Bennett and I vote by proxy now, precisely so we *don't* have to go to the clubhouse. Plus, there are ten months until the next election. Unless someone stages a coup, but who does something like that?

Panic thrums in my fingertips as I type out a response.

Me: *You want me to meet you at the clubhouse?*

Maybe by *clubhouse*, she meant my house. That would be less weird. It's only four letters off, so a definite possibility.

Marnie: *It's not just you, Carrie. It's a development-wide meeting to discuss Sienna Berman and community safety.*

Shit. Shit. Shit.

I stare at the phone, my feet frozen to the spot. Is this it? Is Marnie going to release the footage? Even if TJ didn't do anything to Sienna, the video looks bad — *extremely* bad. Plus, he lied in a polygraph. He perjured himself to the police. No one is going to believe a word he says after that. My fingers tingle with anxiety, as they hover over my phone.

"Carrie?"

I whip around at the sound of Bennett's voice.

"I hate that the call did this to you," he says, resting his hands on my shoulders. "You're incredibly jumpy. Are you okay?"

No, I'm not okay. We are not okay. The words are on the tip of my tongue, but I can't make them surface. I'm speechless.

"What is it?" Bennett's forehead furrows with concern. "Did you get another call?" His lips curl into a sneer.

My eyes flick down to my phone on the table, where the text from Marnie threatens to upturn our entire lives. Bennett follows my gaze. He picks up the phone, reads the text, then shakes his head at me.

"What the hell is she going to do?"

I chew on my lip. The truth is, I have no idea. I *wish* I knew. At one time, I thought I knew my best friend, but as it turns out, I don't know her at all.

"I have no idea, Bennett. Maybe nothing. Maybe something. But we need to get there."

Just not this second, though, as the doorbell rings.

"*Seriously?* What now?" Bennett stomps from the room to answer it.

Moments later, he's back with TJ by his side. I don't have time to consider why my stepson used the front door and not the garage, or who drove him home, for that matter. Despite him living here for the past few months, I've never actually met any of his friends. Those are questions for later.

"Come on. Let's go," Bennett says, an unfamiliar quiver in his voice.

I hold my breath as I follow my husband outside.

His hands shake as he locks the front door behind us.

CHAPTER TWENTY-SIX

We are packed into the clubhouse like sardines. Every seat is taken, and a standing-room-only crowd is rapidly gathering around the perimeter of the room. The last time the clubhouse was crowded like this was at the annual HOA elections. It was a contentious meeting, primarily for former president Ryan Altman, but nothing like this.

The time *before* last time, we gathered to discuss the drowning of seventeen-year-old Sofia Swanson. The vibe then was more along the lines of a tête-à-tête than a desperate call for community action. When news of Sofia's death broke, we had no idea what we were looking at.

Now, there's a train barreling toward us, and we can't look away.

There are no snacks set out on a table, no coffee or vodka-spiked lemonade like the last time. Perhaps because we know all too intimately what the outcome of this mystery may well be. A disconcerting sense of déjà vu strikes me, and I don't seem to be alone. The room buzzes with frenetic energy, zaps of electricity hopping from person to person.

Marnie taps her fingers against the microphone, and the room goes silent, except for the clicking sounds emanating from the clubhouse entrance. I whip my head around, and I notice the

TV cameras — at least a half dozen pointing at the podium like a firing squad. In a place like this, it's the equivalent of a White House press junket.

How *did* the press get wind of this?

I'd have thought, with all the controversy surrounding The Estates, this would have been a closed meeting. It must have been Marnie — always trying to stretch her fifteen minutes of fame. What *wouldn't* she do to keep herself in the limelight? She probably contacted the media herself and personally escorted them through our exclusive gates.

My gaze darts about the room, studying the professional faces with station identification badges, the steady hands with pens poised to take notes, the fingers hovering over record buttons on video cameras . . .

An unsettling thought slithers through my mind. Could one of *these* people be the one who warned me to watch my back? Does one of these reporters know something I don't? But I struggle to comprehend why they would be so cryptic about it. I shiver as I think about the hand slapped against my driver's side window.

Someone clearly means business.

Bennett taps my shoulder, bringing my attention back to Marnie. I watch as her eyes find Damian in the crowd, sitting a few rows behind us. She smiles down at him and waves. He blows her a kiss, which colors her cheeks hot pink. There's a twinkle in her eye. She's quite the celebrity — Damian the Travis to her Taylor, supporting her from the crowd. Of course, once the metaphorical football season starts, their roles will be reversed, and Marnie will be in the stands supporting him in whatever it is that he does, because I'd bet my left arm it's not flipping houses.

When she's done making eyes at her new beau, Marnie clears her throat and begins addressing the crowd. "Friends, neighbors.

I wish it weren't such troubling circumstances that have us gathered here today. As many of you may already have heard, Sienna Berman is missing. She was last seen approximately forty-eight hours ago and has not been accounted for since."

My frantic thoughts pound through me like a jackhammer. *Forty-eight hours. The last time Sienna was seen. With my stepson.*

Marnie pauses, and my entire body tenses. A chill runs up and down my spine. This is it — the moment Marnie exposes TJ to the paparazzi-filled crowd. Sweat drips from my clenched palms onto my pants.

I raise my eyes, meeting Marnie's. It feels like she can see right through me. As if sensing my fear and playing on it, Marnie hovers her fingers over a remote on the podium. Her gaze flicks from mine to the seventy-two-inch television hanging in the center of the room.

She's actually going to do it.

No, no, no.

I close my eyes tightly as if pretending this isn't about to happen will keep it from happening. The silence stretches taut like a rubber band ready to snap.

"As I was saying . . ."

I open one eye, then the other to find Marnie's hands folded on the podium. The remote is set off to the side. My heartbeat slows slightly.

"We are asking *anyone*," she stares in my direction, an unreadable expression on her face, "with information to please get in touch with Detective Johnson of the Armonk PD. His cards are on the table by the door. There is also a signup sheet for volunteers to help look for Sienna. I think I can speak for us all when I say that we just want to bring Sienna home safely. I will turn the podium over now to Detective Johnson for any questions you might have about the investigation."

With that, Marnie passes Detective Johnson the microphone and joins us in the crowd, settling into the seat next to Damian. He wraps a protective arm around her shoulder, and she looks up at him, eyes wide like a cartoon deer.

Meanwhile, reporters clamor to get their questions out, shutters clicking, video rolling.

I zone out as Detective Johnson fires off whatever answers he can without 'compromising the investigation.'

I steal a glance at Marnie. Her hands are covering her face. Through her fingers, I see her eyes, her cheeks. She appears to be crying, but the odd thing is, I don't see a single tear.

Come to think of it, I don't think I've ever actually seen her cry.

CHAPTER TWENTY-SEVEN

The positive is that the meeting ends without TJ being taken away in cuffs.

To say my family is relieved would be an understatement. Our development-wide meeting could have ended very badly for TJ — think fire and brimstone. Not that we're by any means out of the woods, but at least TJ's secret rendezvous with Sienna is safe . . . for now.

I definitely have my work cut out for me, though. Twenty-seven days feels like a freaking decade. At this rate, I don't know if I can put up with Marnie for another twenty-seven seconds.

The most pressing matter, though, is cornering my stepson about the journal. But I can't do that until—

"Carrie? Are you even listening to me?"

"I'm sorry, what?"

My husband shoots me a flabbergasted look. "I have to go into the office to sign some papers. Do you want to come with me?"

"To sign some papers?"

Bennett chews on his lower lip. "I guess that doesn't sound like much fun. But . . ."

"But what?"

"Will you be all right here?"

"I'll be fine," I tell him. I mean, I *hope* I'll be fine.

"Okay." Bennett nods, not looking very convinced. "Well, I'll ask TJ to stick around in case you run into any trouble. Until we figure out what's going on around here, I don't want you staying alone."

"I'm good," I say, placing a hand on Bennett's arm. "Don't worry about me."

The corners of Bennett's lips rise, forming a perfect smile. "It's my job to worry about you, Carrie. What kind of husband would I be if I didn't?"

Despite the stress pressing down on us like a pile of bricks, I smile back. "The kind of husband who has an *actual*, important job to do that doesn't involve his wife."

"Fine, then," he agrees. "I'll be back as soon as possible. Let me know if there are any developments while I'm gone."

"Of course."

With that, Bennett kisses my forehead and leaves me in the foyer, alone with my thoughts. And my stepson. I follow the sound of TJ banging around in the kitchen.

"Whatcha doing?" I ask, catching him by surprise.

"Jeez, Carrie!" TJ brings a hand to his chest. "Don't sneak up on me like that."

I can't tell from his expression whether he's joking or serious. Maybe the recent events have made me paranoid, but I suddenly that realize I can't glean anything from his expressions at all. Forget lawyer or professional chef — TJ may have a future in poker. Just hopefully not in the jail yard.

"Sorry, I didn't mean to startle you." I hold up both hands, showing him I meant no harm. "I just wanted to talk. Can we talk?"

TJ's brow furrows. He picks up a dishrag and wipes his hands. "I was just getting started on dinner, but yeah, we can talk."

I motion toward the table, where we sit down across from one another. TJ folds his hands between us.

"What is it, Carrie?"

Nervousness washes over me like a deluge. My palms leak sweat, and my heart gallops fast and hard. "How are you doing?" I ask, regretting the question as soon as the words fall from my lips. What a lame offering considering there's a missing girl in our development who he's suspected of kidnapping.

TJ raises an eyebrow. "How am I *doing?*" Clearly the most ridiculous question ever. "Let's see . . . the whole community — my *family* — suspects me of kidnapping one of our neighbors . . . I'd say I'm just grand."

"I don't suspect—" I start to argue, but I'm not fooling anyone here.

"Yes, you do, Carrie. It's so obvious. You're afraid of me. Admit it."

I shake my head emphatically. "I'm not afraid of you, TJ."

"You're a terrible liar."

I *am* a terrible liar, so I throw my hands up in submission. "Okay, maybe I'm *a little* afraid . . ."

TJ flinches at my admission as though I've stabbed him in the heart.

"Look," he says, leaning toward me. "I swear to you. I did not do anything to Sienna."

He looks so sincere, eyes soft, hands relaxed, I almost believe him.

Almost.

"Lydia Berman came by again. She brought Sienna's journal." I pause, watching TJ's face for any signs of panic. He doesn't look worried. If anything, just confused, but to be honest, I'm not even sure about that. I'd have a better shot at reading Braille. "She wrote about you in it," I continue.

TJ shrugs. "She was harassing me, Carrie. Like, obsessed. I'm sorry, but I'm not shocked she wrote about me in her little diary."

It's not the fact that she wrote about him. It's *what* she wrote about him. I'm not sure I can hammer out the distinction without letting TJ read it for himself. It could potentially be a serious mistake turning the journal over to him.

I guess we will find out.

"Wait here," I tell him as I leave to get the journal.

My legs shake as I ascend the stairs to my bedroom. I wonder whether this will be the moment when TJ's mask falls off, revealing who truly resides beneath. Or is this all some terrible mistake conjured up by a deranged woman and her equally deranged daughter?

With TJ waiting for me downstairs, it's too late to turn back now.

I take a deep breath as I make my way to the bed. I slip a hand beneath the duvet, sliding my fingers between the mattress and box spring. I shift left and right, the knot in my stomach growing. The only other thing I feel is the tight embrace of foam and springs.

There's no journal.

CHAPTER TWENTY-EIGHT

Panic courses through my veins as I frantically search for the journal. I'm the only one who knows about it. I didn't tell anyone. Not even Marnie. *Especially* not Marnie.

At least, I *thought* I was the only one who knew about it. But this wouldn't be the first time I was wrong.

My mind flashes to the warning — *Watch your back, Carrie.* The hairs on the back of my neck prickle. I whip my head around, almost expecting to find someone in the bedroom with me.

But there's no one. I'm utterly alone, with only the sound of my heart throbbing in my ears for company.

I desperately continue my search, lifting the edge of the mattress to peer beneath it. *How can this be?* I slump to the floor, my arm jutting farther into the void.

And then, sweet relief.

My hand collides with the worn leather book. I must have buried it deeper than I remembered. Even though I'm fairly certain I may be losing it, I allow myself to inhale. *Of course*, the journal is here.

Slowly, my heartbeat returns to normal.

I clutch the journal to my chest, mentally preparing myself to confront TJ with Sienna's words. They play through my head on a loop like a record stuck on repeat.

I can't take this anymore. He's been following me everywhere — like some sort of sick stalker. I don't know what he wants from me. I just know I need to stay away from him. TJ Winter is dangerous. I don't care what the police say. I know he killed Sofia and Lila. I just know it. And he's going to kill me, too, if I don't stop him. I am going to stop him.

I'm not sure how TJ will be able to talk his way out of this one.

I grasp the handrail tightly as I make my way back down the stairs. I pause at the entryway to the kitchen, silently watching my stepson. He's still sitting exactly where I left him at the table, his head resting in his hands. He looks exhausted, but then how could he not be? Life in The Estates is exhausting.

No, it's more than just exhausting.

It's *deadly*.

I try to shake the thoughts of what happened to those other poor teenage girls because we don't know for sure that anything terrible has happened to Sienna. It doesn't have to be a foregone conclusion that she's been harmed, even if our neighborhood's track record would indicate such.

I slip into the seat next to TJ and rest a hand on his shoulder. "TJ?" I say quietly, not wanting to startle him again.

His gaze shoots up, meeting mine over the journal. "What is *that?*" he asks, eying Sienna's journal like it's a bomb he's been asked to diffuse.

"It's Sienna's 'little diary.'" I try to infuse light into my words, but there is no light to be found here. Only darkness. The only way it could be any darker is if . . . I don't allow myself to complete the thought. Sienna Berman is probably fine. Maybe if I keep telling myself she's run away, I'll somehow manifest it.

I nudge the journal in TJ's direction. "Here. Have a look."

TJ cautiously picks it up. His expression is stoic as he scans through a few pages. Then he shakes his head and drops the journal like it's been set on fire.

He shoves it back in my direction. "This is bullshit, Carrie. Complete bullshit."

God, how badly I want to believe him. But . . .

"You don't believe me, do you?"

When I don't respond, TJ explodes, startling me with a sudden surge of anger. "Right, so I guess if Sienna says it, it must be true. Never mind that I didn't do anything." He slams his hands down, shaking the table.

I suck in a sharp breath. "I want to believe you, TJ. I *do*. But why would Sienna write this in *her* journal that only *she* sees if there's no truth to it?"

"You're asking me to analyze the actions of a crazy person? I'm sorry, but I can't do that. I don't know *why* she would write any of this. Or why she hates me so much, for that matter."

I get what he's saying. Despite all the uncertainty swirling around us like a hurricane, one thing is certain — TJ has never gotten a fair shake.

Not then.

Not now.

Not ever.

I can't help but empathize with him. It wasn't that long ago when I was lost at sea in a similar boat. And now here we are together, our eyes lingering over the journal that could destroy any chance at a future my stepson has. And destroy my darling husband in the process.

The doorbell chimes, yanking us both back to the present. TJ jerks his head up, his gaze meeting mine.

"Who?" he asks, barely a whisper.

I fumble for my phone, pulling up the Ring app. My stomach somersaults. I can't find my voice. I flip the screen so TJ can see the raven-haired figure looming on our doorstep for himself.

"Did you have plans?" he asks.

I shake my head, chewing on my lower lip. Usually, I'd think nothing of an unannounced Marnie drop-by. But after how things went last night, Marnie is just about the last person I'm expecting (or hoping) to find standing on my porch.

"You're not going to tell her, are you?" TJ gapes at me with a look of sheer terror on his face. At least, I think that's the expression I'm registering. He should be terrified. The footage is one thing. *This?* Sienna, describing in her own words how dangerous TJ is, is quite another.

"No, no," I answer. "Of course not." I rise from the table onto shaky legs, heading to the nearest drawer — the one that houses our wine openers. I shove the journal deep inside. "You should probably . . ."

I turn to look at TJ. All the color has drained from his face, leaving him whiter than the kitchen walls. "I don't . . . I can't see her."

I don't know what it is between the two of them, but even I sense TJ *shouldn't* see her right now. The chair legs screech against the kitchen tiles as he rises to his feet, sending a chill down my spine.

"Go upstairs," I say. "I'll let you know when she's gone."

I don't have to tell him twice. He's already jogging up the back staircase.

I take a calming breath before heading to the front door. Here goes nothing.

CHAPTER TWENTY-NINE

"What the hell, Carrie?" Marnie barks in lieu of a formal greeting.

"Hello to you, too." I try to disguise the edge in my voice. Instead of greeting Marnie with a punch in the face, which is tempting, I force myself to smile widely.

She doesn't smile back, not so much as a lip quiver. Her rage perplexes me. "Well, are you going to invite me in?" Marnie moves her hands to her hips as if her pinched facial expression alone isn't telling enough.

I clench and unclench my fists behind my back. "Yes, of course. Come in."

I step aside for a visibly agitated Marnie. She's like one of those cartoon characters with smoke blowing from its ears. She pushes past me, her heels scratching across the marble floor. Why the heck is she wearing stiletto heels to walk across the street to my house anyway?

"Do you want something to drink?" I offer, knowing that it usually helps smooth out the edges in Marnie Black.

Just not this time. Marnie spins around to face me, her cheeks blazing like cherry tomatoes under the summer sun. "No, I don't want something to drink. I want you to tell me what you were doing at Damian's house last night!"

Well, I can't very well do that . . .

I involuntarily cough, thankful I'm not currently having a drink, or it would be an Ocean Spray. "Whatever do you mean?" I ask in the most innocent voice I can muster, considering I'm evidently the worst liar ever. "I went to Damian's house to get the bottle opener so we could have some wine. *Remember?* And then I got lost."

"*Lost?*" Marnie repeats, the mocking tone lending a sharp edge to her voice. "You honestly expect me to believe you got lost in his house? My God, Carrie. How long have you been living next door to it?"

I shrug. "Two years. But you know, I hadn't been over there since the whole penis incident at book club." I joined The Estates book club at Marnie's behest when I first moved in, only to get blackballed when I suggested a Colleen Hoover book. *Too racy*, they claimed. These women wouldn't know a good book if I hit them over the head with one. I'm not sure how they produced offspring, with their blatant abhorrence for sex with their husbands.

Marnie impatiently taps her foot on the floor.

"Anyway," I continue. "I had *way* too much to drink last night. I got disoriented. I'm sorry, but I don't know what else you want me to tell you."

"How about the truth?"

"That *is* the truth," I press. I will *not* back down.

The corners of Marnie's lips dip. Her eyebrows turn in. I stare at her awkwardly, nodding like a bobblehead doll.

"It seems you and I have a very different understanding of the truth, then," she scoffs.

Just like how you tried to pass off takeout as your own home-cooked meal? I yearn to spit in her direction. But I guess we can both have our little secrets for now.

When I say nothing, she continues. "Fine, I'll have a drink. You're so frustrating, Carrie. You're, like, literally *driving* me to drink." Marnie abruptly turns on a sharp heel toward the kitchen.

Oh no.

I scamper after her, my gaze desperately flicking to *the* drawer — the one that doesn't just house our wine openers now.

My heart seizes as her hand connects with the handle. She must be looking for a corkscrew. I could tell her that we never found them. But Marnie would still look for herself. What then?

"*Wait*," I practically scream.

Marnie freezes, her hand hovering over the drawer.

"I got it. Make yourself comfortable." I stumble over my words, just barely getting them out. I squeeze my hands together to stop them from shaking.

And then I feel a sharp stab of panic as Marnie hesitates. A sickly feeling washes over me.

"Fine," she decides, tearing her hand away.

Oh, thank God. One crisis averted.

Marnie stomps over to the table and plops down onto a chair. She folds her arms angrily across her chest. "You better start talking, Carrie. Or I swear, I will."

On to the next one.

I try to hide the shake in my step as I walk to the fridge and pull out a bottle of Pinot Grigio. Wine usually puts Marnie in a happy mood. However, Marnie does not look happy. Her lips are turned down, and a deep crease has settled between her eyes.

It's going to take a heck of a lot more than a glass of Pinot this time. *What else have I got?* I feel Marnie's eyes boring into me as I discreetly shove the journal deeper into the drawer while grabbing the wine opener. I gently close the drawer behind me. I wish it had a dang lock.

"I see you found the wine opener," she says, voice dripping with insinuation. "How convenient."

I turn my back to her, unable to formulate a response. I focus on the wine bottle instead. Despite my best efforts, my hands tremble as I try to uncork it. It takes several attempts to pierce the cork, and I wind up twisting so erratically that bits and pieces break off into the wine. I pour the cork-filled wine into two glasses, hoping Marnie doesn't notice the debris. I don't need to give her any additional reasons to be upset. It would seem she's got plenty, at least in her mind. My legs wobble as I carry the glasses to the table. It's like I'm walking on stilts.

Marnie pulls the glass from my hand before I have the chance to sit. Apparently, manners have gone out the window. She takes a hearty sip, not dragging her eyes away from me for a second. The silence consumes me, and I struggle to figure out what she wants me to do — offer her my firstborn? TJ might not count, and something tells me she doesn't want him anyway . . .

"Marnie . . ." I place a hand over hers, but she jerks it away, as if scorched. As upset as I am with her for her recent behavior, the rejection burns. I fight the sting of hot tears in my eyes but push forward. "I'm sorry you're so upset with me. I promise you, I really did get lost."

Marnie's eyebrows knit together. "I don't know, Carrie. It just seems weird."

"I get it, okay? I do. But I don't know what happened. Maybe the stress was just getting to me. Coupled with all the wine. We drank *a lot* of wine."

Marnie looks me square in the face. "Well, to be honest, it seems to me you don't want me to be happy. It's like you have Munchausen's or something."

My eyes widen in shock. "*Munchausen's?* Like I want to make you *sick?*" I can't believe she is serious.

"No . . . like you want me to stay unhappy," she shoots back coldly.

"Why in the world would I want you to stay unhappy, Marnie?"

"Because you're jealous? Because I'm less available now? Who knows with you . . ." She throws her hands in the air. A flash of light reflects off her cocktail ring, momentarily rendering me blinded. Disoriented.

"I . . . That's not . . ." For a moment, I wonder if she could be right. But no, I am not a happiness killer. A husband killer, fine. But happiness? No way. That's ridiculous.

"I'm worried about you, is all. You and Damian — it's all happening so fast. I just want you to be careful. You barely know this guy."

Marnie folds her arms across her chest. "I know what I need to know, Carrie. I care about him, and he cares about me."

"Fine. I promise I want you to be happy, Marnie. It's all I've ever wanted. You're my best friend."

With a slight curl to her lip, Marnie doesn't look like she believes me.

But I've got bigger problems than whether or not she thinks I want her to be happy. Namely, I don't know *who* this person is sitting across from me.

And that makes her dangerous.

CHAPTER THIRTY

Soon after, Marnie storms off in a plume of false eyelashes, her departure bringing both an incompatible sense of relief and dread. I spend the next few minutes cleaning fallen lashes from the floor and poring over what the hell just happened.

I can't for the life of me understand why she's so worked up or why she's been so cold toward me for the past two days. It's not my fault Sienna Berman is missing *again*. And it's not my fault that Lydia Berman suspects my stepson *again*. It's certainly not my fault our new neighbor had a box ominously labeled *DO NOT OPEN* that I couldn't resist opening.

Okay, maybe that part was a little my fault.

Does Marnie think I have the hots for Damian and was rifling around in his underwear drawer or something last night? That would be even more ludicrous than her accusing me of having Munchausen's. I'm not interested in our new neighbor, at least not for the reason she clearly is. Damian Mankiewicz is hot, yes, but I've got a perfectly good-looking, successful man at home, thank you very much.

I've been nothing but amicable to Damian — platonically friendly. I've tried to be warm and welcoming. *Neighborly*, we call it. It was *my* idea to go over there and introduce ourselves!

While I may not be wrong (about thinking I've done *almost* nothing wrong), I have to make this right. There's just no telling what Marnie will do if I don't.

Perhaps I'll just come clean. Share my suspicions with Marnie and let her do what she wants with them. That's a great idea, maybe twenty-seven days from now.

Unless I delete the footage from her phone. Then Marnie can't prove anything without evidence. Without it, it would be her word against mine. So, that's what I'll do. I'm so upset that I may even take down the whole app while I'm at it. Marnie can twiddle her thumbs until the next day's footage loads, for all I care.

I just need to get a hold of her phone.

But the question remains as to how.

My own phone rings, and I rush back into the kitchen to pick it up before it goes to voicemail. I knew Marnie couldn't actually stay mad at me for this long. It's crazy. We've been inseparable for the past two years. I supported her through her husband's death, granted, after I accidentally killed him, but still . . .

Except, my phone is not where I left it. I grab an AirPod off the counter, sticking it in my ear.

I hesitate a moment before answering because I'm not sure I can stomach another one of *those* calls. But then I think, *what if it's Marnie, upset about how we left off?* Thinking I'm ignoring her call might push her over the edge she's precariously teetering on. I can't let that happen. I have to answer it.

"Is she gone?"

"TJ?"

"Yeah. Is the coast clear?"

So it's not Marnie, after all.

"She's gone." I exhale slowly, trying to temper my disappointment.

"I'll be down in a minute," he tells me. "If we're done talking about the diary for now, I'd like to get a jump on dinner."

"Okay, sure." I end the call. There's nothing more to discuss about the journal for now. TJ says it isn't true, and I have no way to prove otherwise. I'll have to let that one lie for now. Besides, it'll be nice to have a break from cooking tonight so I can pour all my time and energy into figuring out how to deal with the problems piling up faster than the Amazon packages on my doorstep.

Speaking of which, I head to the front door to retrieve said packages. But as I crack it open, my latest haul is not what catches my attention.

I stare out onto the street, my feet glued to the floor. My eyes bulge and my mouth falls open. I can't believe what I'm seeing. Marnie Black and Lydia Berman are standing in the road in front of my house. No, they're not just standing there — Lydia *is* pointing at my house. As for Marnie, she's nodding along, eating up whatever nonsense Lydia is feeding her.

I quietly slip the door closed before they see me. I collapse back against it, my knees buckling. There's no conceivable explanation for what they're doing out there. Marnie and Lydia despise one another.

There's just one person they despise more than each other.

I locate my phone on the entry table and pull up the call log to fire off a call to TJ and let him know what I just witnessed. To be fair, I'm not entirely sure *what* I just witnessed, but I saw enough to know that Marnie and Lydia were talking about someone in my house. And, by association, my stepson.

An unsettling thought creeps through the underbrush of my mind. Marnie could be telling Lydia about the footage, and, in exchange, Lydia could be informing a riveted Marnie about the journal.

Oh God. Either way, TJ is completely screwed.

My finger hovers over the phone screen, ready to hit the call button.

Except TJ's name does not pop up on my recent calls list. My last call was from an unknown number.

Son of a bitch.

CHAPTER THIRTY-ONE

My world feels like it's been knocked off its axis. The room spins as I try to make sense of my call log. Why would TJ call from an unknown number?

Has it been my *stepson* harassing me all along?

"Carrie?" I startle at the sound of TJ's voice ringing from the kitchen. It's chilling, like invisible fingers scraping across my skin.

My gaze flits down to the phone in my hand. My knuckles are white. I'm not just saying that. They're *actually* white. I'm clutching the phone so tightly I'm surprised it hasn't shattered. Just like the glass in the kitchen TJ broke when he was doing *what* exactly . . .

The most awful, sinking feeling swarms in the pit of my gut. Black dots dance before my eyes as the shock of what this might mean settles in. Try as I might, I can't come up with a single rational explanation for why TJ would call from an unknown number. He has a cell phone with a perfectly good *listed* number assigned to it. He would have to dial *67 to block that number to call me. That seems like some serious effort to place a call from upstairs. Another possibility dances at the back of my mind — he has another phone.

A *burner* phone.

Just like what Bennett suggested Sienna might have.

My mind is now spinning so fast I can't see straight. I lean against the wall for support.

"Carrie?"

This time, TJ's voice is followed by heavy footsteps. *Oh, God.* I can't let him find me like this. If I can't even wrap my head around these thoughts, how can I possibly articulate them?

"I'm in here," I call out in a voice that's unnaturally high.

"What are you doing?" he asks, looking me over skeptically. He fidgets with the dish towel in his fingers, pulling it back and forth between his hands. The way he's wringing it, it looks like a ligature.

He wouldn't strangle me with my own dish towel, *would* he? No, this is ridiculous. But the narrowing of his eyes, the tension in his posture as if he's a predator readying itself to pounce . . . I consider confronting him about the unknown number call, yet something in the way he moves reminds me of a caged animal. And caged animals are prone to attack.

My eyes remain fixed on that dish towel as I stammer, "I . . . um . . . I was just grabbing the packages from outside."

The corner of TJ's mouth quirks up. "Where are they?"

"Where are who?"

"The packages you were grabbing from outside?" He cocks an eyebrow as he surveys my empty hands.

"Oh." I laugh nervously. "Delivery hasn't come yet."

TJ smacks his lips. "Right."

He so does *not* believe me. To be fair, I wouldn't believe me either.

"You're acting really weird, Carrie." Funny, Marnie said the exact same thing. Self-consciousness slithers into my chest like a snake in a vegetable garden. *Am I?* TJ takes a step forward, closing the space between us.

"I'm just feeling a little tired," I say. It's basically the *only* thing I've said that's true in this entire conversation. Living here is utterly exhausting. This is *not* the life I imagined when Bennett swept me off my feet and moved me into The Estates. Then, of course, I hadn't known about TJ. Or bitter best friends. Or househusbands behaving badly.

Upscale suburbia can be one hell of a nightmare.

"Maybe I'll lie down for a bit if you don't need any help with dinner."

TJ's shoulders relax. He throws the ligature — er, dish towel — over a shoulder. "Nah, I'm good. Can I make you some tea?"

Tea does sound nice, but . . . I'm not sure that's the best idea, considering I thought, however briefly, he was about to strangle me. "No, but thank you."

TJ smiles widely, dimples forming on his cheeks. "I guess I'll get to it then."

I exhale loudly as his back disappears from sight. Along with the checkered dish towel that I'll never look at in the same way again.

I shuffle up the stairs as quickly as I can. I need to put some space between me and my stepson. Except TJ's voice trails after me as I climb the winding staircase. He's not trying to stop me from going upstairs.

He's just humming.

Now, that's odd. There's a missing girl in our development. TJ was caught *on camera* with the missing girl and named in her journal as a threat, and now he's *humming?* Like a freaking songbird? Me, with my near-coronaries, can't comprehend how he's so darn calm. Like father, like son, I guess . . .

Just not like stepmother. I'm a walking disaster. Anxious, disheveled. Hot, cold. Burning from deep within my core, with goosebumps lining my flesh.

I let myself into the bedroom, gently closing the grand doors behind me. The doors weigh at least eighty-five pounds apiece.

They're made of solid pine imported from some bougie province in French Canada. The doors cost Bennett a small fortune when he designed the house — one of the many *extras* he splurged on to set his, or rather *our*, mansion apart from the rest. It cost him even more to replace the one that crushed Mark Black to death.

On that note, I twist the lock, securing myself inside. When Mark first died, I had a difficult time coming in here. I kept seeing the look of madness on his face as he chased me into the bedroom. His mouth moved as he denied being a psychopath, but all the while his body moved to kill me. The door rattled on its hinge before falling to the ground and suffocating him under its weight. I slept in one of our guest rooms for an entire month after they released me from the hospital.

Then, slowly, I came to accept that I was safe here.

At least, I *thought* I was safe here.

I reach into my pocket for my phone. I need to call Bennett to find out when he'll be done signing his papers. I take back what I said. *This* is the most important business we've got. The business of TJ, Damian, Marnie, Sienna, Lydia . . . The list goes on and on and on.

I move my hand around one pocket, then the other. My stomach sinks. I left my phone downstairs. I am so *not* going down to get it. I'm not leaving this room until Bennett comes home.

I just need to figure out what to do with myself. I'm mentally exhausted but too wired to nap. Maybe I'll read a book. I could use the distraction — some spice and an ugly cry. *It Starts with Us*. Take that, book club. I reach into my nightstand drawer to retrieve the book.

As I'm reaching for the book, something tangles around my fingers.

What the . . . ?

I pull my hand from the drawer.

How did Marnie's necklace wind up in my drawer?

My heart lodges in my throat as I examine the delicate gold chain. It's caked with rust. No, not rust. Blood. It's caked with *blood*. My stomach bottoms out. This isn't Marnie's necklace.

It's Andrea Winter's.

It is the very same necklace that Mark Black gave to her. The one that she was likely wearing when she was pushed to her death. Last I heard, this necklace was sitting in an evidence box at the Armonk Police Department.

And now it's sitting in my bedside drawer.

CHAPTER THIRTY-TWO

A full-blown panic attack consumes me. My heart is racing, and I'm sweating like I've just finished Zumba, followed by a nine-ty-minute hot yoga class. My pulse is dangerously high. I pace my bedroom, frantically trying to figure out how evidence from the Armonk Police Station has wound up in my nightstand.

This. Is. Not. Possible.

"Carrie?" I nearly jump out of my skin at the sound of my name and banging on the bedroom door.

Great. It's TJ. Did *he* plant this necklace in my drawer?

Do I answer? Let him in? What if he's come back with the dish towel?

I haven't felt frightened like this since, well, since twenty min-utes ago when he cornered me downstairs . . .

"Carrie, answer me. Please. That detective is back. He's in our house, waiting for you downstairs."

Detective Johnson? Waiting for *me?*

I scramble to the door, reluctantly unlocking it. "What's going on?" I whisper, convinced Detective Johnson is eavesdropping on our conversation from downstairs. *Why would TJ let him in the house in the first place?* I'm starting to think my stepson may not be the sharpest tool in the shed. Or maybe he's more calculating than I've given him credit for.

TJ shrugs. "I don't know. He just said he needs to talk to you, and that it's 'urgent'." TJ makes air quotes around the word *urgent*. My head swims with unsavory possibilities.

"Please tell him I'll be down in a minute. Don't say anything else, okay?"

"Okay, but he doesn't seem all that interested in talking to me. Only *you*." TJ points a finger at my chest, stopping just shy of poking me in it.

I stand momentarily frozen in place as my stepson disappears down the hall.

Then I hurry from the room and hasten down the stairs, clutching the railing tightly — it's the only thing keeping me upright. My legs feel like the overcooked spaghetti Marnie would have probably made the other night if she knew how to cook.

I find the detective standing inside the foyer by the front door. His face is ashen, his expression serious. There's not even a shadow of a smile on his face. He looks like he just found out someone died. Dread pools in my stomach.

My first thought is Bennett. Where is my husband?

"There's been an accident—"

"No." My legs give out, and I sink to the floor.

"*Bennett?*" Big black dots dance through the air. Hot tears spring to my eyes. It can't be Bennett. Something can't have happened to my husband.

Detective Johnson's eyes meet mine. There's something hard in them. Something cold. It chills me to the core.

"Your husband is fine, Mrs. Winter."

Oh, thank God. I slowly allow myself to breathe.

The detective reaches out a hand and helps me to my feet. "Can we sit down?" I don't point out the fact that I was just sitting. It seems inappropriate, considering.

Instead, I nod and motion toward the sitting room adjacent to our foyer. No one ever actually sits in here. The couches are made of stark white leather imported from Italy, and the accent pieces cost a gazillion dollars apiece. It's always felt like an extension of our marble mausoleum. And now, like an interrogation room.

All of a sudden, I hate my house. I hate this freaking *place*.

Once seated, Detective Johnson draws a sharp breath. "It's your neighbor—"

"*Marnie?*" I interrupt. *Oh God, has something happened to Marnie?*

Detective Johnson's gaze locks on mine. "No, Mrs. Black is unharmed."

I exhale a sigh of relief. So Bennett and Marnie are fine. TJ is home. Is it the *new* neighbor? "Well, who is it then?"

"Lydia Berman . . ." Detective Johnson's voice trails off.

My breath catches in my throat. Lydia was just outside with Marnie no more than an hour ago. *Unharmed.*

"What happened?" I squeak out.

"She was in a car accident. She crashed a few blocks outside of your development. She drove head-on into a tree. The damage was . . ." He pauses, his eyes pulling up as if searching for the right word. "Catastrophic."

My mouth falls open. "Is she . . ."

"She's badly injured, but the doctors are hopeful that she'll pull through. She was lucky a good Samaritan helped pull her from her vehicle before it burst into flames."

Burst into flames? "That's just . . . that's awful."

Detective Johnson nods somberly. "It is quite awful." He doesn't say anything else as his eyes bore into mine. It's almost as if he's assessing my reaction to this news.

After what feels like an eternity of silence, he adds, "There's something else."

"Something *else?*" I'm not sure I want to hear what he's about to say. It feels like that moment when the ocean ebbs before a tsunami hits.

The detective leans forward in the chair, as if he's about to let me in on a secret. "We have reason to believe Lydia Berman's brake lines were cut."

And here comes the wave. Crash.

"Cut?" My eyes widen in shock. "Like on *purpose?*"

"Like on purpose," he confirms.

Of course, because it's not like you would cut someone's brakes *by accident.* I nearly scoff at myself. How could I be so dense?

The room spins violently as the news of Lydia's accident sinks in. Detective Johnson waits for me to respond, but I don't know what to say. I don't need to ask *why* someone would want to harm Lydia Berman — half the development can't stand her, and the other half barely tolerates her — but that doesn't necessarily mean that someone would try to *kill* her.

Suddenly, I'm not so sure.

Detective Johnson watches silently as I try to make sense of what has happened. But I can't make it make sense. With Mark Black cold in the ground, I can't think of who among my neighbors is capable of something so despicable.

And then it registers. Why Detective Johnson came here to personally deliver this news about a neighbor he knows I have bad blood with.

"Mrs. Winter?"

"Yes?" My voice cracks in my throat.

"Where were you this afternoon?" It's a loaded question that sounds more like an accusation. His tone has changed, any hint of pleasantry gone. There's an atmospheric shift in the room that has the hairs on my neck standing up.

This day has officially spiraled completely out of control. It feels like I'm being buried in a hole I can't dig my way out of. But I didn't *do* anything. He can't place me at Lydia's house if I was never there. Unless, somehow, he can.

"I . . . I . . . was home. I've been home since the meeting at the clubhouse. TJ was here as well, so he could vouch for me."

"Where is TJ, Mrs. Winter?"

"He's upstairs."

Detective Johnson scratches the silver stubble on his chin. "I see. So he may not have known if you snuck out the house for a bit."

"No, I didn't say that—" I start, before the detective interrupts me.

"Well, see, here's the problem. I received a call from a potential witness placing you at Lydia Berman's house this afternoon. Care to share *what* were you doing at her house this afternoon?"

I shake my head, horrified by the implication. I can't believe what I'm hearing. It feels like my ears have malfunctioned. "I have no idea what you're talking about, Detective. I wasn't at her house. I haven't been to Lydia's house in months," I insist. "Why would someone say something like that?"

"I can't say," he answers, fiddling with the handcuffs dangling from his holster. "But I'm going to need you to come down to the station for questioning."

The room spins, slowly at first, and then so quickly I can barely keep my head upright. I'm dizzy and disoriented, like I've just stepped off a roller coaster. "For *questioning?* Are you kidding me? I would never . . . I don't even know where to find the brakes in a car, let alone sabotage them. What would I even cut them with — my nail clippers?" *A cheese grater,* my traitorous inner voice suggests unhelpfully.

Detective Johnson looks unimpressed. I'm sure he's heard all this and more before. Not that he's seen many (or any) other intentional brake cuttings in Armonk, but the way he's staring at me with unwavering eyes is downright unnerving. I'm back in my sixteen-year-old body getting caught breaking curfew, only worse. I'm accused of breaking brakes. "Am I under arrest? Do I need a lawyer?"

He narrows his steely eyes on me. "You're under suspicion of tampering with her brakes. Barring any charges, you'll be free to leave after we're done questioning you."

"Barring any *charges?* But I swear, I didn't do anything."

"That's to be determined, Mrs. Winter."

CHAPTER THIRTY-THREE

"Can I at least drive myself there?" The last thing I need is for Marnie and our other neighbors to watch me being hauled away by the police. It's not a good look, especially in a place like this.

Detective Johnson nods, his arms folded tightly across his chest. "You can drive yourself. I'll meet you at the station. You know where it is, *right?*" He arches an eyebrow inquisitively, though it's not really a question.

Of course, I know where the station is. It's the same place where I endured hours of interrogation after Mark Black's death. He also knows I have GPS in my car, like every other person with a vehicle produced after 2015 or a gosh darn *phone*. He's trying to get under my skin, and it's *working*. It makes me despise him even more.

But not more than whichever neighbor ratted me out to the police. And with a false story, no less!

I feel sick. Someone is trying to frame me.

"I need to grab my purse and keys, and I'll head over." I try, unsuccessfully, to disguise the apprehension in my voice. I'm stuck in a place between unadulterated rage and crippling fear. Hot lava flows through my veins while cold panic churns in my gut — a perfect storm of uncertainty.

"Fine." Detective Johnson glances at his watch. "I'll expect you in about thirty minutes."

To be honest, I'm shocked he's letting me drive myself. *You're not under arrest*, I remind myself. He can't force me to go *with* him. I'm not even sure if he can force me to go down to the station at all.

I walk the detective to the front door. My stomach roils as my life, my *freedom*, flashes before my eyes. Is this karma for not being straight with the police when I learned about the video or about the diary? I was just trying to do the right thing for my family. It feels like the secrets I've kept are wrapping themselves around my neck and squeezing.

Detective Johnson turns back to face me, his gray eyes steely. "I'll see you in twenty-nine minutes, Mrs. Winter." His voice is colder than ice, sending shivers down my spine.

Once the door clicks shut behind him, I quickly gather my things. I call out to TJ, but there's no answer. Perhaps he went for a walk to clear his mind or is hiding out upstairs, waiting to make sure Detective Johnson has left. I can't help but think this is all his fault. If that video hadn't existed in the first place, if he hadn't pissed Sienna off (or worse), my life wouldn't be crumbling all around me.

I check the kitchen on my way out, but it's decidedly empty and quiet. It looks like TJ isn't cooking dinner tonight. A horrific thought paralyzes me: will I even make it back for dinner? I quickly dial Bennett's number, but his phone goes straight to voicemail.

I slip the phone into my purse. I'll have to try Bennett again from the road. I really need to go. The police station is twenty minutes from my house, and the clock is ticking so loudly it's all I can hear. *Tick. Tick. Tick.*

I hit the key fob on my BMW, unlocking it from the kitchen. Then I move through the mudroom and into the garage. I'm about to get in the car when a shimmer of something on the garage floor catches my attention. I'm not sure what it is. Oil, maybe? That's just great. Now one of our cars has an oil leak on top of everything else.

When it rains, it pours, and unless there's a leak in the roof or in a car, something has dripped onto the concrete.

My eyes flit up and then down. No leak in the roof. It's oil. It has to be oil.

I repeat this over and over despite my instincts screaming for me to get the hell out of the garage.

I approach the spot tentatively. It certainly looks like oil. Yet I can't shake the dread clinging to every inch of my body like insidious vines choking a tree. I take a deep breath through my nose — my garage doesn't smell like an auto shop. As I step cautiously closer, the less the puddle looks like oil.

A few more steps, and I'm standing directly over the spot, a red glint so deep, it's almost imperceptible. It's not oil, after all.

It's blood.

I don't have time right now to consider the countless questions pinging around in my frantic mind.

I lean against the car to steady myself. My heart is beating so loudly that I'm sure TJ can hear it wherever he is. With shaking hands, I check the time on my phone. I've got nineteen minutes to make it down to the station.

My eyes scan the room, looking for something to cover the blood. I can't let anyone see it until I know where it came from, and I can't find that out right now since there's a detective awaiting my arrival at the police station. I spot a can of garage concrete-floor paint and place it over the bloody concrete. The top slides off, and my finger dips into the cold black. I quickly wipe it off on the side of the can and leave it be.

That'll have to do. There's no more time to consider how I've become an accomplice to whatever transpired in this garage — or to think about *what* transpired in this garage, or to contemplate whether the blood could possibly belong to our AWOL teenage girl, or whether my stepson has been fooling us all along.

I slip into the car and open the garage door. I pull out into the driveway, closing the garage door behind me. I take one last long look at my house as I pull away down the street. I've got a police interrogation to attend.

CHAPTER THIRTY-FOUR

Despite driving twenty miles above the speed limit down the long, windy roads of backwoods Armonk, I'm five minutes late for my interrogation. I almost drop dead from shock when I don't find Detective Johnson waiting impatiently outside the station.

I slip my BMW into a visitor's spot by the front entrance. I'm just a visitor, gosh darn it. I have no intention of staying. I haven't done anything wrong other than hide the existence of an incriminating surveillance video and a missing girl's journal. It's not like I tampered with Lydia Berman's brakes.

But someone clearly did . . .

On that note, I grasp the wrought-iron handrail tightly and walk up the stairs to the imposing building I swore I'd never return to again. Not after the last time.

Try as I might to live my life on the right side of the law, it would seem The Estates has other plans for my family and me.

The door clatters loudly behind me as I step inside the police station. A chime signifies my arrival, and a uniformed officer glances up from behind a plexiglass partition. The officer motions for me to approach the desk. My footsteps echo through the intimidating space like gunshots. The only thing louder is the sound of my heart beating out of my chest. I'm certain she can hear it from behind the plexiglass.

Oh boy, I'm having second thoughts. *This was a bad idea. A really bad idea.* I tried calling Bennett the entire way to the police station, but his phone kept going to voicemail. I should have waited for him to call me back . . .

I freeze, debating whether I should turn around and leave the way I came in — as a free woman! But fleeing would certainly make me look guilty, like I'm shoplifting my freedom. Could they trigger some alarm system that locks me inside and forces me to stay? This entire ordeal is nothing short of crazy.

The officer-receptionist stops waving and picks up the phone. I vaguely entertain the notion that she could be calling backup. Does she think I'm some common criminal who stumbled into the police station? I can't hear what she's saying, but her expression is serious. Her eyes are narrowed on me, her lips pinched in a tight line.

I smile weakly, but she doesn't smile back.

A loud, beeping sound fills the room, causing me to jump. A heavy metal door slowly opens, and my heart skips in my chest as Detective Johnson emerges and strides across the lobby with purpose.

His lips are curled into a grim smile. His posture and expression are strong and serious — it's almost as if he's letting me know that we are on his turf now. As if the uniforms and guns didn't give that away.

"Glad you could make it, Mrs. Winter. It took you a little longer than I expected, though . . ." He looks at his watch and then back up at me like I've broken the law by showing up five minutes late. *Five* minutes, for goodness' sake! It takes longer than that to walk from the parking lot into the station.

"Traffic," I manage. The lie comes out whiny and small. I wish I sounded more convincing. Wish I *felt* more convincing.

Detective Johnson raises a skeptical eyebrow. I don't love the way he's glaring at me like he's convinced I've done something dodgy *in addition* to showing up five minutes late. He's not wrong, obviously. It's just not what he thinks it is. It's nothing to do with Lydia Berman's brakes. I glance down at my hands and spot a smear of black garage paint. I quickly bury my palms in my pockets.

My pulse quickens as the detective gestures toward the heavy door he emerged from moments ago. I can't leave now. I draw a deep breath and follow him. I flinch as the door slams shut behind us, physically trapping me inside the police station.

We walk silently down a long, dimly lit corridor with closed-door rooms on either side.

Detective Johnson stops in front of one and opens it widely so I can step inside. It's an interrogation room roughly the size of a Manhattan studio apartment. It might as well be a prison cell. It already feels like the walls are closing in on me. I've been in this room before, when I was questioned in the aftermath of Mark Black's death. Except this time, it's Lydia Berman's attempted murder I'm suspected of.

I'm hit with a whirlwind of emotions, threatening to knock me off my feet.

"You know the drill." Detective Johnson points to a beat-up metal table flanked by chairs. Once again, he's not wrong. Unfortunately, I *do* know the drill. But it doesn't make Detective Johnson any less of a jerk for pointing it out. And it doesn't make me any less fearful of what this interview might bring.

I pull out a chair, the metal legs screeching against the concrete floor like nails on a chalkboard. The hairs on my arms shoot up. The room is unforgivingly hot — stifling, even. Fluorescent lights flicker overhead, casting a spotlight over me. My hands tremble as I stare at the one-way mirror, and I wonder who is watching on the other side.

God, I hate this place.

Detective Johnson takes a seat across from me and pushes a tape recorder toward the center of the table. It's one of those old-fashioned ones with actual ribbon tape. I haven't seen one of these bad boys since 2000. No, make that since the last time I was here. It feels a little too *official* for my liking. "Do I have your permission to record this interview?"

I don't know. I blink at him owlishly. *Does* he?

Against my better judgment, I give a slight nod to indicate my consent. *If I act like I've nothing to hide, Detective Johnson will believe I've nothing to hide. Right?* Isn't that what Bennett said? Why he let TJ take a lie-detector test? Unlike my stepson (probably, definitely, maybe), I'm such a bad liar that I don't even believe myself. Worse, I can't shake the feeling that talking to Detective Johnson may backfire spectacularly . . .

"So . . ." he starts, folding his hands on the table.

"So . . ."

"You're here, Mrs. Winter, because we received a tip placing you at Lydia Berman's house this afternoon, just shortly before her brakes failed, causing her near-fatal collision." He pauses, leaning forward. "Before they were *cut.*"

I inhale a sharp breath. Detective Johnson has gotten right to the point. There's no small talk. No good cop, bad cop. Only bad. *Very* bad. "Yes, and I told you I wasn't there. I don't know a thing about brakes. And even if I did, I would never intentionally try to hurt my neighbor." I fold my own hands, mirroring his posture. "My husband and I are upstanding members of our community, Detective Johnson."

Detective Johnson clears his throat. "So you've said."

"It's the truth." I take a deep breath, attempting to project calm. I'm anything but.

"How would you describe your relationship with Lydia Berman?"

My stomach turns. *Terrible, awful, the worst* all come to mind. But I can't tell him that, *obviously*.

"We're neighbors, Detective. We've had our ups and downs. You already know she doesn't care for my family."

"And how do you feel about her? About *her* family?"

I wonder what he's implying. Does Detective Johnson think I had something to do with Sienna's disappearance *and* Lydia's sliced brake line?

I shrug, trying not to overreact or to get ahead of myself. "She is who she is. You can't be best friends with everyone, Detective."

"If you're not friends, why was she at your house yesterday?"

My hands curl into fists on the table, nails digging into the flesh of my palms. *How could he possibly know that?*

As if reading my mind, Detective Johnson opens a manilla folder on the table and hands me a stack of photos. I thumb through them, slowly at first, but then quickly, my heart beating out of my chest.

They're stills of Lydia and me from yesterday. They appear to have been taken from a Ring camera — a Ring camera with a straight-on view of my front porch.

There's only one house with a straight-on view of my front porch.

Damn you, Marnie Black.

CHAPTER THIRTY-FIVE

I've gone completely numb. It's as if all the oxygen has been sucked from the air. The room spins, and I grasp the edges of the table to hold myself upright.

Marnie fucking *Black*.

I reel as I struggle to piece together why she would do something like this. Was she also the one who made the call claiming I was at Lydia's earlier today? I seriously can't believe that.

"*Well?*"

I'm about to tell Detective Johnson some watered-down version of Lydia's visit when a commotion erupts outside the door.

"You can't go in there!" a female voice screams.

"Fuck," Detective Johnson mutters, clenching his fists on the table.

A second later, the door flies open, and Bennett bursts through the frame. The whole scene is quite comical if I'm being honest. Not that being suspected of attempted murder is comical.

I briefly wonder, *How did Bennett know I was here*, but immediately dismiss the thought as Bennett erupts into a volley of shouts.

"You mess with my son, that's one thing." Bennett jabs an accusing finger at Detective Johnson. "You mess with my wife, that's *quite* another."

The female officer from reception enters behind my husband, frazzled, looking like her jaw is about to unhinge. "I tried to stop

177

him, Detective," she gasps. If she wasn't smiling before, she is definitely *not* smiling now. And I don't think it's because she suffers from facial paralysis.

It feels like we're starring in an episode of *Cops*.

"I could arrest you, Mr. Winter." Detective Johnson's upper lip trembles as he says this with little conviction. "Pushing past police security. Barging into an interrogation room during an active investigation."

"On what grounds, Detective? I'm fully entitled to be present as Carrie Winter's *lawyer*. The lawyer she should have been offered before being dragged down here."

"Whoa, whoa, whoa." Detective Johnson jumps up from his chair, nearly knocking it to the ground. "I did not drag Mrs. Winter down here." He whirls round to me, seeking validation. "Did I drag you down here?"

As if I might side with this man. I keep my mouth glued shut.

"You drove your own car, for God's sake!" he screams, his husky voice echoing through the room.

"That's irrelevant!" Bennett shouts. "Did you offer her legal representation?" Something tells me Detective Johnson is *not* going to win this argument. If I were him, I'd bow out gracefully, apologize for the misunderstanding, and call it a day.

"Well, no," he admits.

Bennett shoots the detective a venomous glare. I've never seen my husband this angry. I don't think I've ever seen any human this angry. Not even Marnie. Although clearly, she had to have been pretty upset to put me in this position in the first place.

"Mr. Winter, with all due respect, your wife is suspected of cutting Lydia Berman's brakes. The woman almost died."

"What evidence do you have for her alleged involvement?"

"A neighbor claims to have seen Mrs. Winter lurking around Mrs. Berman's house before the accident."

"Okay . . ." Bennett takes a long pause. I perch on the edge of the chair, waiting to hear what he'll say next. It's pretty incriminating that someone saw me there, except for the fact, of course, that it's a complete lie.

"May I ask who offered this accusation?"

"I'm sorry, but I'm not at liberty to release that information."

"Have you considered the possibility that the person who made this allegation is responsible for committing the crime? Perhaps trying to draw attention away from themselves and onto my wi— my *client?*"

"Look, Mr. Winter. Obviously, I'm taking this tip with a grain of salt. But we have to take all accusations seriously. Especially with your development's history . . ."

Bennett grits his teeth, and a muscle in his jaw twitches. "This is a witch hunt. Someone obviously has it in for my family. If she's not under arrest, I'm afraid Mrs. Winter is not at liberty to answer any further questions. Unless you can present us with some actual *evidence* other than hearsay from an anonymous source, our conversation is over." Bennett reaches into his suit pocket and pulls out a business card. "You can contact me personally when you've conducted a *legitimate* investigation."

With that, Bennett reaches out a hand and helps me to my feet. "Let's go," he instructs.

I'm practically paralyzed with shock, but somehow, my limbs move as my husband leads me out of the interrogation room.

We're almost out of earshot when Detective Johnson mutters, "You're going to regret this, Mr. Winter."

CHAPTER THIRTY-SIX

"*You're going to regret this, Mr. Winter,*" Bennett mimics as we walk out of the police station and step into the parking lot. "Is he freaking kidding me?"

The scary part — he's clearly *not*.

"I'll send someone to pick up your car later," Bennett continues, calming down slightly the farther we get from the police station doors.

I nod in agreement. He opens the Porsche door for me, and I collapse into the custom leather interior. To be honest, I've never been so happy to be inside my husband's car. Usually, he drives too fast, and the car is so low to the ground that I feel every last twist in the road, gravity yanking me mercilessly in all directions. But right now, Bennett could pop wheelies on speed humps for all I care, so long as I never have to set foot in that police station again.

My husband pulls out of the station slowly before ripping the gas on the open road. His hand squeezes mine so tightly I nearly lose feeling in my pinky. It's as if he is holding on for dear life. I can't blame him.

But one single question continues to chip away at me.

"How did you know I was at the police station?" I ask. When I left the house, Bennett was still at work, phone turned off, and TJ had disappeared, I assume, somewhere upstairs.

So, who told him I was there?

"I got pulled into a meeting," Bennett says, flicking on his turn signal before whipping onto a side road. "I listened to all your voicemails when I got out."

Of course. I called him about a hundred times on my way to the station.

Now that we have that settled, my thoughts turn to Marnie. She must have been the one who gave those pictures to Detective Johnson. There's simply no other explanation for how he got them. And she's probably the one who claimed to see me outside Lydia's house, though I can't imagine why she would say something so horrifically untrue.

I flash to Marnie and Lydia talking in the street in front of my house and wonder whether they orchestrated this little stunt. Was *Marnie* the one who cut Lydia's brakes? Did Lydia cut her own brakes and have Marnie report me for it? No, that doesn't make sense. Lydia wouldn't cut her own brakes.

I take a deep breath, fighting to rein in the thoughts running amok in my head. "There's something I need to tell you, Bennett. Something important."

Bennett rubs a thumb over my knuckles, his eyes steeled on the road ahead. "What is it, Carrie?"

Here goes . . . "Lydia came by the house."

"Before her accident?" His eyes flick from the road to mine, a panicked expression on his face.

"Well, obviously *before* the accident, Bennett. She couldn't have come by *after* the accident. I've been at the police station." Needless to say. "Not to mention that Lydia's been clinging to life at the hospital! And, it was yesterday," I add, almost as an afterthought.

"Please tell me you didn't . . ." My husband whispers.

"Oh, my God, *no!* I swear, I did *not* cut her brakes."

"Of course not," Bennett says, exhaling a loud breath. "But you'd tell me if you did, *right?*"

Well, that's just dandy. My husband thinks I'm capable of cutting another woman's brakes.

"Yes, I would tell you if I did. But there's nothing to tell. Lydia drives a Tesla. Don't you need your phone connected just to pop the hood on that? I wouldn't know where to even find the brakes. I don't know how to change the oil in my own car!" I'm not sure why Detective Johnson and my husband have mistaken me for Mario Andretti. I'm good at many things, but car maintenance is not one of them. Car sabotage is, clearly, *not* in my wheelhouse.

"So what did you want to tell me about Lydia coming by, then?"

"Maybe you should pull over for this."

Bennett jerks the wheel toward the curb so quickly I'm certain I have whiplash. Perhaps I shouldn't have told him to pull over . . .

"What is it, Carrie?"

On the side of a road somewhere in Armonk, I fill Bennett in on Lydia's unexpected visit with Sienna's journal, the incriminating contents of which identify his son by name.

"Is that it?" he asks.

"Is that it?" I squawk, parroting him. "Sienna accused TJ of threatening her, Bennett." If ever there were an *if something happens to me, look at so and so* moment, this is it.

"*And?* Detective Johnson accused *you* of cutting Lydia Berman's brakes."

Heat rises to my cheeks. "What's your point?"

"My point is: you said you *didn't* cut Lydia's brakes. Just because Sienna claimed TJ was harassing her doesn't make it true."

I'm not sure we're talking about the same thing here. Because the *blood* . . . I'm about to tell Bennett what I found in the garage when my phone pings loudly in my purse.

It's a text from Marnie, of all people. She's got some nerve.

Marnie: *Whatcha doing?*

Me: *What am I doing? Driving home from the police station. But you already know that, don't you?*

Three little dots dance on the screen. Dance. Disappear. Dance. Disappear.

My phone suddenly rings. *Go ahead and ring*, I think treacherously.

"Are you going to answer that?" There's a palpable edge to Bennett's voice. Heck, we're all on edge.

"Fine," I huff, accepting the call and lifting the phone to my ear. "Hello?"

"What in the world is going on? I saw the police car outside your house. And then I saw you take off right after. Are you okay? Why were the police there?"

Maybe because you gave them photos of Lydia and me on my front porch, I want to screech into the receiver, *and called to tell them you saw me outside her house before her brakes were cut.* Marnie Black is one hell of an actress. She should open a school for aspiring pathological liars — *Marnie's School of Mythomania* has a nice ring to it.

I'm dying to call her out, but it's a conversation better to have in private, not with Bennett listening and gripping the steering wheel like he wants to rip it straight off the dash. I'd like to try and make it home alive.

"Have you heard what happened to Lydia?"

"No," Marnie hesitates. "What happened to Lydia?" She sounds genuinely surprised. Could she *really* not know?

"She was in a car accident. Crashed into a tree down the road."

Marnie lets out a loud gasp, followed by a few beats of silence as the news sinks in. "Oh, my gosh, that's terrible. Is she okay?"

I take a deep breath. "It was pretty bad, but she should be."

Another stretch of silence ensues. I glance out the car window at the sky, the turbulent weather rolling through. My stomach tightens with dread.

Finally, Marnie speaks, pulling my attention back from the dark, dense clouds ominously hovering over us. "But . . ."

"But what?"

"What does that have to do with you being at the police station?"

It is as if she doesn't know this already since she's the one who had to have provided the police with the pictures.

I'm going to call her out *in person* this time. "I think we should sit down and have a nice, long chat, Marnie."

Marnie lets out a deep sigh. "Fine," she says, disappointment saturating her voice. "You can tell me tonight."

"Tonight?"

"Damian wants you and Bennett to come for dinner. He said he'd order Chinese so I don't have to cook. He really is so sweet and thoughtful."

'*So I don't have to cook.*' This *woman*. I fight the urge to throw up in my mouth.

"What's tonight?" Bennett whispers from the driver's seat.

"Hold on, Marnie." I cup a hand over the phone and turn to Bennett. "Damian and Marnie want us to come over tonight."

Bennett smiles widely. "I'd say we could use the distraction, wouldn't you?"

I usually would, but Marnie Black might be the whole reason we need a distraction.

CHAPTER THIRTY-SEVEN

We plan to meet up at Damian's house at six. That should be fun, considering how pissed I am at Marnie and how I don't entirely trust our new neighbor.

In the meantime, Bennett and I buckle down to have a serious conversation with TJ.

"TJ," Bennett calls out before we've fully stepped through the door.

TJ emerges from the kitchen, looking completely nonplussed. He's dressed in cotton pajama pants, his hair still damp from the shower. A reminder that he's not the one who just spent several hours at the police station.

"What's this I hear about a journal?" Bennett asks.

TJ clenches his jaw and shoots me a pointed look. I roll my eyes — as if I wasn't going to eventually tell his father about the journal.

"I'll show you." I walk to the island, open the drawer with the wine-bottle openers, and . . . what the . . .

The journal isn't there.

My legs just about give out from under me. I frantically pull corkscrews from the drawer, laying them out on the island until the drawer is empty. We have an obscene number of corkscrews.

Still no journal.

I turn to Bennett and TJ, flabbergasted. My legs once again sway beneath me. I should probably sit down. "Did you take the journal, TJ?"

TJ shakes his head. The corners of his lips dip as if he's insulted that I would ask such a thing. Meanwhile, he was the only one other than Sienna, Lydia, and me who knew about the journal in the first place. Sienna is missing, Lydia is in the hospital after having her brakes cut, and I was at the police station accused of cutting her brakes. That leaves — let's see — *him*.

Unless Lydia informed Marnie about the journal, but I saw them talking *after* she came over here. TJ certainly wouldn't have let her into the house to rummage around in our drawers. Or at all.

"Then where is it? I hid it in here—" I stab emphatically at the drawer — "when Marnie dropped by unannounced."

TJ lifts a shoulder. "How would I know what you did with it, Carrie? I went upstairs to my room when Marnie dropped by unannounced. Remember?" He shakes his head. "You told me to go!"

I'm not too fond of TJ's tone. If I were his birth mother, I'd slap him upside the head.

Bennett's eyes, meanwhile, dart so quickly between TJ and mine that it's actually making me dizzy. Finally, they land on his son. "TJ, promise me you didn't touch the journal. I've given you the benefit of the doubt, but if Carrie says it was there . . ."

"I don't know *where* she put it," TJ huffs. "But I promise you, I didn't touch it."

Bennett's shoulders sag with relief. "I believe you."

I stand there, mouth agape. Bennett really just sided with TJ over me. I know where I left the freaking journal — in the god-damn drawer! I'm so mad I could scream and throw the journal at both of them . . . if I could find it.

"I'm telling you it was in there. But, fine. Whatever." I fold my arms across my chest, completely dismayed. Bennett and I don't fight. At least, we never used to fight until TJ showed up on our doorstep. Since then, it would seem all bets are off.

Why won't my stepson just tell the *truth?* He *has* to have taken that journal. There's no other possible explanation.

"TJ," Bennett says. "I think you should lay low for a bit. Let this blow over."

"I'm not the one they think messed with Lydia's brakes." He mumbles, loud enough that I hear it. Then he shoots me another look like I'm the Evil Stepmother.

"No," Bennett agrees. "But if someone finds Sienna's journal claiming she was afraid of you, I'm afraid you *will* be the one they think had something to do with her disappearance."

"Or worse," I add for good measure. It's almost been seventy-two hours since she went missing. The chances of finding her are dropping by the second.

"Whatever." TJ shrugs. "I didn't do anything to her."

I think about the missing journal, the blood in the garage, the necklace in my drawer, TJ's phone call from an unknown number . . . and I'm no longer so sure.

TJ pushes out of his chair and rises to his feet. "I'll go chill out upstairs," he says, turning and walking away, but not before he narrows his eyes on me one last time. Within a few days, I've gone from stepmother of the year to Lady Tremaine. Though, I'd hardly compare TJ to Cinderella. He drives his dad's Porsche, for Christs' sake — the Porsche that Bennett won't even let *me* drive.

Once TJ has left the room and his footsteps have disappeared up the stairs, Bennett turns to me. "Let's try to have a nice night, okay?"

I'm not sure how that's possible, but I reluctantly agree. Bennett kisses me on the forehead and heads upstairs to get some work done and get ready for what is sure to be a *nice* night.

Or so he says.

I should get ready as well, but there's something I need to do first. One by one, I go through every last drawer and cabinet in the kitchen, removing and replacing items. By the time I'm finished, there's no doubt in my mind that TJ has done something with Sienna Berman's journal. He's the only one who knew it was there. One of the only ones who even knew it existed.

And I can't help but wonder, if he's done something to her journal, is it because he's also done something to her?

CHAPTER THIRTY-EIGHT

I check my reflection in the full-length foyer mirror before we head out to have dinner with Damian and Marnie.

I look awful — *beyond* awful. If awful had a fraternal twin who was the rougher-looking of the pair, *that* would be me. My hair hangs limply above my shoulders as if I'm the victim in a true-crime documentary. When I cut it a few months ago, stacked bobs were all the rage. With my sun-kissed highlights and prominent cheekbones, the cut was quite flattering. Now, I look like a shaggy dog. My hair won't even stay in a ponytail as the pesky front pieces keep popping out.

It doesn't help that I've got deep, purple circles under my eyes that all the products in Sephora couldn't cover up. Whatever. This is the least of my problems.

As I contemplate the evening ahead, the need to figure out who, exactly, Damian Mankiewicz is and what he's doing here presses against my ribcage. My thoughts flit to Marnie, who has become my worst nightmare since her supposed knight in shining armor arrived in The Estates. Maybe it's Damian *who has* something to do with Marnie turning me in to the police.

At least Bennett looks effortlessly dashing, as always. His dark hair is perfectly full and shiny. I bet *his* hair would stay in a ponytail if it were long enough.

I almost stamp my feet in frustration. It's so *unfair!*

"Carrie? Are you ready?"

I pull my gaze from my reflection. It's not getting any better than this, especially since the pink bulb lighting in here is doing nothing to enhance my appearance.

"Yeah, let's go." I grab the bottle of Riesling that Bennett has hand-selected for our evening out. Apparently, Riesling pairs exceptionally well with Chinese food. I couldn't care less what we drink tonight. Moo goo gai pan and white wine don't rank too high on my list of concerns.

We walk in silence to Damian's house. Bennett and I usually have an abundance of things to say to one another, especially now that we have a (man) child to talk about, but the air between us bubbles with tension. Still, I'm grateful to be out of the house away from TJ. Not that Marnie is such a pleasant Plan B, though.

Bennett brings a finger up to the bell, but before he can ring it, the door swings open. Marnie stands in the frame, looking a heck of a lot better than I do. She wasn't dragged down to the police station for an interrogation earlier today, however, which is all I can say to console myself.

"Hey, girl," Marnie chirps, kissing my cheek.

Hey yourself, traitor.

Instead, I clear my throat. "Hi, Marnie."

"You look lovely, Marnie." I shoot a sideways glance at my husband. Leave it to Bennett to smooth out the tension with his charm. That's one benefit of marrying a lawyer, I suppose. The guy always seems to know what to say. "This is for you," he adds, passing Marnie the bottle of Riesling.

"Oh, Bennett," she coos, touching his shoulder with her blood-red nails. "It's as if you read my mind. I'm guessing you hand-picked this. Carrie, did you know that Riesling is the number one top wine pairing for Chinese food?"

"I do now," I growl through gritted teeth.

Marnie smiles, but there's a hard look in her eyes that makes me uneasy. But what about today — about my so-called best friend — *hasn't* made me uneasy?

"Come in," she says, stepping aside so Bennett and I can enter Damian's house. The way she was waiting for us at the door, it would seem she'd confused this house with her own. Not that it's any of my business. It just seems like things are moving faster between the two of them than a Daytona 500.

"Carrie. Bennett, my man." Damian joins us in the entryway, his dimples on full display. He gives Bennett a fist pump, then pulls me in for a hug. I stiffen at his touch. Not that he or Marnie seem to notice.

It would appear, based on the way they're eyeing each other like moonstruck teenagers, that they started drinking without us. Or engaged in some other form of entertainment before our arrival. I cringe at the thought.

And then there's their outfits. They're dressed in — dear *God* — matching sweater vests. It looks like they've just enjoyed a competitive game of pickleball or golf. I'm waiting for the announcement that they bought stock together in Ralph Lauren.

Damian and Bennett set off for the kitchen, leaving me alone with Marnie.

"So what were you up to, today?" I ask.

"Oh, you know, just getting ready for tonight," she responds nonchalantly.

"Getting ready? I thought we were ordering Chinese . . ."

Marnie takes an exaggerated breath and rolls her eyes. "We are, Carrie."

"Well, I guess I'm just not understanding what you needed to do all day to get ready to order Chinese food."

Marnie lets out a loud huff. "What's with the interrogation, Carrie?"

The word *interrogation* spurs a fresh spark of anger, setting me alight. I'm done playing this game.

"Did you know I was at the police station, Marnie? You're the one who called Detective Johnson, aren't you?"

Marnie attempts to raise her eyebrows, but her forehead doesn't move. She must *really* be head over heels for Damian. It appears she's gotten Botox. She purses her lips at me, and wow, it looks like she may have gotten filler as well. I guess she really *was* busy today. "What are you talking about, Carrie? Why in the world would I call Detective Johnson?"

"That's what I would like to know." I bring my hands to my hips.

"Come on, let's go get a drink," she says far too breezily, considering the gravity of this conversation. Of *my* situation.

As if she can distract me with a drink . . .

Marnie doesn't wait for a response. She turns on her heels and heads toward the kitchen. I reluctantly follow her, expecting to find Bennett and Damian there, but evidently, they've already ventured off to the game room. I indulge in a hearty eye roll. *Men*.

Marnie pours us each a glass of Riesling, which I will never, ever forget pairs well with Chinese food. Not that I plan on *ever* having Chinese food again with Marnie and Damian after tonight.

Or possibly ever speaking to her, depending upon what she has to say for herself.

Marnie gestures for me to have a seat on a stool at the island. I take a large gulp from the glass and sit, my eyes narrowed on her.

"Detective Johnson showed me the pictures, Marnie. They're from *your* Ring camera." I point an accusing finger at her, and she steps back as if I've poked her in the chest.

"What pictures, Carrie? I literally have *no clue* what you are talking about."

Such a good little liar. "Pictures of Lydia and me on my front porch, taken from directly across the street."

"When was Lydia on your front porch?"

I chug the remaining wine and hold the glass out for a refill, thirsty, not distracted. "Just tell me the truth, Marnie. What did I do to you to make you so mad at me that you'd try to frame me for Lydia's attempted *murder?*"

"Whoa, whoa, whoa." Marnie holds out both hands. "Attempted murder? You said she was in a car accident."

"She was. *After* someone cut her brakes. Did you tell the police I was at Lydia's house? That I cut her brakes?" I slam my palms against the island, unable to contain my frustration.

Marnie looks like she's seen a ghost. She's gone completely ashen, as if all of the blood has instantly drained from her body.

"Someone cut her brakes? I think . . . I think I need to sit down." Marnie slurs. She attempts to grab the countertop but misses, bashing her head against it as she slides down to the floor, leaving a dark streak of bright red on the white marble.

"*Marnie!*" I scream, hopping up from my seat with lightning speed and rushing around the island to make sure she's okay. I'm mad as hell, yes, but I don't want anything bad to happen to anyone else.

Not today.

A wave of worry washes over me as I catch sight of Marnie splayed helplessly on the tile floor.

While she still may be an Oscar hopeful, Marnie isn't acting right now. She is most definitely passed out.

CHAPTER THIRTY-NINE

I scramble through the kitchen, looking for anything and everything I can find to assist Marnie, all the while screaming at the top of my lungs.

Thankfully, Damian has thought of everything. He appears incredibly organized and well-stocked for a single guy. Not that a single guy can't be well-stocked and organized, but I can't think of one man I know who has actual smelling salts in his kitchen.

Marnie still lies unconscious on the floor, apparently having fainted from the news that Lydia Berman's accident was *no* accident. That *someone*, allegedly me, wanted her to crash that car.

I continue screaming out to Damian and Bennett while searching Damian's drawers for a washcloth to wet and place on Marnie's forehead. It's in one of those drawers that I find the smelling salts. I crack them open and hold them under Marnie's nose. Within seconds, her eyes shoot open, filled with a look of horror like she's just been attacked.

"What happened?" she asks, bringing a hand to her head.

"You fainted," I tell her. She attempts to stand on her own, but I stop her. "Here, let me help."

I link an arm under hers and hoist Marnie to her feet. She leans on me as I guide her to the kitchen table, where she slumps in a chair and drops her head into her hands. I wonder if she has a concussion. Maybe I should call an ambulance. I mean, her head is literally bleeding. Not gushing, but definitely bleeding. She might require a stitch or two to close it up. I bet Damian has liquid bandage around here somewhere. I mean, the guy's got smelling salts.

Enough about Marnie's head and Damian's excessive first-aid supplies, I chide myself. *Get a grip, Carrie.*

I grab Marnie a cold glass of water and sit beside her at the table. "Do you know your name?" I ask. "Address? Are you dizzy? Nauseous? How many fingers am I holding up?" I hold up four fingers, wiggling them to assess her pupils.

Marnie regards me curiously. "Four," she says with conviction. "I'm *fine*, Carrie. But that was some bombshell you just dropped. You could have at least told me to sit down . . . Like I did when I showed you the video footage of TJ and Sienna," she mumbles. Clearly, Marnie is just fine.

"I thought you knew."

"How would I possibly know?"

I'm starting to believe she really *didn't* know. This is an awful lot of effort to play dumb.

Maybe I have been wrong about this all along. Is Marnie (*gasp*) innocent?

"Well, I just assumed when Detective Johnson showed me pictures taken from *your* Ring camera and then brought me down to the station because someone said they saw me at Lydia's house this afternoon . . ."

"So you just assumed it was me? Your *best friend?*" Marnie shakes her head, visibly offended. Great — now I've made her mad. If she did do all this, who knows what a mad Marnie is capable of? I certainly don't want to find out.

But I'm not entirely off base here. "I saw you, Marnie, outside with Lydia. She was pointing at my house, and you were nodding along."

Now Marnie is staring at me like *I'm* the one who's crazy. "Oh, Carrie, you really shouldn't let your imagination run away with you. Lydia was talking about your grass."

"My grass?" My shoulders slump. I'm dumbstruck.

"She said it's not fair that not only do you have the nicest house on the block, but you've also got impossibly green grass."

I feel a tinge of flattery from the compliment, but *no*. Am I to believe Lydia Berman was coveting my lawn when her only child is *missing?* That would be crazy even for a certifiably crazy lady.

"So, who gave Detective Johnson the pictures from *your* Ring camera if it wasn't you?"

Marnie flips her hair over a shoulder. It looks like black spun silk. I want to run my fingers through it. God, I miss my hair. "I swear, I have no idea who gave the police the pictures, Carrie. If I knew, I'd tell you."

I narrow my eyes at her. Marnie recoils, as if she can hear the questions hammering around in my thoughts.

"Seriously," she continues. "It couldn't have been me. My Ring camera has been malfunctioning. Damian tried to help me with the app, but then wound up rewiring it today."

My stomach twists in a knot. Damian helped her with the app. Rewired it, even.

The perfect opportunity to make a copy of the footage.

But if Damian was the one who gave Detective Johnson the pictures of Lydia and me, the question remains — what did I ever do to him?

CHAPTER FORTY

Despite her injury, I'm the one shaking when Damian and Bennett finally blaze into the room, worry streaking their faces. But no one is looking at me. Shock tugs their eyebrows skyward when they catch sight of Marnie crumpled at the table with her head in her hands, blood streaking the pristine marble.

Damian rushes over, rubbing a soothing hand across Marnie's back. "What happened? Are you okay?"

Marnie's eyes flick up, a helpless look on her face. She's certainly gotten good at playing the damsel in distress. "It was so scary, Damian. Carrie told me about Lydia and . . . and . . . I fainted. I hit my head pretty bad."

Damian examines Marnie's head, his brow wrinkled in concern. "Let's clean you up," he says. I watch as Damian walks over to the island and rummages around a drawer, coming up with an extra-large Band-Aid and some antiseptic ointment. He kneels down next to Marnie, gently caring for her wound. I must admit, he does do an impressive job patching her up. Despite her injury, she bats her eyelashes at him flirtatiously. Three more extensions fall to the floor. Damian will have to purchase a robot vacuum if this relationship continues for much longer.

"Do you think I'll need stitches, Damian?"

"No, you're going to be just fine, beautiful."

Damian's bedside manner is impeccable. For a moment, I wonder if he's actually a nurse.

That's the thing. You never really can know anyone, even when you think you do.

Once everything has calmed down, Damian asks, "So what happened to Lydia?"

"It's just terrible," Marnie says. "She was in a car accident. Someone cut her brake lines."

Damian lets out an exaggerated gasp. "Do they have any idea who might have done it?"

I examine Damian's face, his expression now relaxed. Something isn't tracking. He's asking all the right questions, but if I had to guess, it seems like he somehow already knew about Lydia. Did the police go to his house as well? Or is *he* the one who called the police in the first place?

It takes every ounce of strength I have not to call him out.

Once Marnie has assured us all that she is feeling back to normal, Damian suggests we move our party to the living room. After all the excitement in the kitchen, I'd say that's a brilliant idea.

We're all settled in with drinks in hand when the doorbell rings. My entire body stiffens. I bite the inside of my cheek just hard enough to draw blood. I'm guessing blood does *not* pair well with Chinese food.

The doorbell chimes for a second time.

"Are you going to answer that?" I squeak. Because I sure as hell am *not*.

"You okay, Carrie?" Damian asks, making no move toward the door. "You look a little green."

I fight the urge to sneer at him, *Oh, I do, Damian, do I?* How perceptive. I feel like Kermit the frog. My intestines are tangled in such a tight knot, there might as well be a fist shoved deep inside my torso.

"I just thought maybe you didn't hear the doorbell. It's rang twice already."

As if on cue, the bell rings for the third time.

Damian raises an eyebrow at me skeptically. "I heard the bell, Carrie. Don't worry so much — I'm going to answer the door *now*. He glances down at his phone. P.S.," he adds as he turns to walk away. "It's just the Chinese food."

My cheeks go hot. How could I forget about the Chinese food? While I'm drinking the Riesling that pairs so perfectly with Chinese food, no less.

Clearly, I need to calm down. It's just Chinese food that Damian ordered for dinner. Detective Johnson is not coming to Damian's house to haul me off to jail.

My inner panic somewhat settled, I look on as Damian returns a few minutes later with two *very* full bags of food. If I had to guess, he quite possibly ordered the entire menu. My stomach rumbles loudly. Despite the events of the day — of the past *four* days — I'm utterly ravenous.

"Let's do buffet style," Marnie suggests.

"That's a great idea!" I agree enthusiastically. I would very much like to stuff my face full of each item off the menu.

I look at Damian, and oddly, he's the only one in the room who's not smiling. A crease has formed between his otherwise perfect eyes. He looks almost . . . *angry*. But there's no possible reason he could be angry. We have Riesling and Chinese food, for God's sake!

"Can we chip in for the food?" I ask. Maybe he thinks Bennett and I are freeloaders or something, and it has him annoyed. This is the second meal he's hosted over the first few days he's lived here, after all. Though I assume Marnie covered the expenses for the last, because it would be a cold day in hell before she admitted it was takeout.

"No way," he says, shooing away my offer. "It's on me."

Okay, so it's not *that*. Then *what* is it? I can't imagine what has Damian so perturbed. It's not like he was the one accused of cutting Lydia Berman's brakes.

"Thanks, man." Bennett pats Damian on the back. "Here," he adds, "let me help you get everything set up." With that, the men set off for the dining room to set up our smorgasbord-style meal.

As soon as I'm confident they're out of earshot, I seize the opportunity to grill Marnie. "Is everything all right with Damian? With *you* and Damian?" I ask, trying to tread lightly.

Marnie sucks in a breath. "What do you mean by *that*, Carrie?"

So much for treading lightly. I've thrown on my combat boots and stomped all over the damn place. Super. I've clearly offended Marnie *again*.

"Nothing, nothing . . ." I hold up both hands to stop her from attacking me. If her fierce expression is any indication, it's not such a far-fetched possibility. Not only are her eyelashes a potential hazard, but her long, pointed, and blood-red nails could be weaponized. And that damn cocktail ring . . . "Damian just seems upset is all. And obviously, he would be upset if something was off with the two of you."

Marnie folds her arms across her chest.

"Seeing how *into* you he is," I add.

Thankfully, that seems to do the trick. Marnie's shoulders relax slightly so they're no longer lodged in her ears. "You're right, Carrie. Damian is *very* into me. Do you want to know what he told me?"

I nod enthusiastically. "Of course I do!"

"He said he can't remember the last time he felt this way about a woman. And you know he's a recent widower, so that means he feels even stronger for me than he did for his wife."

That's one way to interpret it, I guess.

But it just doesn't make sense — Damian swooping in here and falling head over heels for Marnie Black over the course of a few days, loving her more than his late wife, to whom he has dedicated an entire medium-sized U-Haul box full of photos.

And a gun.

No, there's something we're *all* missing here. Damian has a secret, one that extends deeper than that *DO NOT OPEN* box.

I'm determined to find out what it is.

"Carrie, Marnie," Bennett calls from the dining room. "Sup is on."

I *will* to find out what it is. The tantalizing scent of garlic and ginger wafts beneath my nostrils. After I eat my Chinese food, that is.

CHAPTER FORTY-ONE

I immediately pile my plate with lo mein noodles, sweet and sour chicken, boneless ribs, and every other delicacy from the spread. The only problem is that the table is so full of hot dishes, there's nowhere to sit.

"We can eat in the living room," Marnie suggests. "Maybe watch a movie or something?"

"Leave it to you to come up with the most brilliant idea." Damian taps Marnie on the tip of her nose lovingly.

"Get a room," Bennett jokes and the three of them burst out laughing. I'm the only one not laughing. I'm not even smiling. Not that anyone seems to notice.

And I don't feel like watching a movie with them. I feel like inhaling a plate of Chinese food and possibly going back for a second plate and inhaling that one as well. After that, I want to go home.

Call me crazy, but I'm not getting the best vibe here tonight. With the matter of who gave Detective Johnson those photos and made that call to consider, I can't help but wonder: am I eating Chinese food and drinking Riesling in his house right now?

I follow the three musketeers into Damian's living room, which is nicely decorated with a maroon wraparound leather couch and a bearskin rug. A fire burns brightly in his fireplace, embers dancing in the air. The whole scene is very rustic chic. A dark, metallic object above Damian's fireplace catches my attention.

A rifle.

What is Damian Mankiewicz, suburban house flipper, doing with a rifle above his fireplace?

"Do you hunt?" Bennett asks nonchalantly as if it's perfectly normal to have a rifle hanging front and center on your living room wall. Maybe in the mountains, but *here?* In The Estates?

I wonder if it's loaded. Like the gun I found upstairs in Damian's *DO NOT OPEN* box. I haven't told anyone about that yet, but I think we may need to be careful around this man.

Perhaps not right this second, though. I sink into the couch and start forking large bites of food into my mouth while Damian recounts his experience deer hunting. Apparently, it was one time, many years ago. So having the rifle so readily accessible on display is for what, a *second* time, many, many years later?

I plunge deeper into my dinner, aggressively piercing a piece of chicken. This Chinese food is so dang good that I almost forget about everything that happened today.

Marnie lifts the remote off the coffee table and clicks on the television. The remote has a thousand buttons, and she struggles to figure out how to select a movie.

"Hit the voice option," Damian says through a mouthful of food.

I watch as she presses the microphone icon. "*Moo-vees,*" she says, annunciating the word with her mouth practically resting against the remote. She tries several times before throwing up her hands in frustration.

"It won't *listen* to me. Maybe it only recognizes your voice, Damian."

"It's not programmed to recognize only one person's voice, Marnie. Try again, or just hand me the remote."

While Marnie and Damian go back and forth about the intricacies of the microphone button on the remote control, the local news plays in the background.

I recognize the anchor — Matt something or other. He stands in the woods, a very somber expression carved onto his face. That very somber expression is highlighted by the red and blue lights twirling in the background.

I nearly choke on an egg roll, but yet again, no one notices. I could probably take my shirt off right now, and no one would notice. Everyone's eyes are glued to the screen.

"Turn it up," Damian tells Marnie.

"I . . . I . . . I can't figure out the volume," she whines, a tomato-like blush creeping into her cheeks. Damian grabs the remote from her and cranks up the volume.

"Tonight, on Channel 12 News. The body of a young woman has been found in the woods surrounding the tragedy-plagued Estates. According to an inside source, authorities strongly believe the remains could belong to missing teenager, Sienna Berman. Sienna went missing four days ago and has not been seen or heard from since. The cause of death will be released pending an autopsy, but sources close to the case have confirmed that the victim was shot at least once. We will provide updated information just as soon as it's received."

The camera cuts from the reporter, and a commercial for cat litter pops up on the screen. *Ugh, seriously?* I almost mutter around a mouthful of lo mein. The remains of a young woman, quite possibly Sienna Berman, have been found, and the network thought it was a good idea to cut to cat litter. Cat Appreciation Day isn't even until the end of October!

The only thing less tasteful would be to cut to a commercial for guns. My eyes dart instinctively to the fireplace mantel.

As I slow my chewing, contemplating, a vision of the gun in Damian's secret box flits across my mind.

We've got two guns, a mysterious new neighbor, *and* a dead girl.

I place my plate on the coffee table. I've completely lost my appetite.

CHAPTER FORTY-TWO

Now, no one is eating the Chinese food or drinking the Riesling. We're all sitting in stunned silence, staring at the television.

This *can't* be happening. Not again.

A ticker flashes across the bottom of the screen, the same information running over and over again. *The body of a young woman was found shot dead in the woods. It is believed to be that of missing teenager Sienna Berman.*

This time, when the doorbell chimes, I don't ask Damian if he's going to answer it. I'd rather he *didn't* answer it, to be honest. But that's not an option. We all know who's waiting on the other side of that door.

"I'll go with you," Bennett offers.

Damian gives Bennett a nod. "Thanks, man. This is just crazy." Our new neighbor has no idea what crazy is.

But I can't help feeling as though he might be more closely acquainted with crazy than he's letting on.

"Do you think that's a good idea, Damian?" Marnie interjects. "For the police to know we're all together? They already think TJ kidnapped—" she clears her throat — "*murdered* Sienna, and that Carrie cut Lydia's brakes."

Good God, she's making us sound like the Manson family.

"They think *what?*" Damian's eyes widen dramatically. He's looking at me like I actually cut Lydia's brakes. I can't check the oil in a car. I don't even like pumping my own gas. Yet somehow, I can locate and cut a brake line?

I don't feel like discussing this again, but I have to say something. "Someone claimed to have seen me outside of Lydia's house this afternoon. Before her accident."

Damian raises an eyebrow. "Were you there?"

"No, I wasn't!"

I study Damian's face. I can't tell if he believes me. Or if he already knows I wasn't there because he's the one who lied about seeing me there.

"Exactly," Bennett says, running a hand through his hair. "So you have nothing to worry about then."

Usually, I believe whatever my husband tells me, especially regarding the law. As one of the top picks in Westchester's Forty Under Forty, there's no denying that he *really* knows his stuff. But this time, I'm not so blindly confident. I'd say I have plenty to worry about.

The expressions on Marnie's and Damian's faces, the way they keep glancing at me and then stealing looks at one another, would indicate they agree. Despite emphatically stressing to Marnie that it *wasn't* true, she obviously thinks I've done something wrong. And now Damian thinks that, too.

Once the men have left to answer the door, I turn to Marnie. "Just so you know, Marnie, TJ was cleared in Sienna's disappearance. He passed a polygraph test!"

Marnie lets out an unimpressed sigh. "Everyone knows polygraph tests mean nothing. They're not even admissible in court."

All true, but . . . "Still, he *passed*. And I didn't do anything to Lydia. Why would you say something like that?"

Marnie rolls her eyes. "Stop being so dramatic, Carrie."

She can't be serious. "I'm *not* being dramatic." I stomp a foot on the floor dramatically. "This is my freedom we're talking about, Marnie. You're making me look *really* bad. Someone is trying to frame me. Is it *you?* Are *you* trying to frame me? Is that why you're acting so nonchalant about all this?"

Marnie bares her teeth. "*Frame* you? Are you kidding me? I'm just trying to live my life, Carrie." She pauses, as if gathering ammunition. "I'm the one who lost my husband, not *you!* I've finally found someone who's crazy about me, and you're ruining *everything!* All you care about is yourself." Spittle flies from her mouth as she says this.

Her accusation — that *I'm* the selfish one — stings like a crack across the cheek. "You're trying to get me thrown in jail!" I spit back.

"Well, you're trying to make sure I'm single again! Acting all weird around Damian. Making snide comments."

"I'm the one making snide comments?" I shake my head. "You seriously think I'm trying to uncouple you? Really? You know what, Marnie. You and Damian can go have a beautiful life together for all I care. I don't need to be a part of it. How does *that* sound?"

"The best news I've heard all day."' Marnie jumps to her feet, her dark eyes burning with disdain. "I seriously can't with you, Carrie. I'm going to get another drink. Seems like I need them when you're around." She storms out of Damian's living room. The clap of her high heels echoes like gunshots down the hallway.

As Marnie's footsteps recede, I take a moment to absorb what's just happened, but I can't make sense of it. I've spent the past two years doing everything with Marnie. She was my partner in crime (too soon?). I sit still, struggling to process it all — how could she possibly hate me this much?

My eyes flit to the couch where Marnie has left her phone. I pick it up, turning it over in my hands, wondering how things have gone so terribly wrong. How — *if* — I can ever make them right. Surely, there's *something* I can do. I sit like this for what feels like hours but is likely only minutes.

I'm going to be sick. But not because I just lost my best friend.

The sound of another familiar set of footsteps approaching makes my skin crawl. I look toward the living room archway, and lo and behold, I'm staring at Detective Johnson.

Let's just say it does *not* look like he's here for a courtesy call.

CHAPTER FORTY-THREE

"Mrs. Winter."

"Detective Johnson."

This is the extent to which I acknowledge the detective, though proper etiquette would dictate that I should probably stand. I'm not trying to be rude. I'm terrified that if I attempt to balance on my feet right now, my legs will buckle beneath me. As it is, my hands are shaking. I bury them between my trembling legs, hoping he doesn't notice.

"Please, Detective." Damian motions toward his couch. "Have a seat."

The detective moves toward the wraparound couch, sitting close to me, but not *too close*. Thank God for small favors. Damian and Bennett remain standing. As if her Spidey senses told her she was missing out on something, Marnie suddenly appears in the living room, drink in hand. She sits as far away from me as possible on the other side of Detective Johnson.

"So I understand you've heard the news," he says, motioning toward the television which is running the news on repeat.

"It's just awful," I say, meaning it. After everything that's happened here, to have something like this happen again. It's not just awful. It's unfathomable.

Detective Johnson nods in agreement. "Awful, yes. But this is, unfortunately, the reality we're dealing with."

Reality sucks, I want to scream, but I bite my tongue.

"How can we help, Detective?"

"Right." Detective Johnson pulls his trusty notepad from his jacket pocket. I wonder what he's already written about me. About my family. Will he be asking everyone else in this room the same questions? Maybe he interviewed Bennett and Damian at the door, and now he's moving along to me. Marnie's probably next.

That *must* be it. He's interviewing everyone in the development, trying to piece together who last saw Sienna Berman. My stomach clenches. The answer to that question is probably TJ.

"Where were you on the evening of April 8th?"

I rack my brain. What's today's date? The 12th, I think? I glance up at the television, finding the date and time on the corner of the screen. Today is the 12th, 8:30 p.m. It's been four days since Sienna went missing. Four days before she was found *dead*.

A lump forms in my throat. I don't love the Bermans, but I feel for that poor girl. She didn't deserve to die. And her mom, as crazy as she may be, doesn't deserve to lose a child. I wonder if a kind nurse has broken the news to Lydia, lying helpless in the hospital as she recovers, or whether Lydia watched the discovery of her daughter's body play out in real time on television, just like the rest of us. Maybe it's better if she hasn't regained consciousness yet. The thoughts gut me. "I was at home, Detective."

"Is there anyone who can vouch for your whereabouts?"

"I can," Bennett interjects. "She was at home with me."

"Of course she was," Marnie mumbles.

I clench my fists in my lap. This means *war*.

"And TJ . . ." he says, glancing down at something written on a page. I try to look, but he snaps the notebook shut.

"What about TJ?" Bennett asks, a defense edge to his voice.

Detective Johnson shifts his attention to my husband. "Where was your son on the night of April 8th?"

"He was at home with my wife and me," Bennett answers with conviction.

Detective Johnson shakes his head. He obviously thinks we're lying and believes we are covering for TJ.

A sudden feeling strikes me. I. Don't. Care. Detective Johnson can speculate all he wants, but he can't prove anything.

Except, someone else can . . .

"He wasn't at home with them. That's a lie!" Marnie shouts. For a moment, the room falls completely silent. It is so quiet, I swear I can hear the blood coursing through my veins. With what resembles a scowl on her overly injected face, Marnie shatters that quiet, "TJ was with Sienna Berman before she went missing. And I have *proof*."

CHAPTER FORTY-FOUR

My eyes widen in shock.

She wouldn't.

"Where's my phone?" Marnie shouts, frantically searching for her cell phone.

Apparently, she would.

Marnie starts pacing around the living room like a madwoman. She stomps off to the kitchen, returning a few minutes later *without* her phone. Then she starts moving plates around and overturning couch cushions.

I glance at Damian. He's never seen Marnie like this. With his nose turned up and jaw hanging, he looks mortified. I realize now that Marnie hasn't told him what she has on her phone. Perhaps she did intend to keep our little secret.

All bets are out the window now.

After a few minutes of her huffing and puffing and cursing like a sailor, I decide it's been long enough. I pull her phone out from underneath me. "Marnie," I say, holding out her phone.

"What are you doing with my phone?" she seethes. An angry vein pops on her forehead.

"I'm not doing *anything* with your phone," I say innocently. "You left it in here when you went to get a drink."

Marnie grits her teeth and grabs the phone out of my hand. Her cocktail ring scratches against my skin, leaving a long red streak in its wake, just shallow enough not to draw blood. That freaking ring. I chomp down on my lower lip to stop myself from screaming.

It works. I don't scream, and I don't say anything else. There is nothing else to say. My *former* best friend is hellbent on destroying my stepson. A part of me wonders if this is all my fault. If I'd just been a little nicer, a little more supportive, and a little less *weird* around Damian, maybe we wouldn't be here right now. Instead, we'd be happily noshing on our aromatic Chinese food while drinking our perfectly paired Riesling.

Instead, Marnie is busy explaining to Detective Johnson how she is the only one with access to all of the surveillance footage in The Estates. "And there's something you need to see," she says as she jabs at her phone. "Something, I've *just* discovered tonight," she adds, which is so *not* true.

Her eyebrows knit together as she presses this and that, trying to locate the clubhouse footage from the night of April 8th — the footage of TJ having a heated conversation with Sienna before she went missing.

Before she turned up in the woods — dead.

My eyes flick to Bennett. He looks like he's seen a ghost. I'm sure he's thinking Marnie is about to expose TJ. Detective Johnson will march next door to our house and place my stepson under arrest for the murder of Sienna Berman. TJ will spend the rest of his life rotting away in a prison cell.

Except, I know something my husband doesn't know.

"Well?" Detective Johnson asks, tapping his pen against his notepad. "What did you want to show me?"

"I have a surveillance video of TJ and Sienna. He was with her before she disappeared."

Detective Johnson's eyes light up. "Okay, let's see it."

"April 8th, right?" Marnie types the date into her phone. Her jaw tightens as her finger moves feverishly across the screen. "I swear, I have it. It's here somewhere . . ."

We all stare at Marnie as she becomes increasingly distressed, attempting to locate the video. "I don't understand," she mutters to herself. "I have the 7th, the 9th. Where the *hell* is the 8th?"

I glance at Bennett again, this time catching his eye. And then I wink. Marnie's not going to find the surveillance video from April 8th. Detective Johnson will never see TJ and Sienna arguing or my stepson grabbing her too roughly by the shoulder and following her as she stormed off. No one will ever see the footage.

I deleted it.

Then, I completely wiped the deleted footage from the recently deleted file. That video may as well have never existed. And good thing, too. Marnie and Detective Johnson clearly have it in for TJ. My stepson would never get a fair trial because, between the detective and Marnie, they would throw the book at him. I have my own suspicions, but until there's solid forensic evidence linking TJ to the crime, Marnie can suck it.

She really should have had the foresight to take her phone to the kitchen with her instead of leaving it with me in the living room after we unceremoniously put an end to our two-year friendship.

Marnie's eyes shoot up to the ceiling as the realization dawns on her. Several extensions fall from her lids and stick to the sides of her face.

"You!" she screeches, jabbing a finger in my direction. "*You* deleted the footage!"

"I did *what?* How would I even know you had footage? Didn't you say you *just* discovered it?" I try to sound as demure and innocent as possible. "Really, whatever are you talking about, Marnie?"

Marnie jumps from the couch and lunges for me. "She's lying!" she shouts, grabbing for my hair.

Detective Johnson steps between us. "Ladies, I've had enough of this. Mrs. Black, lying to law enforcement is a serious offense."

"But I—"

Detective Johnson holds up a hand to stop her. "And Mrs. Winter, if what Mrs. Black says is true, and there *is*, in fact, video evidence of TJ and Sienna, know that I *will* find it. Everything is traceable."

"Except the harassing phone calls my wife has been receiving, right?" Bennett chimes in. "Why don't you check Marnie's phone for that? She clearly seems to have it in for our family."

We continue hurling arguments back and forth. It feels like this nightmare will never end.

The only one who's awfully quiet is Damian.

I peer at him standing in a corner of the room, watching the chaos unfold. Somehow, he doesn't look upset at all.

In fact, I think he's *smiling*.

CHAPTER FORTY-FIVE

Despite Detective Johnson trying his damnedest to separate us, Marnie cannot be deterred. She's still trying to claw my eyes out, hauling herself over the detective's shoulder, scrabbling for my hair and any piece of me she can get her hands on. I fear I've unleashed the beast. All I want is to go home, but Marnie has my arm in a kung-fu grip, those blood-red nails digging into my skin.

Detective Johnson yells for Marnie to release my arm, but I'm not even sure that she can hear him. Her eyes are practically bulging from her head, her voice loud and deep as she bellows that she's going to kill me. It's no exaggeration to say that the woman looks like she's possessed — deranged, even.

Detective Johnson gives Marnie one final stern warning, "Cease and desist, Mrs. Black, or else," before her body goes completely limp, and she collapses into a heap on the floor.

What the hell just happened?

I watch on in horror as Detective Johnson pulls out his walkie-talkie. "I need backup at 267 Main Street in The Estates. Hostile individual has been tased. Send a medical team."

Wait, what? Tased?

Cemented to the spot, I watch as Marnie convulses on the floor, Taser barbs protruding from her clothing, her skin. Detective

Johnson crouches on his knees, hovering over her. "Damnit," he mutters under his breath.

He momentarily looks up at us. "You need to return to your house *now* and *wait* for me there. I'll be interviewing your son again. I've been at this long enough to know when someone is hiding something."

I snatch my purse off the table, my hands shaking, but my stubborn feet refuse to move. I just keep staring at Marnie, wondering if she'll be okay, wondering how we got to this point in the first place, and wondering how Marnie and I were ever best friends. *With friends like these*, I think wryly to myself, *who needs enemies?*

I suppose that's what we are now — *enemies*.

My thoughts are interrupted by the whoosh of EMTs rushing into the room. They immediately jump into action, tending to Marnie — taking vitals, administering fluids, and asking questions. I overhear one of the workers telling Damian that it's rare, but in some instances, tasing can cause neurological problems and brain damage. *How comforting*, I think.

"Come on," Bennett says, taking my arm in his. "I think we should go."

"Shouldn't we wait to see if she's okay?" I could kill Marnie Black myself right now, but an (admittedly small) part of me still wants her to be okay. Old habits die hard, it would seem.

"Let the professionals take care of her. And please don't be mad at me for saying this, Carrie," Bennett holds up his hands as if warding off an attack, "but I think you may be the last person she's going to want to see when she comes to."

I nod, realizing he's right.

I follow Bennett out of the living room, toward the front door. We pass by Damian on the way out. He's watching from the sidelines, letting the EMTs do their job. I try to interpret the expression on his face, but it's unreadable.

"I'm so sorry about this, man. I have no idea what the fuck just happened," Bennett offers.

Damian lifts a shoulder, his lips pressed into a thin line. "You and I both. Not your fault at all, though. Clearly, I need to have a nice, long conversation with Marnie." We all look down at Marnie lying motionless on the bearskin rug. Drool slides out the corner of her mouth, and her eyelashes are freaking everywhere. "Once she regains consciousness," he adds with a shrug, though it goes without saying. Bennett just shakes his head.

I walk out the door without saying a word.

CHAPTER FORTY-SIX

Bennett and I speed walk to our house. It will only be a matter of time before Detective Johnson is back on our doorstep, wanting answers.

We don't have answers. At least, *not* ones that we can give him. Not yet.

I wonder what will happen to Marnie when she comes to. Will she go to jail for *assault?* Will the police buy her story that I deleted an incriminating surveillance video of TJ and Sienna from her phone?

Detective Johnson's ominous words hit me again. Can the police actually recover anything? What if the footage comes to light? No one can prove I erased it, but they could build a pretty damning circumstantial case against my stepson with it. I struggle to envision an outcome that doesn't involve TJ in a maximum-security prison.

Bennett fumbles with the door lock, his hands shaking. My poor husband. I'm not faring much better, but I take the keys from him and manage to unlock the door. Bennett pushes against it, causing it to swing open violently like he's executing a police raid. The door smashes against the mirrored accent table, which lets out a piercing squeal as it shatters into a million pieces.

I study Bennett's face. He doesn't appear at all fazed by what he's just done. He's not looking at the shards of our thousand-dollar accent table that are strewn across the marble floor of the foyer. He doesn't even remove his shoes as he pushes deeper into the house, screaming TJ's name. Bennett *never* wears shoes in the house.

I stare at him, dumbfounded. Who is this man?

I quickly close the door behind us. Aside from Bennett screaming his head off, the house is eerily quiet. It doesn't sound like anyone is home. *Unless, TJ could be in his room . . .*

Seemingly having the same thought, Bennett dashes up the stairs, taking two at a time. All the while, he shouts TJ's name like it's a matter of life or death. I guess it kind of is after what the police uncovered tonight.

The house echoes with the sound of my husband's voice. "TJ, *TJ*," he bellows, over and over. There's no response. If TJ is home, he's not answering. And if he's not home, the question of where, exactly, he is will have to be addressed when we come to it.

I listen to the shuffling upstairs as Bennett frantically goes from room to room, searching for his son.

"Carrie," he yells, "check the garage." Clearly, no luck.

I run into the kitchen, stumbling through the mudroom. My hands quiver as my fingers brush against the cool steel of the knob.

I rip open the door. Frozen in place, I let out a breathless gasp.

"Bennett," I scream out, my voice cracking. Within seconds, Bennett dashes into the garage, completely out of breath. His hair is wild, mirroring the look in his eyes. And then he sees it, too. He grasps the wall for support.

"Your Porsche," I cry. "He took your Porsche."

Bennett slaps a palm against the garage wall. "He never takes it without asking. *Why?*"

I blink at Bennett. TJ taking the Porsche without asking is the least of our problems right now. Concern thrums through me alongside countless questions. Where did he go with the Porsche? Has he fled Armonk? New York? The country? And *why?* The doorbell rings. Bennett and I freeze. The police have arrived even faster than expected. Detective Johnson must be chomping at the bit to interrogate my stepson. "What are we going to do, Bennett? Where could he be?"

"I honestly don't know. Call him, Carrie. Keep calling until you get him on the phone. I'll deal with Detective Johnson."

I'm not sure how he plans on dealing with Detective Johnson when we've no idea where TJ has gone. Despite passing the polygraph, I'm sure he's still on the shortlist of suspects. Actually, after what Marnie just pulled, he is probably *the* shortlist. Once the seed is planted, it's got nowhere to go but to grow.

I shove my hand into my purse and yank out my phone, thumbing through my contacts list and selecting TJ. I wait with bated breath as the phone rings.

And rings. And rings.

Straight to voicemail.

Shit.

I quickly redial him, but this time, the call goes directly to voicemail without ringing. I try a third time with the same result.

Damnit. TJ's phone can't die at a time like this. Unless he's turned it off . . .

"Carrie?" I startle at the sound of Bennett's voice.

I shake my head. "There's no answer, Bennett. TJ's phone is going straight to voicemail." I don't mention the call I made where it rang and rang *before* going to voicemail. That doesn't necessarily mean anything. Besides, my husband has broken into a full-blown sweat, with red splotches climbing his neck like vines. I don't think he could handle even the possibility that TJ would intentionally reject our calls.

"What did Detective Johnson say?" I ask, afraid to ask.

"Like he told us at Damian's house, he wants to talk to TJ. I told him he was out for the night. That bought us a little time.

He's not under arrest. Just wanted for questioning." Bennett runs a hand through his hair. "They're rushing the lab work on the body they found. The face was . . ." He pauses, drawing a deep breath. "It was severely beaten beyond recognition, but the body . . . there were defensive wounds — hairs and fibers and scrapings taken from underneath her fingernails. If TJ had something to do with this . . . if it *is* Sienna . . . oh, God." Bennett collapses into my arms.

That cool confidence my husband carries around like a brief-case is gone. Just like his son.

"We'll find him, Bennett," I say with way more conviction than I feel. I pray to whomever might be listening that they don't find his DNA on Sienna Berman because, while I can hide a journal and delete a video, I can't fix that.

Here's hoping that we're not too late.

CHAPTER FORTY-SEVEN

"I'll drive," Bennett says, grabbing the keys to my BMW off the hook in the mudroom.

Thank goodness Bennett had the foresight to have one of his couriers pick it up from the station and deliver it to our home. Otherwise, we'd be completely stranded. It's not like I could ask Marnie for a ride at this point.

"Are you sure that's a good idea, Bennett? I mean, you're visibly distressed. I don't think you should drive like this."

My husband is upset enough already, and he doesn't even know half of it yet — the unknown number call I received from TJ, the blood in our garage. Then again, I was just attacked by my crazy ex-best friend with razor eyelashes and ice-pick nails.

"I'll drive," I insist.

"Fine." Bennett tosses me the keys, but the reluctance doesn't go unnoticed.

As we make our way to the car, I glance down at the spot I covered up earlier today. The can is still there, concealing the blood Bennett doesn't notice. I imagine once we paint over it, no one will ever know there was blood there. Unless a forensics team tested for it . . . A shiver of panic runs through me. I'm sure the garage concrete paint is no match for luminol.

Oh, God. We have to find TJ.

I back out of the garage, waiting for the door to fully close before pulling down our driveway. No one can ever get inside that garage.

It's pitch black in The Estates, one of those nights where even the stars aren't visible. There are street lamps, but the board voted long ago against using them after 9 p.m. This is the type of development where peace and privacy are valued far more than kids playing outside at night. And The Estates is so safe. I roll my eyes. Perhaps if it weren't so freaking dark at night, we would have seen the carnage happening right under our noses.

But I guess we will never know.

For now, though, I appreciate the darkness. It is in darkness that you can hide. I'd rather not have anyone watch us leaving the development. Not least of all because we are setting off in search of my stepson, who is wanted for questioning in connection with a murder.

Surprisingly, Detective Johnson's unmarked police car isn't parked across the street from our house. As we drive farther down the road, it becomes evident that his vehicle is not parked on our street *at all*. That's odd. Has he returned to the crime scene? Or is he just like us? Out searching for the prime suspect?

We use the service entrance to exit the development. Thankfully, no reporters are waiting for us in the bushes this time. I'm sure they're all camped out by the woods where the body was found. I can't believe a dead body was found by our development. *Again.*

"So what's the plan?" I ask Bennett as the gate clicks closed behind us. Hopefully, my husband has more insight into where TJ might be because I haven't a freaking clue.

"Head toward Yonkers," he says as he frantically types out a text to his son. "I don't understand. He always responds to me . . ." He trails off. I shift my eyes, examining Bennett's profile in the low light of the BMW. His brow is furrowed, lining his forehead. His hands are knitted into a tight knot in his lap.

I'm not sure if Bennett would agree, but I'm starting to think it's a good thing that TJ took the Porsche without permission. You don't come across many Special Edition 911s on the average suburban street, if any. At least we know what to look for, if not where. I guess Yonkers is a start. Maybe he's gone to see a friend, and his phone really did die. It could be an Occam's razor thing, where the simplest explanation is the right one. It doesn't have to be wrong, just because a girl suspected of being Sienna Berman was found murdered in the woods, and TJ is the one suspected of murdering her. Doubt, nonetheless, worms its way into my mind.

I carefully maneuver the car down the dark and windy roads of Armonk. There's not another vehicle in sight. Nothing happens in a hamlet like this after 9 p.m.

Until TJ showed up on our doorstep. Until Mark Black unleashed his fury on our development. Until our dashingly handsome but likely deceptive neighbor moved into the house next door to ours.

I glance at my husband, who has thrown his phone into his lap in frustration. Now is as good a time as ever. "Can I ask you something, Bennett?" Bennett turns to face me. I have his full attention. "Do you find it weird that Damian has a rifle in his living room?"

Bennett's eyebrows shoot up. He looks surprised by my question, but I still think it's weird, especially since he's only been hunting once.

Especially since Sienna Berman was likely shot to death.

"I find it weird that he's with Marnie. The gun," he shrugs, "not so much."

"You've been hunting at least a dozen times before, Bennett, and *we* don't have a gun on our mantel."

Bennett lifts a noncommittal shoulder, seemingly unbothered by my astute observation.

I continue, "Look, I don't disagree with you on the Marnie thing, but maybe the question we should be asking ourselves is *why* Damian is with Marnie? And what is he doing in our development?"

"Carrie, you know he got that house for a steal."

"True, but can you honestly tell me you would move into The Estates because you got a house there for a steal, knowing what you know?"

He goes silent as he mulls this over. "No, I guess I wouldn't."

"So why do you think he's here?"

Bennett pinches the bridge of his nose. "I don't know, Carrie. What is your issue with Damian, anyway? He seems like a perfectly nice guy to me."

I take a deep breath and tighten my grip on the wheel. "I don't trust him, Bennett. I feel like . . ."

"Like what?"

"Like he's hiding something big from us."

CHAPTER FORTY-EIGHT

"Turn here," Bennett orders, and I take a sharp right turn onto a quaint tree-lined street. Unlike our neighborhood, the street lamps burn brightly in this part of town.

The part of town where Andrea Winter lived before she was murdered.

I'm not sure why I didn't think of this. Of course, this should be the first place we look. It's where TJ spent his entire childhood. Perhaps TJ was craving a sense of comfort and nostalgia, away from the prying eyes of the neighbors and police at The Estates. Maybe he even came here to ponder how things could have gone so terribly wrong outside the suffocating confines of our picture-perfect development.

However, as we cruise by Andrea Winter's former house, which *still* has the For Sale sign displayed on its lawn, my stomach sinks. There's no sign of Bennett's Porsche. Not here, and not anywhere else on the street.

But there is something I hadn't picked up on before — a bold, white sign advertising redeveloper Damian Mankiewicz with a phone number. How could I not have noticed that before? I pull over to the side of the road and quickly jot down the number. Bennett is too busy punching at his phone to notice what I'm doing.

"He's not here," I say, stating the obvious, still peering at the sign.

"Keep driving," Bennett says. I steal another glance at my husband, his face now highlighted by the street lamps. His jaw is clenched, and a vein pumps quite fiercely in his neck. I'm struck again with that same foreboding feeling that we are on the precipice of something terrible.

For the next three hours, Bennett directs me down every main road and side street in Yonkers. We drive past baseball diamonds, bars, and bodegas. But there's no sign of Bennett's Porsche or Bennett's son.

After circling the same streets at least a half dozen times, I tell Bennett, "I think we should go home. Wait for TJ there. I'm sure he'll come back." The truth is, the only thing I'm sure of is that we have no idea where TJ is. For all we know, he could be in Canada by now. At some point, the police will probably put out a BOLO for Bennett's Porsche and an APB for TJ. I shudder at the image of my stepson's face plastered all over the news.

But for now, all we can do is wait.

Bennett taps his fingers against the dash, thinking. "Fine, drive home."

We drive back to The Estates in total silence.

The development is *unusually* dark. I know I said it's dark, but it would appear there's been a development-wide power outage.

"This is kind of creepy," I tell Bennett as we drive through the deserted black.

"Yeah," he agrees.

I push the remote to the garage, but nothing happens. I try again. A third time. And then I give up. "It's not working."

"There must have been a power outage or something," Bennett offers. "Just park in the driveway."

How odd. I don't think we've ever had so much as a power flicker since I moved in here. Certainly not a full-blown power outage.

After parking the car in the driveway, we use the lights from our phones to make our way to the front door. Once inside, Bennett resumes heartily screaming TJ's name, but unsurprisingly, there's no answer.

"I'm going to stay down here in case TJ comes home," Bennett says. "Do you want to stay with me?"

"I'm exhausted." I let out a loud yawn for effect. "I'm going to head up to bed."

Bennett kisses me goodnight, and we part ways in the foyer.

As soon as I'm upstairs in our bedroom, with the door closed, I pull out the number I copied from the redeveloper sign.

"Hello?" a raspy voice answers.

"Is this Damian Mankiewicz?" I ask, my heart beating out of my chest. It certainly doesn't *sound* like the Damian Mankiewicz who I shared a hearty plate of lo mein with only hours before. Perhaps I've woken him up. All the excitement of the night has been exhausting. Heck, living here is exhausting.

"This is him."

"Damian Mankiewicz of 267 Main Street in Armonk."

There's a long pause. "No, sorry, you have the wrong Damian Mankiewicz. Who knew I had such a popular name?"

"I'm sorry for the inconvenience," I say, quickly ending the call. I almost let a triumphant fist pump fly because surprise, surprise, I was right.

My new neighbor Damian Mankiewicz is *not* who he says he is.

CHAPTER FORTY-NINE

I pace back and forth in my bedroom, adrenaline churning in my body like water in rapids. Despite the fact that I *knew* Damian was lying, the confirmation lands hard. I struggle to arrange the pieces — why he's lying, why he's here, and who the *hell* this man masquerading as a house redeveloper is — in a cohesive picture.

And what has he done to Marnie?

As often happens when I think about Marnie, as if she has some sort of strange telepathic insight into my inner thoughts, my phone chimes with a text. I hesitantly turn the phone over in my hands before reading it.

Marnie: *Carrie . . . I'm sorry about how out of control things got tonight. That jolt really knocked some sense into me. Who knew all it would take was a Taser, lol? Please, come back to Damian's so we can talk. Let's make things right between us. I don't want to go to sleep in a fight.*

I stay rooted to the spot for a few moments, just staring at my phone, lost in thought. Relief and dread both fill me like hot and cold water in a tub. I want more than anything to go back to the way things *were* with Marnie. This might be our only chance. But the thought of going back to Damian's house, now that I know what I know — and everything I *don't* know — sends shivers down through my very bones.

Still, I can't leave her there *alone*.

I'm about to write back when another text comes through.

Marnie: *Please don't tell Bennett. I'm so mortified.*

I take a deep breath. A niggle of worry nags at me. With everything going on here, I should tell Bennett. But if I tell him I'm going over there, he will insist on coming, which could set Marnie off all over again.

So I make a decision that I may come to regret.

I tiptoe out of the bedroom and into the hallway. Our living room is set off to the side of the house. If I'm quiet enough, Bennett shouldn't hear me. I make my way down the winding staircase toward the front door. The house is black and silent, the power still off. I reconsider for a moment, stuck between checking in with Bennett and walking out our front door.

With one foot placed in front of the other, I make my choice.

Letting myself out the front door, I take a deep breath of the late-night air. It's unnervingly dark outside, suddenly cold. I wrap my arms around my body and shiver.

I focus my eyes on the house next door, the place where tonight's disastrous evening began. The place where this nightmare was seemingly set in motion less than a week ago. The place where my former best friend was tased by a police officer.

I take deliberate, measured steps away from the safety of my home. I don't know what to expect. Marnie Black never apologizes for anything or to anyone. Maybe she was right — the Taser could have actually jolted some sense into her.

Only the future knows that for certain.

I approach the door with trepidation, a knot forming in my stomach. I lift a hand and knock gently, waiting a few moments before I knock again.

No answer.

I try the doorbell next, pressing a finger against the ringer. It takes a few moments for the realization to set in that with no power, there's no functioning doorbell. I knock again, but still, no one comes to the door.

I think about Marnie's penchant for scaring me, and I wonder for a moment if this is one of her sick jokes. I debate turning around and going back to my house, telling Bennett everything.

But a noise from inside stops me.

I bring my hand to the doorknob, remembering that Damian doesn't lock his front door. I hesitate for a moment before I twist. The handle turns, and I push open the front door.

I step inside the house, quietly closing the door behind me.

"Hello?" I call out. "Marnie? Damian?"

I stand in the foyer, struck with an overwhelming sense of foreboding. The house is as quiet as a crypt. I could have misread the text. Maybe they've gone to Marnie's house. Yet I can't explain the atmosphere here. Every cell in my body screams *run*.

I can't—

I feel it before I hear it. A hand pressed against my mouth. Hot breath in my ear.

Damian's voice, "Don't scream."

CHAPTER FIFTY

I scream, a piercing shriek that could wake all of The Estates.

He quickly silences me, his hand pushing harder into my mouth, his fingers lacing across my nose so I can't breathe. Now, I couldn't scream again even if I wanted to. He jabs something solid against my back. It feels like the barrel of a gun.

I instantly go quiet, still.

"That's better," Damian whispers, his voice unnervingly calm. "Now walk."

He pushes me forward through the dark, the object biting into my back my only guide.

I take slow, soft steps through the pitch-black, unable to see anything. To breathe. To think straight.

He's going to kill me. This can't be how it all ends.

My knee hits against something hard, and I wince in pain, gasping. And then Damian's hands are on my shoulder, pushing me down until I'm sitting.

Damian flicks on the flashlight on his phone, casting the room in an eerie glow. My eyes dart up to the mantle above his fireplace. The rifle is gone.

I whip my head around, expecting to find Marnie sitting next to me. She's also nowhere to be found.

"Marnie?" I manage. "Where's Marnie?"

"I can explain," Damian begins, voice shaking. "I just . . . I just want to talk."

"Where is she?" My voice cracks.

"She's home, in bed. Sleeping off what happened."

"But she texted me . . ."

Damian reaches into his back pocket, pulling out her phone. Panic thrums in my chest, my mind taking a minute to catch up.

"*You* texted me from Marnie's phone? What do you want from me?"

"I just need to talk, Carrie."

I shake my head, but a fresh surge of adrenaline emboldens me. "You can't trick me into coming here, and expect me to talk. What do you really want? And I know you're not Damian Mankiewicz. Who are you, really?"

Damian sinks into an adjacent loveseat, dropping his head into his hands. "Jones. Damian Jones."

So his introduction as 'Damian Brown' wasn't just a playful quip — he's a compulsive liar about *who* he is. And *what* is he? "Are you even a house flipper?"

"Well, no," he admits. "I told you, I'm pretty boring."

Pretty freaking nuts is more like it. Instead, I stammer, "Wh . . . what?"

"Look, I didn't want anyone to figure out who I was. I thought if anyone looked me up, they'd figure I was telling the truth. No way to prove otherwise since there are no pictures online of the real Damian Mankiewicz."

Hiding his identity just doesn't make any sense. I rack my brain, trying to place him. Jones . . . Jones . . . I don't know a Damian Jones.

But I do know of a Jessica Jones.

"Oh my God," I whisper, realization setting in. "Any relation to Jessica Jones? From the *Westchester Sentinel?*"

Damian nods, slow and even. "Jessica is . . . *was*—" he hesitates, drawing in a measured breath — "my wife."

My mind darts to the pictures in the *DO NOT OPEN* box. The gun that I took from the box and hid beneath my mattress. I'm not even sure why I stole the gun. I don't even know how to hold a gun, let alone shoot one. At the end of the day, I guess the thought of leaving that weapon in the hands of my mysterious new neighbor troubled me more than taking it. I should feel vindicated that my gut is to be trusted, but all I feel is completely shaken.

I inhale sharply, panic flowing through my body. "I . . . I don't understand. What are you doing here?"

"It's simple," Damian starts, a look of determination passing across his face. "I came here to find out who killed her. And to make them pay."

"I'm sorry, but I don't understand. Mark Black killed Jessica Jones. Didn't he?"

"For a smart woman, you really are clueless," Damian quips, handing me Marnie's phone. My eyes dart between him and the phone, unsure what to do or what to make of all this. What could Marnie possibly have to do with Jessica Jones, other than being married to the man who killed her?

"Read the texts," he tells me.

My eyes focus on the chain of texts between Marnie and an undisclosed number.

Marnie: *Is it done? You know what will happen if it's not . . .*

Undisclosed number: The Sentinel *is closed for business.*

Marnie: *Jessica?*

Undisclosed number: *I thought we weren't naming names . . . but yes.*

The room violently spins. I bring a hand to my mouth, gagging. This can't be.

Marnie had Jessica Jones killed.

But the questions remain: Why? And by who?

"I had no idea," I gasp. "I mean, I knew Marnie had her things, but *this?* I can't imagine her doing something so terrible." Ousting someone from book club is one thing. Putting a hit out on someone, quite another.

"There's more. Those other girls, Andrea Winter . . . Mark wasn't the one who killed them. It's all in there."

A wave of dizziness washes over me. The spin on the room gains velocity. Marnie wouldn't do something like this. But doubt has a way of finding me, even in the dark.

"I need you to help me figure out who these texts were with," Damian continues. "Who killed my beautiful wife?" His voice — always so sure and even — suddenly breaks.

I suddenly think about the unknown number call from TJ, the thought of burner phones hurtling to the forefront of my mind. He could be the one communicating with Marnie. Is *this* the reason they evade one another at all costs? A darker, more sinister question stalks me, and I struggle to shove it to the wayside. Did my stepson commit murder? No, there must be another explanation. TJ isn't capable of *that*.

Suddenly, it's not my thoughts of TJ or Damian's desperate plea for answers that have my attention. Out of nowhere, a figure emerges from the darkness.

And she's clutching the rifle.

CHAPTER FIFTY-ONE

"Damian, look out!" I scream, but it's too late. The barrel of the gun comes crashing down onto his head. He goes limp in the chair, blood dripping from a gaping wound. I turn to look at the person holding the rifle.

"*You?*"

"Hey, Carrie."

I stare incredulously at Sienna Berman as she props the rifle on her shoulder.

"You're alive?"

Sienna laughs, a cold, unnerving sound. "Obviously."

I don't understand. Like, advanced calculus don't understand. "But the girl they found . . ."

"Yeah," Sienna says without a hint of remorse in her voice. "Unfortunate for her."

I'm shocked. Confused. *Horrified.* "Who . . . who was she?"

"Just a girl from another development who was sleeping with my boyfriend," she responds nonchalantly.

"Your boyfriend?" I blink at her like a deer caught in a flash of high beams.

"Mark Black, Carrie. Get with the fucking program."

My heart leaps into my throat. Then it jumps to my feet. It's everywhere in my body, pinging wildly around. Fear spirals through me like a bloody corkscrew. "What are you doing, Sienna?"

"What I should have done a long time ago. Getting back at you and your family, Carrie. This is all your fault. And Marnie's."

It feels like I'm the one who's been hit over the head. Sienna couldn't possibly know, unless she overheard Damian expose Marnie for the murders. I can't help but wonder, though: has she known all along?

I watch in horror as Sienna repositions the rifle, aiming it straight at my chest. She stares at me with her soulless, dark eyes that look almost black, and a smirk on her face as she watches me attempt to arrange the pieces of this damned puzzle.

"Feels like you're going a little crazy, doesn't it?" Sienna tilts her head and looks me over like I'm the one who's gone mad.

It's as if she can see inside of my head. That's almost unsettling a thought as what she plans on doing with the gun she's got pointed at me.

Before I have a chance to respond, Sienna cackles loudly, and every nerve in my body seizes. It feels like *I've* been tased. "Oh Carrie. Surely you've been wondering about all the strange things happening." She hesitates, as if waiting for me to fill in the blanks. "The missing diary, the necklace, the *blood* in your garage. Come on, girl, have you figured it out yet?"

"Y . . . y . . . you did all that? But how?"

"I stole your spare key from Marnie's house. Super easy, considering she leaves her own key under her flower pot. With everything that's happened here, you'd think she'd be a little more careful. Anyway, once I had the key it was just a matter of sneaking in and out at the right times. I used the back door, naturally."

My mind runs in erratic circles, struggling to make sense of a seventeen-year-old pulling this off. But try as I might, I can't wrap my head around it. I need to keep her talking. The longer she's talking, the longer she's not shooting.

"I don't understand—"

"What don't you understand, Carrie? How I got my diary back, or how I slipped the necklace in your drawer?"

Well, both . . .

"But . . . but . . ."

"But . . . but . . ." Sienna mocks.

"How did you get the necklace from the police station?"

"That was *my* necklace. Mark gave it to me."

My follow-up question screeches to a halt in my throat. Mark bought *three* of the same necklaces. How many more are there out there? More importantly, "Why did you leave blood in my garage?"

Sienna seems to mull this over. "Well, I had to make the necklace look authentic, right? And then when I cut myself a little too deeply, I decided to make good use of it instead of cleaning it up. Worst-case scenario, I figured one of you would get thrown in jail if I never resurfaced. Brilliant, right?" She cocks the gun, any hint of a smile instantly sliding off her face. "And turning everyone against you made this extra fun, Carrie!" I watch in horror as she giddily jumps up and down in place, the rifle quivering.

"Please, Sienna. You don't want to do this. Your mom. She's been so worried about you. She's in the hospital, fighting for her life. You should be with her. It doesn't have to end like this."

Sienna blinks rapidly, her lips a razor-thin line. "You think I'm not aware of this, Carrie? Who do you think cut her brakes?"

I gasp as if I've taken a shot to the chest. An icy chill seeps into my bones. And I thought Lydia was crazy. "You cut your mother's brakes?"

Sienna nods her head, her dark, tousled curls bouncing in the low light of Damian's wayward iPhone flashlight. "You wouldn't understand what it's like having a mother like her. She wouldn't leave me alone — she's suffocating. If it wasn't for her and her big mouth, Mark and I might still have been together. *I* was the one he wanted to be with. And *you*," she hisses with ice in her voice, "killed him." She stares at me with such venom that it actually feels like I've been poisoned.

Then she takes a step closer, her finger hovering over the trigger.

"Please, Sienna. I'll do whatever you want. Just don't shoot me. I didn't mean to kill him. The door, it fell . . ."

"*Shut up!*" She screams, coming closer. "Lie face down and put your hands behind your back."

"Sienna."

"*Do it!*"

I quickly do as she says, my heart pumping fiercely in my ears. Just as swiftly as I've repositioned myself on the couch, I hear the rip of duct tape and feel its bite as she wraps it tightly around my wrists. Sienna works surprisingly fast, binding my hands and feet.

I turn my head to the side, watching as she does the same to an unconscious Damian.

We are so incredibly screwed.

Sienna hums to herself as she finishes off Damian, though, by the looks of him, he's not going anywhere for a while — or, potentially, ever. I wonder why she hasn't shot us yet. Given the surprises of the evening, I can't conceive of what she plans to do before she kills us both. If Damian is still alive, that is.

"Don't go anywhere," she chirps wickedly, laughing. And just as quickly as she appeared, I hear the click of the front door as Sienna disappears into the night. My skin prickles at the image of Sienna out there with the shotgun.

No one in this development is safe.

"Damian." I release a strangled whisper once certain she's gone. "Damian."

I'm only met with silence. Panic rushes through me. He has to be alive — he just has to be.

I roll myself off the couch, hitting the ground with a painful thud. I take a deep breath, slowly inching my body toward him.

Damian is hunched over in the chair, his head hanging limply to the side, unmoving. Oh God, he looks dead.

"Damian," I plead, louder this time. But still, he doesn't answer. It looks like I'm on my own.

CHAPTER FIFTY-TWO

Fear paralyzes me. I've never been so afraid in my entire life. Damian is unconscious, possibly dead. And I've been bound by a psychopath who's coming back God only knows when. I have to do something to find a way out of this mess before Sienna returns to finish us off. I try to draw in more oxygen, but my breathing is shallow, as if my lungs have forgotten how to function.

I stare desperately at the window. The sky is just starting to lighten as the sun is beginning to rise. I roll back and forth on the bearskin rug, trying desperately to loosen my restraints. And then it hits me.

The box cutter.

I slip my hand into the back pocket of my jeans, stretching my fingers until I make contact with it. My hands tremble as I fumble with the blade. Red-hot pain shoots through me as it slices into my hand, and the warmth of fresh blood pulses in my fingers.

But I won't stop. I *can't* stop.

Time seems to crawl excruciatingly, but somehow, I manage to remove the box cutter from my jeans and slip it in between my wrists and the duct tape. With my pulse throbbing in my wrists, I slide the boxcutter back and forth, slowly and *carefully*. My heart skips a beat as I feel the restraint loosening. A few more seconds . . .

Halle-freaking-lujah.

I quickly cut the tape on my ankles, then pull myself up so I'm at eye level with Damian.

"Damian." I place both hands on his cheeks, lifting his head gingerly so I can examine his wound. Recalling the plethora of medical supplies in the kitchen, I stumble through the semi-darkness, hoping to find what I need. When I return, Damian's head lolls to the side once again.

I hold the smelling salts in my hand, giving them a crack and bringing them under his nose. Within seconds, Damian lets out a loud gasp, his eyes flying open in shock.

His gaze shoots frantically all over the place. I hope he doesn't have a concussion. "Wh . . . what . . . ?" He stumbles over his words. Or, rather, I hope he doesn't have a *serious* concussion. The guy definitely has a concussion.

"Shh . . ." I caution him. "You need to be quiet."

His brows furrow together, and then he squeezes his eyes shut in visible pain.

"What happened?" he finally manages.

"Sienna Berman was here. She hit you over the head with your rifle." *Why did you have to have a rifle over your mantle in the first place?* I internally lament.

"She's *alive?*"

My sentiments exactly. "Alive and well. And hellbent on revenge, apparently."

Damian's eyes go wide.

"Look, I'll explain it all to you later. Right now, we need to get help. Sienna stormed out with your rifle. I don't know where she went or what she's gone to do. Only, she's *going* to come back. Can you stand?"

Damian attempts to rise to his feet, immediately falling back against the chair. He brings both hands to his head as if trying to contain the pain that's radiating off of him in waves. If it were possible to catch a headache, I'd be long gone.

I chew on my lip, puzzling over what to do. I could call the police, but I doubt they could even get here in time. Can I leave Damian here to risk heading next door to my house on my own? Sienna could see me, though, and I wouldn't make it one piece. Then what will happen to Damian? He's clearly injured, confused.

But what choice do I have?

I'm about to tell Damian about my plan, when a furious bang rips through the night, startling us both.

Sienna is back. She's going to kill us both. She's . . .

A few moments of silence pass as my mind tumbles through how terrible my last moments on this planet will be. My heart thumps against my ribcage as I listen for her footsteps.

Except, that's not what I hear.

Just screams.

CHAPTER FIFTY-THREE

I rush to Damian's living room window, staring out onto the street at the orange lights on the horizon. It's a beautiful early spring morning. However, it's far too busy on the street in front of our houses for such an occasion. A crowd rapidly gathers in a circle, heads bent down toward the concrete, eyes trained on the street. I catch a glimpse of something lying on the concrete.

Someone.

I picture Sienna with the rifle and my blood turns to ice. What has she done?

There's no time to think. I run from Damian's house, swinging the front door wide open so violently that it nearly falls off the hinges. I sprint onto the street, pushing past neighbors, friends. I've never run so fast in my entire life. My chest tightens as I search the crowd for my husband. My stepson. My best friend.

No, no, no, my mind wails.

I nearly hurtle headlong into TJ and Bennett, who are huddled together among the circle of residents, and a sigh of sheer relief rips itself from my throat. "Thank God, you're both okay," I cry as Bennett wraps me in his arms. He holds me so tightly, I can't move. I can hardly breathe. I fidget in his grasp, but he won't let go. It's almost as if he doesn't want me to turn around to look where all my neighbors are looking.

Some of the tension drains out of my body, but the reprieve is momentary. "*Bennett?*" Tears stream down my face. Everything that's happened over the past few hours, the past few *days*, comes rushing to the surface.

The question remains of who lies unmoving in the street.

I can't take much more. I push against his chest. I need to see who's lying there. Finally, he lets me go. I whip around, staring at the figure.

A lump forms in the back of my throat.

"*Marnie?*"

My eyes rake over her body, bent in an unusual position, and dark hair fanned across the pavement. A light breeze blows through the air, the sun shining brightly on her bloodied face.

I move closer. Bennett touches my elbow to stop me, but I shrug him off.

My eyes sting. I bend down, hovering over her body. There's blood everywhere. A spent shell casing. She's completely still. A chalk figure at a crime scene. The neighborhood buzzes around me, but all I hear are my jagged breaths.

Marnie is impossibly, irrevocably dead.

Marnie and I have had our ups and downs over the past two years. In friendships and in *any* relationship, you have to take the good with the bad. Yes, Marnie was loud and nosy and demanding and — I could go on *all* day — but she was loyal. I wasn't truthful about my past when my husband and I first met. Marnie found out, but she never did tell.

She always kept my secrets.

But the moment she tried to show Detective Johnson the video footage of TJ on her phone last night, I knew I could never trust her again, even if we recovered from our fight. I also knew that if given the chance, Marnie Black would do anything to destroy TJ, even if she took me down with him. At the end of the day, her hatred toward my stepson was stronger than her friendship toward me. I may never understand that. I realize then at this moment that I never will understand that.

Marnie is gone.

And Sienna Berman is the one who killed her.

Bile rises in my throat. I turn to Bennett and TJ. "Sienna. She's . . ." I start to say, and then I see it. The mark right below his left eye — it's red, angry, and wasn't there last night. I think of all the things that could cause such a mark, but keep coming back to one — Marnie's cocktail ring.

The missing gun from beneath my mattress streaks through my thoughts like a blazing comet.

At once, the puzzle is complete.

EPILOGUE

Marnie Black

I woke up in a complete panic this morning, having realized in the wake of being tased that I'd left my phone in Damian's house. He must have brought me home last night. You'd think he would have stayed to make sure I was okay, but he's not here for me.

Just like I'm not here for him.

I'm smarter than Damian gave me credit for — than *anyone* gave me credit for. After getting completely hoodwinked by a philandering husband, how could anyone believe I would throw myself at our complete stranger of a new neighbor and ignore all the obvious red flags?

Exactly.

Damian isn't as smart as he thinks he is. I knew exactly who he was when I sprinted up to his door. Despite his bulging muscles and easy-flowing lies, the guy is not in construction or house flipping or anything even remotely to do with interior design. He's a flipping accountant, of all things. But, more importantly, he's the next of kin for Jessica Jones. I recognized him immediately from the piece the *Westchester Sentinel* ran on the reporter's funeral.

Some of us still read the newspaper.

So why did I throw myself at Damian Mankiewicz. Sorry, Damian *Jones?*

It was all about damage control. I needed to know what he knew and to stop him from finding out what I'd done. Plain and simple.

Until I got tased and left my damn phone at his house.

Anyway, I was on my way to get my phone this morning, praying Damian hadn't gone through it. There's some pretty incriminating evidence on that phone. For me *and* TJ. Not gonna lie, I'm surprised Carrie never once pieced together *why* TJ and I can't stand to be anywhere near each other. Perhaps because we were both guilty of murder? For TJ, the death of his mom meant a better life. I mean, look at the kid. He's living in the lap of luxury, interning at a prestigious law firm, and driving his daddy's Porsche. For me, the deaths of Andrea Winter, Sofia Swanson, and Lila Lockwood meant sweet revenge for my lying, cheating, underage-girl-preying bastard of a husband. As for Jessica Jones, if she could only have kept her nose out of where it didn't belong. But then again, we wouldn't have had the pleasure of Damian's shirtless arrival.

I mull over my relationship with Carrie and how she's so afraid of making me mad. How she always lets her questions about my strained relationship with TJ go when I refuse to give her answers. I, for one, would never take no for an answer. Perhaps Carrie was worried I had a little bit of Mark Black in me.

As it turns out, we all have a little Mark Black in us.

Take Sienna Berman, for example — ripping through the streets with a rifle slung over her shoulder like a freaking cowboy, her eyes wild and glazed, the gun shaking violently against her underdeveloped teeny bopper body. When she saw me, she lifted the barrel and aimed it at my head. I closed my eyes and held my breath as she took a shot. But when my eyes shot open a few moments later, no pearly gates shimmered in my vision.

I stared at Sienna who was rooted to the spot, still as a painting. As both she and I realized I hadn't been hit, she raised the gun up and down, up and down, seemingly considering whether she should try her luck and shoot again. But she didn't. Instead, Sienna took off, running in the opposite direction. I would later hear through the haze that the police had caught up to her, tackled her to the ground, *and* arrested her for murder.

Except, that's not what happened.

The morning had certainly *not* gone according to plan. I didn't plan on getting shot at by one neighbor and then shot by another. At least, not by *that* neighbor.

Bennett Winter wouldn't hurt a fly. But he would hurt a Marnie Black, apparently.

Had I the strength to talk, I would have told him he should stick to lawyering. The guy is good at everything except, apparently, operating a firearm. I'm pretty sure he just grazed my ear.

If Bennett wanted me dead, he should have aimed a little better. Not that a bullet could stop me.

I'm Marnie *fucking* Black.

Too bad I don't have Nurse Damian trying to patch me up. *Men.* They're never there when you need them, are they?

These are the thoughts flitting through my mind as the ambulance rushes me from The Estates, the flashing red and white lights reflecting off the crumpled faces of my horrified neighbors.

They all think I'm dead. I'm not surprised. I'm one heck of an actress.

"BP 140 over 90, Pulse Sat 90%," one of the EMTs recites as he sticks a needle in my arm. "Starting fluid IV bag, .5 mg of morphine for pain." I squeeze my eyes tight as the EMTs work on stemming the blood flow from my ear. I've got plenty to think about. For starters, who knew Bennett Winter had it in him?

I guess it is true what they say: like father like son.

Bennett was dressed as if out for a run, except he wasn't all that sweaty, and Bennett always runs the trail behind his house. I couldn't help but notice that he was headed straight for *my* house.

"Hey, Bennett." I brought up a hand and waved at him, thankful for a friendly face to tell about Sienna Berman. We needed to call the police — have her apprehended before she hurt, or worse, killed someone.

Except Bennett's face didn't look all that friendly. In fact, he didn't wave back.

Something about his cold expression caught me completely off guard. He was shivering as if he was spiking a fever. It wasn't even that chilly outside. His color was off too, a sort of green hue tingeing his usually tanned, handsome face.

There were no greetings from his end, either. Only, "I know everything."

"What are you talking about, Bennett?" I wrung my hands together to keep them from trembling. There was no possible way he knew *everything*. Unless Damian had gone through my phone and told him, but if that were the case, I'd hardly expect to find Bennett out here confronting me, alone. Surely, Damian would be right here alongside him. And the only other way he could have found out was if TJ had told him the truth. But that's ridiculous — TJ would never tell *anyone* the truth.

The truth that he was the one (fine, fine, with my encouragement) who murdered three of the Mark Black four. He might as well strap himself into the electric chair.

I told myself this, but Bennett's expression told an entirely different story. He clenched his jaw tightly, narrowing his eyes into tiny slits. A vein pulsed in the side of his temple. I glanced down at his hands. One was curled into a fist. The other, hidden behind his back.

He closed the space between us with a giant step, and I panicked. I threw my hands up to stop him, my cocktail ring connecting with the side of his face. I missed his eye by an inch at most.

I stumbled over my feet as I backed away from him. And then, I watched in horror as his other hand emerged with a gun.

"What . . . what are you doing, Bennett?"

The gun quivered in his hand. "I don't want to do this, Marnie. But I have to protect my family. My son. Surely, you must understand."

So he *does* know.

"The ugly truth dies with you," he said, and then he pulled the trigger.

The shot rang out with the bold certainty of a church bell. If only it were so benign.

My right ear buzzed as my head filled with white-hot pain. I crumpled to the concrete and lay there, still as a statue.

Then Bennett, coward that he is, *actually* ran.

Bits and pieces of the EMT's conversation filters through my thoughts. *Fifty percent chance of survival. Possible paralysis. Likely brain damage.*

A wave of nausea hits so hard, it feels like I'm going to be sick. I try to shift my head to the side, but I can't will it to move. Come to think of it, I can't move at all. Oh goodness, maybe this is worse than I thought.

The Winters had better hope I die.

If not, The Estates won't know what hit them.

THE END

ACKNOWLEDGMENTS

Here we are again — the end of another chapter in this unbelievable journey. I will keep this as short and sweet as possible. First and foremost, a huge shoutout to Sîan Heap for finding me in a saturated sea of thriller writers. Working with the team at Joffe Books has been an amazing experience, and I truly have Sîan and Jasper Joffe to thank for that. And of course, none of this would have come to fruition without the rest of Joffe's team of editors, designers, formatters, social-media geniuses, marketers and production department . . . So thanks to each and every one of you as well. Next, my Booksta girls, ARC readers, TikTokers: you have helped me make my dreams come true. I am so appreciative of every post, of every review, of your willingness to help spread the word and get my books into the hands of as many readers as possible. Grateful doesn't begin to suffice. To my family: thank you for putting up with my obsessive need to write. It brings me so much joy, and I am lucky to have such a supportive cast of leading characters in my life. Last but not least, thank you, reader. I hope you have enjoyed this book. There is so much more to come. If you don't already, you can find me on Instagram @dlfisherthrillers and on TikTok @d.l.fisherthrille for updates. And please, don't hesitate to reach out. I LOVE hearing from you!

All the best,

D.L. Fisher

THE JOFFE BOOKS STORY

We began in 2014 when Jasper agreed to publish his mum's much-rejected romance novel and it became a bestseller.

Since then we've grown into the largest independent publisher in the UK. We're extremely proud to publish some of the very best writers in the world, including Joy Ellis, Faith Martin, Caro Ramsay, Helen Forrester, Simon Brett and Robert Goddard. Everyone at Joffe Books loves reading and we never forget that it all begins with the magic of an author telling a story.

We are proud to publish talented first-time authors, as well as established writers whose books we love introducing to a new generation of readers.

We won Trade Publisher of the Year at the Independent Publishing Awards in 2023 and Best Publisher Award in 2024 at the People's Book Prize. We have been shortlisted for Independent Publisher of the Year at the British Book Awards for the last five years, and were shortlisted for the Diversity and Inclusivity Award at the 2022 Independent Publishing Awards. In 2023 we were shortlisted for Publisher of the Year at the RNA Industry Awards, and in 2024 we were shortlisted at the CWA Daggers for the Best Crime and Mystery Publisher.

We built this company with your help, and we love to hear from you, so please email us about absolutely anything bookish at feedback@joffebooks.com.

If you want to receive free books every Friday and hear about all our new releases, join our mailing list here: www.joffebooks.com/freebooks.

And when you tell your friends about us, just remember: it's pronounced Joffe as in coffee or toffee!